01/11 $16.95

WITHDRAWN

I AM NUCHU

For my children: Brandi, Ashley, Whitney,
Justin and Colton

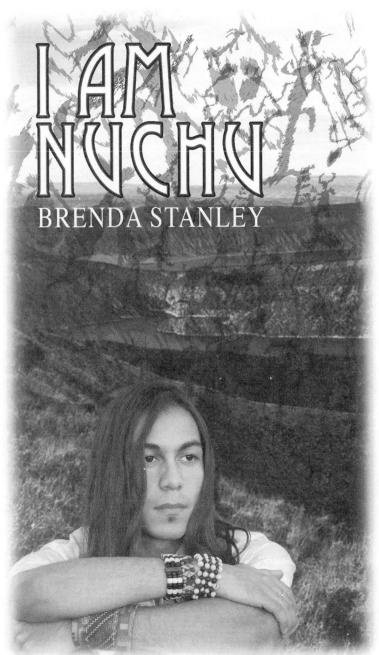

I AM NUCHU

BRENDA STANLEY

WestSide Books
Lodi, New Jersey

Published by WestSide Books
60 Industrial Road
Lodi, NJ 07644
973-458-0485
Fax: 973-458-5289

This is a work of fiction. All characters, places, and events
described are imaginary. Any resemblance to real people,
places and events is entirely coincidental.

Library of Congress Cataloging-in-Publication Data

Stanley, Brenda
  I am Nuchu / Brenda Stanley. -- 1st ed.
    p. cm.
  ISBN 978-1-934813-47-8
[1. Racially mixed people--Fiction. 2. Race relations--Fiction. 3.
Indian reservations--Fiction. 4. Ute Indians--Fiction. 5. Indians of
North America--Utah--Fiction. 6. Divorce--Fiction. 7. Moving,
Household--Fiction. 8. Utah--History--20th century--Fiction.] I. Title.

PZ7.S78686Iah 2010
[Fic]--dc22

                                                              2010031120

International Standard Book Number: 978-1-934813-47-8
School ISBN: 978-1-934813-48-5
Cover design by Amy Kolenut
Interior design by David Lemanowicz

Printed in the United States of America
10 9 8 7 6 5 4 3 2 1

First Edition

I AM NUCHU

1

"Wake up!" Cal said, nudging Doran with one hand while trying to steer the truck with the other.

Doran stirred and adjusted his position against the door.

"Doran. Get up and see this." Cal yelled as he surveyed the area.

Doran slowly pulled his tall lanky frame upright. He squinted, straining to see what was so urgent. "I don't see anything," he mumbled, looking out over the barren, insipid hills.

Cal scoffed and wiped the sweat from his dark brow, "Welcome to hell, little brother. This is our new home."

It was the fall of 2009, and the war in Iraq was entering its seventh year. The entire country felt confused and uncertain, but for Cal the only thing he felt was anger about why he was on a lonely highway, hundreds of miles from home. It had been a long night's drive, and when the morning sun rose, peeling back the darkness to reveal the barren plains of Eastern Utah, Cal wanted someone to confirm that it wasn't all a bad dream.

The two brothers sat silently staring out at the brick colored dirt and unending sky of the Uintah Basin as the old 1973 Chevy truck, piled high with their belongings, rolled along. Desolate red rock cliffs jutted out awkwardly, lifeless with the exception of clinging sagebrush. The air felt like an open oven, and the road shimmered from the heat. Dried out trees dotted the land; gangly masses with rope-like branches that reached out in disarray.

"This isn't it?" asked Doran hopefully.

"If it isn't, we'd better be rounding a bend sometime soon, because the sign back there said, 'Fort Duchesne, 4 miles'"

Doran searched the road ahead of them. "Where's Mom?" he asked.

"She's up there. She's mad at me."

"Why?"

Cal shrugged flippantly, "We stopped about an hour ago for Rachel to pee. You slept through it. I asked her if she was going to try and date the Indian chief or start over with the butcher or the baker."

Doran shook his head. "Why do you have to say things like that? Dad was no angel, either."

Cal scoffed, "Whatever, but at least he'd never bring us to Podunk, Indianville, Utah."

"Where else could she go? This was her home. Aren't you even a little curious about what this place is going to be like?"

"Look around." Cal said, cutting Doran off. "This place is hell."

"What about Grandpa? Aren't you curious about the

Indians? We've been asked about them all our lives," said Doran, motioning to their dark skin. The brothers were used to the questions about their origins. They were born and lived their entire lives in the crystal clean, lush foothills of the Spokane Valley. While both boys were undoubtedly not white, most people guessed Spanish or Italian; rarely did anyone ask if they were Native American.

Cal laughed hard, "What are you, five years old? The Indians! This isn't the old West. That's crap about Grandpa. What the hell kind of grandpa is he? He's visited us once, and I don't think he's ever sent us a birthday card. This place is going to be horrible. That's why Mom lied about it every time we asked. It was her home...if she was proud of it; you'd think she'd tell us the truth about it."

Doran sighed, "I know Mom's pretty upset. I heard her talking to Dad on the phone. She was crying pretty hard. I've never seen her like that."

Cal shrugged, trying to act as if he weren't affected by what his younger brother said. But inside, Cal was devastated by the divorce. Not only was he taken from his father. He also was losing his identity with every mile they drove, a piece of who he was being chipped away and left along the side of the interstate. He had no idea where he was going or how he'd be perceived in the strange and unfamiliar place where he'd soon be living.

"Do you think they might get back together?" asked Doran, wanting to talk.

"I doubt it. Even if they wanted to, it'd be hard with us out here and Dad back in Spokane."

Doran reached down and began to fiddle with the radio.

"Don't bother," Cal said, "There hasn't been a radio station or a sign of life anywhere for the last two hours."

The previous month was a blur to Cal. The problems between his parents seemed to begin when he was injured during one of his football games. He'd intercepted a pass and was hit hard in the stomach. The blow ruptured his spleen, requiring him to have surgery, and it was during his stay in the hospital that his father grew distant. This not only confused Cal, but frustrated him because he was too weak to find out why. Soon after he came home from the hospital, his mother announced they were getting divorced. Almost as bad, she was moving with the children back to where she grew up: the Fort Duchesne Indian Reservation in Eastern Utah.

Horrified with the thought of leaving the only home and friends he'd ever known, Cal at first refused to leave. But his father shunned the idea of him staying, then scolded him for even considering deserting his brother and sister on the reservation. Cal felt ashamed, then became consumed with making his father proud of him once again. But without sports, he felt that it might be hopeless. His injuries kept him from trying for a football scholarship, and now the divorce and move eliminated his chances to go for one in basketball.

While Cal was devastated that his dreams of being a college athlete were in ruins, he vowed he'd go to the University regardless and try to walk on as a red shirt at football tryouts. He spent many sleepless nights plotting and brooding over his situation. The reasons for his parents' failed marriage were a mystery that haunted him. When the divorce was announced, Cal was indignant and pestered his parents with questions, only to find his father more frequently absent and his mother quiet on the topic. He constantly taunted and picked at his mother, hoping to upset her enough to lash out and say something that explained why everything had fallen apart.

A shield of anger soon numbed Cal's pain. He would have crumbled had his father hugged him or his mother insisted that it wasn't his fault. But even as he stood on the cusp of manhood, the boy inside fell asleep each night sobbing and woke up devastated to find that it all wasn't just a bad dream.

As the truck bumped along the small highway, Doran stared out at the dismal land. The majestic, forested mountains of Eastern Washington disappeared, and everything he saw, no matter where he looked, was burnt and dusty.

Doran's height made it hard for him to be comfortable in a car for a long time; although both brothers were tall, Doran had passed Cal by an inch that year. They were alike in other ways, too. Both had identical black hair, healthy bronze skin and engaging, perfect smiles.

The small red Mustang was directly in front of them and Cal saw his younger sister Rachel's black ponytail bobbing as she sat in the seat next to their mom. Rachel seemed older and prettier every time Cal looked at her, and she, too, wanted answers about the divorce. But like Cal's questions, Rachel's were also dodged. She'd sobbed when she found out they were moving, and it broke Cal's heart to see her confusion and not be able to comfort her with answers that made any kind of sense. Only Doran seemed content in not knowing, but that didn't surprise Cal; Doran was never bothered by much of anything and it always drove Cal crazy.

Eventually, a large cluster of triangular shaped adobe buildings appeared at the left. They shot up at odd angles and bore an obvious semblance to a gathering of teepees. The pointed buildings were deserted and worn, but with a prominent sign that read, "Bottle Hollow." Mom flipped on the turn signal and Cal followed her down a small, badly paved road. Both Cal and Doran were surprised to see an immense dark lake appear out of nowhere. No boats or swimmers, just the water surrounded by parched red dirt. The water was an ominous cobalt blue, and so still that the sun reflected like a photograph off the glassy surface of the lake.

Their mom began to slow down and Cal's heart sank. The road dipped and they saw a sign that read, "Entering Fort Duchesne Reservation." He expected to see houses and stores, but instead there was nothing but more scorched and barren road.

"My God, could this be any farther out in the middle of nowhere?" Cal scoffed. He was scared, and he hoped that Doran didn't see it in his eyes.

As they continued to drive, the large ragged trees appeared again, lining the road. Cal gazed into their knotted branches, letting his tired mind wonder. He imagined himself in the trees, first walking through them, carefully stepping over the shabby growth, and then beginning to run. The roots tripped him as he went, and the branches began extending toward him, clinging and trying to hold him as he struggled against their pull.

"Cal!" Doran shouted.

Cal snapped out of his daydream as the truck barreled toward the Mustang; their mom had stopped to make a turn and Cal hadn't noticed. He slammed on the brakes, but it wasn't enough to keep the ponderous old truck from hurtling forward; Mom and Rachel's heads whipped backward as the truck slammed into the rear of the little car.

An odd silence rang in Cal's head as he sat there in the truck, hardly believing what had just happened. Then he and Doran jumped out and ran to the Mustang. Mom was cursing and Rachel sat rubbing her neck.

"Are you okay?" Cal asked, flinging open the door.

"What were you doing? Why weren't you watching where you were going?" Mom yelled.

Seeing that they were fine, Cal was too tired and upset to argue or apologize. After all, he thought, it was his car that was wrecked. He walked back to survey the damage and his stomach heaved when he thought about the hours he and his father spent restoring the 1965 Mustang, sanding, painting, and buffing, and now it was ruined. He imagined the disappointment his father would feel when he found out what had happened.

Unable to look at the damage anymore, Cal turned and leaned against the car. *Things couldn't be worse*, he thought. He'd lost his father, his home, his friends—and now his car. In despair, he covered his face with his hands.

Cal peeked through his fingers as their mom and Rachel slowly pulled themselves from the Mustang. Their mother, Mona, was short and husky, and her coarse black hair was ratted and wiry from the long drive. She stretched and rubbed her neck again, then looked over at Rachel, who was busy tucking loose strands of hair back from her face. Cal couldn't help but notice the differences in their shapes. Rachel stood on pencil-thin legs, and even her neck was long and slender. Mona was proud of Rachel's height, and Cal often heard his mother bragging on the phone to her family about the respective altitudes of each of her tall children.

"We can fix the car," Doran said, trying to comfort his older brother.

Cal started to reply to Doran, but stopped mid-breath and stood with his mouth gaping as he noticed the reservation spread out before him. There the town sat in the belly of the flat, scorched valley. All he could see were small, rundown houses, lined up in perfect rows; many with their door screens swaying, barely hanging on by a string. Their paint was flaked and faded, and blackish green stains ran down the outside walls by some of their windows.

Mona continued to complain to her son, "Didn't you see I was turning?"

Cal waved his hand to quiet her and grunted. He walked past the three of them and toward the town, then stopped and studied the area intently, trying to find something redeeming. *There had to be a "nice" part of town*, he thought. But as he searched, all he found were the dismal signs of poverty and distress.

Cal held out his hands in exhaustion, "This is what you brought us to?" he asked turning back to Mona, who leaned against the car, still rubbing her neck. "I can't believe you made us leave Spokane for this!"

"Don't start with me, Cal! What was I supposed to do? I have no family in Washington. I've never had a job there. At least here I have someone to help me look after you."

"What about Dad? He would have helped."

"I told you before, Cal, your father didn't want me to stay—I tried. I only want to do what's best for all of you."

Cal turned his back on her, knowing it was useless to argue. He'd tried before to convince her to stay in Spokane, but his arguments got him nowhere and now, after driving hundreds of miles, there was no point in arguing more.

Doran stood silently listening, but offering no comments. He truly hated conflict, and like his mother, he avoided it at all costs. When Cal looked him in the eye, Doran just lowered his head as Cal rolled his eyes and kicked the ground in frustration.

"Hey, look!" Rachel called, pointing to the sky.

They all looked above the trees where a large, shadowed wingspan glided silently overhead. Cal shielded his eyes as the bird swooped into the setting sun. It was a bald eagle. Cal watched as the bird soared, then circled above them. Its black body glistened in the sun and seemed even more brilliant than its white head and tail.

What is this beautiful creature doing in a place like this? he thought. Cal wanted to scream out, "Fly away! You can, you know!" He stood and watched the bird soar above him, and then reach its talons for a branch in one of the ragged trees. For a moment he believed the eagle made eye contact as it sat majestically looking down its nose at him. Cal dropped his head forward, took a deep breath, and ran his fingers through his hair. Then he turned and walked back to his family, took a quick look at his car, rolled his eyes and mumbled, "Let's get on with this."

A strong feeling of despair tugged at Cal as he drove the truck slowly into town. Small children romped and played in the non-existent yards of the paltry little homes. Outside, Indian men and women sat on mismatched patio furniture, each of them with a tall bottle of beer resting somewhere close by. Cal looked at them with pity, yet they didn't seem unhappy. They all stared back at him as the truck passed by. The people didn't talk to one another; instead they just studied the two strange vehicles. Although they didn't appear unfriendly, no one smiled or even nodded at the newcomers. Cal noticed that their black hair and rust-colored skin looked very much like his own, but he assured himself that he wasn't like them at all.

"Wow, look at that truck," Doran commented, pointing out his window, "And here's another one. They're brand new!"

"There was a new Camaro back there, too," said Cal. "Seems weird."

"They're not theirs, are they? They can't possibly afford something like that, living here."

"If you could afford something like that, why would you stay?" Cal quipped.

Mona pulled into the driveway of one of the boxy little houses. Cal parked and shut off the truck, and sat in awe as the stocky older man they knew as their grandfather stepped from the house and shaded his eyes from the sun. Cal's disappointment softened as he watched his sister walk up and embrace their grandfather. Just knowing this man

16

was his relative was comforting, especially after the long and uncertain drive.

Raymond lived alone. Mona's mother Dorothy died when Cal was very young so it was hard for him to remember what she looked like. And although Cal only saw his Grandpa Ray once, he was the first familiar face he'd seen in days and he was glad to see his husky, sturdy presence and weathered face.

As the house filled with noise and activity, Raymond stood quietly grinning, with his hands clasped in front of him. Mona told Cal that Grandma Dorothy's father was a Navajo, which is why Mona's face was long and her nose narrow. Since Cal had never seen another Ute Indian besides his mother and pictures of his grandparents, he never understood her obvious pride about her distinct features.

Grandpa Ray's home was small, but considering the rest of the houses Cal saw as they drove into town, it was surprisingly clean. The carpet was soft and worn, and an aroma of baking bread filled the air.

"Do you cook?" Cal asked Raymond.

"Only when I want to eat," Raymond answered in a soft monotone voice. It was so like Mona's voice, distinct and deliberate, yet sometimes almost muted. It was something his friends in Spokane noticed when his mother spoke, but Cal had never thought about it until now.

Cal ignored his grandfather's sarcasm and walked around looking at the pictures of himself and his siblings, carefully placed on almost every wall and table. Cal's heart ached when he looked at the photos of David and Mona, taken when things were happy.

17

"Who are this lady and baby?" Cal asked Mona as she unpacked.

She looked up at the picture, "That's Jackie," she answered quickly.

"My aunt?" Cal bent down closer, "Who's the kid?"

"That's her son."

"Her son? You never told me I had a cousin. What happened to him?"

"Nothing, his father took him after Jackie died."

"Why didn't you ever tell us we had a cousin?"

Mona shrugged.

"What?" Cal pried, "Why didn't you tell us?"

"I don't know."

"Jesus. All these years, you fail to mention I have a cousin? What else haven't you told me?"

Mona looked up at him with exhausted eyes, "Cal, I'll talk to you about it some other time. I'm tired and I want to get unpacked."

Cal picked up another picture with Mona and Jackie sitting close together and smiling. "Nice hairdo Mom...and dig those groovy necklaces. Are those puka shells?" He looked up for a response, but Mona just ignored him. He studied the picture more closely. "God, she was beautiful. Why don't you ever talk about her?"

Mona turned to him, looking annoyed with his questions, "Because it hurts, Cal. It still hurts. Now please come outside and help me unload the trunk of the car."

Cal shrugged off her quickness, knowing that losing her only sister must have been devastating. He placed the picture back on the table and followed Mona from the room. When he stepped outside, he was again hit with the sight of the ramshackle homes of the Fort.

"How can people live like this?" he mumbled to himself.

Mona swung around, "Don't start criticizing everything," she said sternly, "Just because you didn't want to come, doesn't mean you need to start complaining about every little thing."

Cal stared at her strangely, "What's your problem? I realize you're tired, but give me a break. Every little thing? Mom, look around," Cal heaved one of the suitcases from the mangled trunk of the Mustang.

"Cal, you've only been here an hour. Why do you always have to criticize everything?"

"What are you talking about? I don't criticize everything! And if you loved this place so much, why'd you ever leave?" Answers. It's what Cal wanted desperately. *Why did this happen? Why did my life have to change?*

Mona paused and brushed a strand of her coarse hair from her weary face. She began to say something, but then shook her head and continued to unload the car.

"What?" asked Cal, "Are you going to tell me you actually liked living here?"

Mona tried to ignore his question.

"Then what is it? If you loved this place so much, why have we never even come for a visit?"

"Your father hated this place, but he didn't understand things. It's different here. I thought if I left, things would be better. I did it all for you."

"Yes. Things were better."

Mona paused. She took a deep breath and smiled sarcastically, "Different, yes. Better, I'm not so sure."

A small dust devil swirled in the field across the street, diverting Cal's attention. A group of children chased after it, laughing as the wind blew through their clothes and hair. For a moment he felt a rush of warmth fill his chest. He took a deep breath and allowed the cloud of anger to exhale. He watched the children romp and laugh, and he remembered the tiny tots' football team he coached each summer.

It started as a part-time summer job, but it had turned into something that Cal looked forward to each year. He loved kids and they loved him. At first he'd felt awkward, enjoying his role of coach and partial babysitter. Being a high school athlete and having the image of the tough, cool sports star didn't fit with the young man wrestling on the grass with a dozen five-year-olds. But it didn't take long and soon he lost himself in the joy and unabashed emotion of the children. He remembered back to that time of being happy and hopeful as he watched the Fort children giggling and running as the dirt swirled around them.

"It's nice to see someone having a good time," Rachel said, as she stood watching from the front porch, "How long do we have to stay with Grandpa?"

"I don't know," answered Mona. "Please let me at least get unpacked before you start in on me."

"Hey, look at this old gun," called Doran, walking out onto the porch, "He's got more of them inside."

Rachel looked at Doran, and then turned to Cal with an annoyed stare, "Gee, maybe we can all take turns bringing it to show and tell," she said.

Doran's face turned sour and he shrugged. "What?" he asked Cal.

"Nothing," Cal answered, feeling the way he usually did when Doran found the positive in any situation, no matter how dismal it might seem.

Now that they were at Fort Duchesne, Cal was full of questions. His parents' differences were becoming more and more obvious; however he still didn't understand the divorce. After almost twenty years, now they decide to split? It was so sudden, and even though he knew things weren't perfect, it hit him like a guillotine, sharp, cold and quick.

As Cal watched the kids playing in the blustery field, he thought about his own childhood and his perceptions about the Fort and the Ute people his mother talked about. His ideas of being Indian were rapidly changing here at the Fort. When Cal was a child, his mother sat in his room at night and told him stories about the tribe and the teachings of the Creator. Many of the stories talked about animals that possessed human qualities, like jealousy, curiosity, and love. His father had shrugged off the stories as silly folktales and rarely talked about the reservation or the brief time he'd spent living in the nearby town of Roosevelt, working on the oil rigs.

As Cal grew older, he too passed the stories off as childish myths. And while his interest in the Ute teachings faded, the appeal of being Ute was exciting. Cal's distinctive dark skin and hair made him different and he liked it. He often talked about his Ute blood as a way to draw even more attention to his unique characteristics. He embellished the stories his mother told and talked about his heritage, not knowing what that really meant, but neither did anyone else.

Cal was a writer and found it a release and a source of pleasure. He wrote for the school newspaper, and soon found that the stories of his ancestors not only gained him attention throughout the school, but also got him an easy "A" in both his journalism and English classes.

Both Doran and Rachel found they were equally admired for their distinct features, but Cal had one trait that no one else in his family shared: his piercing blue eyes. His friends called him "The Wolf," because during his basketball games, Cal's face grew intense and his eyes flashed, as if stalking his prey. When his crowd of friends saw this happening they always howled, which intimidated the other team and gave Cal a signature few other high school players could claim. It also fostered pride in his Indian roots, which he now found himself questioning on the reservation. Mona had always hated the howling and told Cal to make his friends stop. But since she rarely came to his games anyway, he didn't see the point.

Raymond took his jacket from the hall closet, then told them, "I'll be back later. I'm going to the lodge."

Mona nodded and turned back to the television.

"Where's he going?" Cal asked.

"He has meetings," Mona answered.

"What kind of meetings?"

"Your grandfather is an Elder in the tribe. He makes decisions about the reservation and stuff."

"Decisions about what? How to sit around on your porch and let your house go to hell?" Cal cringed as a jolt of guilt hit him.

"Cal, knock it off! Your grandfather is a very proud man who would be hurt if he heard you say that. Tomorrow's the Bear Dance. They need to prepare for it."

Cal felt foolish and cold-hearted on hearing this so he left the room. He'd heard Mona talk many times about the ceremonies and beliefs of the Ute people. Her dark eyes sparkled as she told about the Bear Dance and the summer night rituals. The way she spoke made it all seem so mystical and special, but Cal knew that it was nothing but a fantasy to mask a childhood she most likely wanted to forget. The historical news articles he wrote with such passion and pride were beginning to feel like he was just dabbling in fiction.

Cal lay down on the small bed in the room that he and Doran shared. He pondered the life he'd been forced to leave and wondered if he'd ever see his home and friends again. He stood up, raised the blind of the small window, and looked out over the field across the street. He studied the homes that surrounded his grandfather's house, their yards speckled with broken toys and trash. It made him mad that Mona never once mentioned anything about the Fort's broken down condition. He felt like he, Doran and Rachel were being punished just having to live there.

"I can't stay here," he mumbled to himself. "I'd rather die than be trapped in this place."

A dull ache nudged at Cal, reminding him of the night before. It had been years since he shared a room with Doran, and his brother's loud breathing, combined with the old mattress, was enough to keep Cal awake, even after the exhausting day they'd been through. But the lack of sleep was not nearly as bad as the thoughts and questions crowding his mind. He dug through his suitcase for a clean pair of jeans and a t-shirt, then quietly headed for the bathroom to take a shower. The hot water hit his shoulders and back, relaxing him for a moment so he could clear his mind. As he stood there, letting the water turn his skin red, he let his guard down and the tears came at last.

Cal was glad he was alone and that the sounds of the water muffled his sobs. He took several deep breaths, allowing the steam to fill his lungs as he worked at bringing himself back from despair. He had to be strong for Doran and Rachel. They had to know that he would get them through this somehow. And he'd promised his dad he'd take care of them, so Cal knew he had to make it all right for them. Even being in such a horrible place, he couldn't be weak. Somehow, he had to convince his father to bring them all back to Spokane; he had to show their dad that he needed them as much as they needed him. Cal would make it right, and then they'd all be happy again. He wasn't sure how he was going to do this, but he knew he had to find a way.

As the sun crept above the unimpressive horizon of the Fort, Cal stepped outside and peered around at the place that figured in his wretched dreams. There were several people outside, but none of them seemed to be doing anything. He noticed their similar boxy shapes and dark complexions, qualities he thought for years were unique to his mother. Earlier that morning, as he stood combing his hair in the mirror, he found himself contemplating his own sense of uniqueness. Like everyone else on the Fort, he too was dark, but he wasn't like them. He was different. He was David Burton's son. It was something he always took pride in.

David was successful and well liked back home. It wasn't just his success in business, but also his ability to charm just about anyone. David was handsome and confident, and at Cal's games, he was often so busy laughing and talking with his many friends, Cal wondered what he was able to see out on the field or on the court. But whenever they returned home after a game, David made it a point to let Cal know what he did right, along with anything he did wrong. His dad kept Cal focused, and losing the chance at an athletic scholarship was as disappointing for David as it had been for Cal. And it also made Cal wonder if David had fought, or even wanted, to keep the kids with him in Spokane after the divorce. Cal couldn't help but blame himself for everything, believing that if he'd played better, if he hadn't been injured, it would have made a difference. Maybe then Dad would have tried to keep them all together.

Cal walked quietly around the house, looking into each of the small rooms and noticing the numerous framed photographs that adorned every surface. There were three bedrooms at the back, and two bathrooms; one in the master bedroom and one in between the other two rooms. Raymond gave the master bedroom to Mona and Rachel, took the smaller of the other two rooms for himself, and left the third for Cal and Doran to share. A small storage area was just off the kitchen; the washer and dryer were in the garage. The kitchen was the largest room in the house. It had a wide metal table and six padded chairs surrounding it. The dining area opened to a family room that held a yellow and brown floral sofa and chair, and a small television propped up on a large wooden bookshelf. Cal studied the pictures and all the trinkets on the shelf.

"I built the cubby holes and shelves because your grandmother never had enough space to put all her pictures on the walls or the tables," said Raymond, who was standing in the entry to the kitchen observing his oldest grandchild.

Cal wondered if his grandmother had possessed the same muted lilt as his mother and Raymond. "Mom said you were a carpenter," Cal said, then glanced at the metal bucket in the corner of the room.

Raymond noticed and told him, "The roof leaks. I should fix it, but I don't do much of that kind of work anymore."

"Why not hire someone?" Cal asked.

Raymond gave him a disappointed shrug and hung his head. "Stupid pride. I'm a carpenter. I should be able to fix it myself. I've been saying that for years now."

"The roof's been leaking for years?"

"It started out with just a drip here and there. Now I have buckets in just about every corner."

Cal was stunned and started to offer his help.

Raymond felt compelled to explain. "I could hire

someone from town, but they don't come out this way too often. I figure some day I'll just have to climb up on this roof."

Cal shook his head and felt uneasy. A twinge of guilt hit him and he wondered why. He stood grasping for words but found nothing.

"I did most of the furniture and finishing work in this house," said Raymond, hoping to break the awkward silence. "I built the tables too," he said, motioning to the end tables. They were unique, with polished tops that showed the rings of the tree, and they had sculpted, curved and knotted legs. The grain was stained, bringing out the brilliant fiery browns and contrasting black veins. Cal had never seen anything like them, but wasn't sure how to react.

"That's nice. It looks good," said Cal. Realizing his comment sounded forced and awkward, he put his head down and brushed by his grandfather. He opened the front door and walked onto the small cement porch. The screen door squeaked before it rattled and slammed shut. Cal couldn't believe he had to hold it up to open it because the hinge was broken and the door hung crooked. He felt the uneasiness of eyes upon him and glanced up to find several people staring at him from across the street. He looked away and stepped off the porch.

Cal cringed as he walked around his precious but gnarled car. It wasn't just a 1965 Mustang; it was a trophy that he and his father restored together, and now it was marred. He'd spent most of the previous sleepless night thinking about how to fix it, and his mood now was somber as he readied himself for the day ahead. His plan was to go into the town of Roosevelt and find a mechanic he trusted. Normally he would do the work himself, but without his father's vast array of tools, it was hopeless.

He revved the engine and backed out slowly.

"Whoa!" Doran yelled, slamming the screen door behind him. He pulled on a jacket and a piece of toast hung from his mouth.

"Do you try to be a slob or are you just naturally disgusting?" asked Cal as Doran threw himself into the car. Doran smiled a toasty grin, and Cal couldn't help but feel glad that Doran was there. They drove through the Fort, turning the heads of all the people who were busy doing nothing.

Across the field Cal spotted four young men, one bouncing a basketball as he walked. The four were rambling slowly, pushing and teasing each other. All three had the same thick torso as the others on the reservation and not one of them was over 5'7" but one was unusually thin.

"Are they our age?" asked Doran optimistically.

"Don't stare," Cal urged. They both looked straight ahead, trying to act as if they didn't notice the group.

The thin one spotted them and stopped the others. They all paused and watched as Cal sped up.

"Hey, boy!" Cal heard the smaller guy yell in a high-pitched slur. Both Cal and Doran turned back to see him jumping and waving as the rest of the group pulled him down.

Cal mumbled under his breath, "Hey, boy?"

Doran shrugged, "Do you think they'll be trouble?"

"Who knows?"

"That guy sounded drunk or stoned."

Cal scoffed, "It's so weird here. This place sucks."

Doran shifted in his seat, and commented, "Maybe the rest of the area is better. We haven't even seen anything outside of the reservation. It can't *all* be like this."

They pulled onto the highway and headed west for the town of Roosevelt. Small, beat-up looking houses dotted dusty open spaces. Fences made of rusted barbed wire and twisted wood sectioned off parcels of land Cal couldn't imagine anyone wanting.

"Nobody's heard of grass around here—there's no green anywhere," Cal said, thinking about the trimmed, verdant hills and flowering gardens of Spokane that he missed so much already.

They rounded a turn and traveled along the main street in Roosevelt. No chain-stores of any kind appeared there and although the shops were small and busy, they all looked tacky to Cal.

Seeing no garage or even a gas station, Cal pulled into the parking lot of an auto-parts store. The lot was filled with pick-up trucks—large ones—some even having four doors. A cowbell clanged as Cal and Doran walked inside, where the store brimmed to the ceiling with everything from camping gear, to spark plugs, to guns. The cash register sat on a long Formica bar, along which sat over a dozen men, all dressed in western snap-front shirts, jeans, boots, and baseball caps with the names of local businesses instead of sports teams above the brim. Steam rose from their cracked, mismatched coffee cups, all of which were held by rough, blackened hands.

The man behind the counter glanced over at the new-comers, showing little interest. After looking around a minute, Cal and Doran walked over to the bar. They noticed a "Help Wanted" sign and Cal nudged Doran for approval.

Doran smiled, "Go for it."

The cashier saw the two waiting and grudgingly pulled himself away from the conversation. "Can I help you?" he asked.

"Yes, we're looking for a garage around town that can do some body work on a '65 Mustang," said Cal politely.

The man leaned back and yelled over the buzz of the bar, "Hey, Henry! Do you know of anyone who can work on a '65 Mustang?"

The men at the bar chuckled and looked over at Cal and Doran.

"Henry there can do the job, but he ain't cheap. He's at the old Gordon's Gas station, down near The Wave."

Cal didn't have a clue where he meant, but didn't want to look stupid and hurt his chances at a job. He smiled, "Thank you." The man began to walk away, eager to finish his previous conversation.

"Excuse me, sir?" asked Cal.

"Yes?" the man replied, clearly annoyed.

"I was also interested in the job on the sign."

The room's low drone slowly turned to silence, and the eyes of everyone at the bar now focused on Cal. The man's furry eyebrows lifted in bewilderment and he sauntered back towards Cal, "What do you want to know?"

"He wants to know what a job is," yelled a tall man with silver hair and dark glasses. The entire group exploded in laughter.

Both Cal and Doran looked over at the men, confused. The man who spoke was the obvious leader. He was tall, with large shoulders and thin legs. His hair was wiry and combed back, away from his face. It had had a sheen that made it look silver, not gray, and he adjusted his sunglasses, took a large chug of coffee, turned and propped his elbows jauntily on the bar, then leaned back, ready to be entertained.

Cal looked over at Doran, who shrugged with confusion, then he turned back to the man, "I was interested in applying, I worked for a garage in Spokane, so I know quite a bit about cars," he explained.

"Spokane?" the cashier asked, as the entire coffee club listened. "Aren't you from the Fort?"

"No," Cal answered sternly, "I'm not from the Fort."

"I wouldn't admit it either," yelled the silver-haired man again.

Cal looked back, annoyed and confused.

The cashier laughed, but hushed the group. "What's your name?" he asked.

"Cal Burton. We had a small accident on the trip here. Normally I'd fix the car myself, but I don't have the tools here."

The cashier's eyebrows furrowed, "Burton?"

"Yes sir," Cal nodded, "My mother is from Fort Duchesne and we just moved here yesterday."

The room went silent and the man's face faded to a stare of disbelief, then he cut off the conversation and turned away.

Cal looked back at the group at the counter, almost all

of whom suddenly became very interested in their coffee. But the man with silver hair stood unchanged; Cal couldn't see his eyes, but he felt the sting of his stare as if he could.

"What happened?" whispered Doran, "What'd you say?"

Cal turned to walk out of the store. "Come on. Let's just go."

Before they reached the door, a voice rose from the center of the group.

"Hey! I hear the Lone Ranger may have an opening." Then the man threw his head back and guffawed.

The silence slowly broke as some of the men laughed uneasily.

Cal's hand was on the door and he stood looking out, then Doran saw his eyes narrow as an icy storm began to churn. Cal turned back to the men and walked slowly to the bar.

He stopped and the group sat glaring at him. Silver Hair pushed through the group and jutted out his jaw, as if waiting to be punched. "You got a problem?" he asked Cal.

Doran flinched.

Cal steadied his stance, "No. No problem. But you just said something that I don't quite understand."

Silver Hair strutted in place, then replied, "I said, 'I hear the Lone Ranger may have an opening.'" Then he smiled.

Cal looked into the empty darkness of Silver Hair's glasses to see his own reflection. There, he looked small and contorted in the shadowed finish. But he took a deep breath and stood straight. "Oh I get it," Cal chuckled sarcastically, "Because my mother's Indian—Tonto. Very funny. Well at least I'm not some big, dumb white ass who sits around with his red-neck friends. I bet you were born and raised in this hellhole. Well, at least I wasn't, and I'd rather work for the Lone Ranger than have a job seeing your lazy butt parked on this bar stool everyday."

Cal walked back to Doran, who stood at the door with a look of astonishment. Cal stopped at the door, then turned back to Silver Hair, "Do you even *have* a job?"

Silver Hair, who up to this point had stood smiling smugly as Cal spoke, reached into his back pocket and pulled out his wallet. He flipped it open and held it out toward Cal. "I'm the Sheriff here, you little shit. You already have one strike against you, with the last name of Burton. Your family has some nerve even showing up around town. Now, because you called my friends here names, you have two strikes. Are you gonna try for three?" Cal's heart sank as the men at the bar all glared in his direction.

The cowbell slammed against the glass door of the store as Cal and Doran climbed back into the car. "What'd we do?" asked Doran. "What did he mean, we have a strike against us because of our last name?"

"What's this crap about being Indian?" said Cal. "Do these people live in the dark ages?"

"Maybe it's something Mom or Dad did."

"What are you talking about?"

"The reason they hate our name."

"Doran, it's been almost twenty years since they lived here. They were our age, then. What could they possibly have done to make someone hate them like that idiot Sheriff in there?"

33

"He probably wasn't the Sheriff back *then*, and he said that stuff about us having the nerve to show our faces in town."

"Maybe he thinks Indians shouldn't come into town," Cal suggested.

"I don't know. It was more than our being Indian that pissed him off," Doran said.

Cal mused for a minute, and then mumbled, "Our being Indian. What's that mean?"

Doran shrugged, knowing Cal didn't expect an answer. The two sat quietly thinking as they drove back to the reservation.

Three shiny new pick-ups were parked in the driveway when Cal and Doran arrived back at their grandfather's house. The trucks stood out awkwardly against the weathered paint and torn screens of the house.

Cal heard talking and laughter as he entered. In the kitchen stood a large Indian man; his hair was long and tied back in a braid, and two Indian women sat at the table. As Cal entered the room, Mona quickly turned toward the sink. The room became quiet as Cal walked over to Mona, who kept her back to him as she tried to hide a beer bottle in the sink.

"What are you doing? It's 10 in the morning!" Cal asked, amazed.

The room was now painfully still. Mona remained silent, unable to face him. As Cal grabbed her arm and turned her around, the beer bottle clanked against the sink, making the two women at the table jump.

"What are you doing, Mom?"

Mona pulled away and said, "Whatever I want, Cal."

Cal slammed his hand against the wall and he pointed toward the women at the table, "This is why we've never been to this hellhole before. I can't believe you made us move here." He stormed out of the house, leaving Doran looking unsure if he should stay or leave with his brother.

The late morning sun beat heavily into the little car as Cal drove so he could be alone to call his dad. He *had* to talk to his father. He had to tell him what was happening, he thought. And then he'd surely find a way to rescue them. During the divorce, his father had all but disappeared, but Cal knew he couldn't ignore this. From a shaded park bench on the side of the highway, he took out his cell and dialed the number to the house he still considered home.

"Cal, that's impossible right now," David tried to explain as Cal ranted, "Your mother caused this, so now *she* can deal with it."

Deal with it? Cal thought, wondering why he suddenly he felt like he was a punishment. His parents weren't fighting over who got custody of the kids, but rather who got the short stick and had to *deal* with them.

"Besides, she has custody, and legally, I can't do anything."

Cal's heart sank hearing his Dad's excuse. "But Dad, this place is horrible. The people here hate us, and Mom's in that house drinking beer at 10 in the morning."

"Who hates you?"

Cal explained about the wreck and the men at the auto parts store.

"Has your mother talked to you at all about...anything?"

"No. Why? What's going on? Why did that man say that stuff about our name?"

"Cal, I never thought I'd ever have to go back to that place, so I never wanted you to know anything about it. There are a lot of things I have to sort through."

"Dad, I can't stay here."

"Be patient. If nothing else, you've got to stay and watch over Doran and Rachel."

"They shouldn't have to live here, either."

"Cal, do you think I like the way things are right now? I didn't ask for this to happen."

"Do you think I did? I feel like my life is over. Why'd you let Mom take us to this awful place?"

"I didn't *allow* anything. She caused all of this. I wasn't the one who was unfaithful."

A sharp pain stabbed at Cal's stomach. He slumped and leaned his head back onto the rough wood of the bench, waiting for his father to continue.

"I'm sorry Cal. I shouldn't bring you kids in the middle of this."

"Who was it?"

"I don't know...please..."

"What? Who was it?" Cal demanded.

"Cal, knock it off. This is between your mother and me. I'm doing the best that I can, Okay?"

Cal stood bleary eyed as a windstorm blew little bits of basin sand against everything standing in its path. "Okay," he mumbled.

The Uintah sun baked the road, melting it off the edge as Cal climbed back into his car. He pulled away from the curb, not knowing where he was headed; just that he wasn't going back to the Fort. As he drove, Cal's mind spun with uncontrollable feelings of hopelessness and thoughts of everything that had happened over the past couple weeks.

He usually felt so confident. His life, up to that point, was filled with one success and happy event after another. Even when something bad happened, he knew it was only temporary and it always passed. But now, he was dwelling on misery and having bad feelings he'd never felt before and it scared him. The stability he'd always felt with his father was gone, and the responsibility of watching over Doran and Rachel was overwhelming. He was turning eighteen next year and could get away from this depressing place, but how could he leave them alone here? Was it possible that he was sentenced to live at the Fort for another three years, waiting for his brother and sister to be old enough to escape, too?

Before his injury, college recruiters had already approached Cal to play football. But his injury shut down their interest, and with the move, any chance at a basketball scholarship was also lost. He wondered if he'd ever go to college, and these thoughts kept running around in his head until he wanted to scream.

Cal continued to drive, weaving his way through tiny tract-house neighborhoods and passing the small high school he'd attend. He wondered what the other students would see in him without knowing who he was. Would they take the time to get to know him, or, like the men in the store, assume he was just one of the Utes on the Fort? He contemplated that thought, and then shook his head, disgusted that he'd even worried about what any of these people thought.

The colors of the late afternoon sky were brilliant oranges and blues. Cal reluctantly turned his precious, damaged Mustang into the reservation. He drove slowly toward the house, feeling weaker and worse the closer he got. The place itself drained him, robbing him of his desire to live.

"Damn this place," he muttered, "Damn it all to hell."

2

Cal and Doran lagged behind, dragging their boat-sized feet as Mona led the way to the tribal arena. In the field surrounding the large wooden bleachers were brushy huts made of poles and dried branches. Inside several of the huts, people gathered, sitting and eating.

The arena was large and desolate, and the old and withering bleachers were in need of paint and repair. In the center was a tall pole standing alone as it stretched upward into the torrid sky. The red dust was everywhere, making the sun seem even more dry and intense.

A small group of people made their way into the arena. The bleachers could hold hundreds, yet for this event, the seats were barely filled. Everyone who came was Indian, and most were older people. They sat in the rows closest to the arena floor, and many of them were dressed in mismatched Indian attire. Mona walked over to a woman and they embraced. She pointed back towards Cal, Doran and Rachel, obviously naming each of them to the woman. She beckoned to Rachel, who pensively walked over and was introduced to a young girl who seemed to be her age standing with the woman. Cal looked around the arena, wondering why nobody his age was there.

The pounding of the drum began and curious, Cal looked up eagerly. Three men sat on metal folding chairs in a circle, each holding a long stick and vigorously keeping the rhythm. A long line of Indian women made its way to the arena floor. Another line of Indian men formed and faced them.

Cal studied them. Most were middle aged; but some were in high school. They were short and round, and very dark, making Cal wonder where the term "red skin" came from. His own skin was a rich, healthy brown, and the faces and arms of the Utes performing looked almost black.

Raymond appeared in the arena and walked to the side of the drummers. He called out to the dancers in a high-pitched wail. Cal wondered what the words meant, and why his grandfather was the center of attention.

The dancers started out with slow, deliberate steps forward, followed by the exact number of steps back. Cal watched intently, waiting for the steps to change. When they didn't, he became bored and his attention was drawn to other parts of the arena. He stared at the faces of the people of the Fort. Most were like expressionless masks as they gazed, engrossed in the dance.

"Are you sure they call this 'the Bear Dance' and not 'the bore dance'?" Cal whispered snidely to Mona.

"If you don't like it, go home," she hissed back quietly.

"Gladly. Jesus, is that all it takes to go back home to Washington?"

"You know what I mean," she grumbled.

Cal stood up and leaned down to her, "If you think I'm ever going to consider this dump my home, you're crazy." Then he walked off.

"Where are you going?" Doran called to him.

Cal swung around and grinned, "With so much to choose from, I can't decide where to go." The music of the dance paused and the people in the bleachers gave a weak round of applause. It caught Cal by surprise, but then he turned back to his mother and clapped loudly, like he did at an important football game. When Mona refused to acknowledge his sarcasm, Cal waved her away and walked off. When he was out of sight of the arena, he slowed his pace and simply drifted along the depressing, downtrodden streets of the reservation.

The sun began to fade and an orange haze rose up over the vista. Cal heard running behind him and turned to find Doran trying to catch up. "Why didn't you stay? You might miss something," Cal said, snidely.

"Mom doesn't want you walking around alone."

Cal shook his head, "Isn't any of this bugging you? Aren't you even a little pissed that we have to live in this shithole?"

Doran shrugged, "I don't like it, but what can we do?"

"Go back to Dad," Cal answered loudly.

"How? I thought we couldn't, with all that legal stuff..."

"That judge had no idea where he was sending us. Dad couldn't have known, either."

"Cal, he used to live in town."

"I don't care. It changed or else he's forgotten. He

41

wouldn't have let this happen if he'd known we were coming to this disgusting place."

They continued walking down a steep decline in the road. They could hear the sound of an engine revving, followed by quick slides and stops in the dirt. Eventually the boys came to the bottom of the sagebrush-covered hill, where a new red truck was being abused in an open field. Two young men were in the cab as a third one flailed around in the back, his long black braid whipped furiously as the truck spun, kicking up red dust into the evening sky.

"What are they doing?" asked Doran.

"Who knows?"

The truck swung around and the young man in the back clung to the roll bar of the truck, his legs flying out. Both Cal and Doran gasped, then the rider flung his legs back in and let out a triumphant yell. Without hesitation, the truck peeled out into a long succession of spins and turns. Several times it had to wait for the dust to settle before continuing.

"Maybe they're practicing for some type of event or race?" Doran suggested optimistically, his eyebrows up.

Cal looked at him, frustrated, as the truck continued to swerve and careen. When it came to a stop, the two brothers looked closely as the red haze fell. The rider in the back was still upright, but he was holding onto the roll bar with both hands. The truck began to rev again, but he called out to them to stop, then threw his head over the side of the truck and vomited. The two inside the cab ran out, hands above their heads in victory.

"Well, I wonder how many times they had to practice

that," Cal said. "I wonder if the amount of puke is figured into the score."

Doran smiled and shrugged at Cal's comment. He was continually feeling chagrin in situations, but it didn't stop him from hoping for the best. As much as Cal hated the thought of Doran being taken advantage of, he admired his ability to always find something positive about anything or anyone.

The brothers made their way back up the hill and out of view of the group in the truck. They walked for a long time, not speaking. It wasn't an uncomfortable silence; both were deep in thought. The evening air felt good, warm, with just enough of a cool breeze. The Fort didn't smell the way Cal had expected, and actually it had no smell at all. The air was clean and filled his lungs easily when he inhaled. He breathed in deeply several times, hoping it would clear his mind and stop the constant chatter of conflicting thoughts that were struggling inside his head.

The night closed in, and soon they were walking in the dark. The yellow glow of the streetlights barely reached the pavement. The Fort was placid except for the distant beating of the Bear Dance drum.

"This sure isn't what I expected," Cal mumbled.

"Me, either," Doran agreed. "Mom made it sound so—" he paused, "I don't know, fascinating. But then again, she really didn't. I made up a lot of the stuff in my head. Maybe I was just hoping it would be something good."

Cal raised his eyebrows and smiled.

"Maybe that's why we've never been here," Doran went on.

"No kidding." Cal said. "It was better when we didn't know anything about this place. I'd die if anyone thought we were from here."

Doran nodded in agreement, "I can't believe Mom had to grow up here."

Cal walked along thinking. "That's why I can't believe she wants us to have to put up with this crap."

Doran shrugged, "I don't know. If you grew up here and you never knew anything else, maybe it wouldn't matter. Maybe it seems normal to her."

"If that's the case, then why'd Aunt Jackie kill herself?"

Doran looked at Cal confused, "Kill herself? I thought Mom said she drowned."

"That's what we were told. Why didn't anyone ever say anything about this mystery cousin of ours we never knew existed? There's something weird about that whole thing. It's like this big family secret. Maybe that's why we never came out here. Maybe something horrible happened and Jackie couldn't stand the thought of living any more."

Doran worried about Cal's comments, realizing his inquisitiveness only led to arguments with their mother.

When they returned to their grandfather's house, it was dark and quiet. The sounds of the drum still pounded away in the distance, and Cal wondered if the steps of the Bear Dance had ever changed.

Doran headed for the kitchen and grabbed a cold drink from the fridge.

Cal walked to the living room and again studied the pictures of the family he never knew. "It all seems so strange," he said, then carefully lifted one of the frames from the wall and turned it toward Doran. "This is our grandmother. I'd never have recognized her. She looks a lot like Mom, and yet she's a total stranger." He put the picture back on the wall and then leaned in closely to examine the photo of Jackie and her baby. "She looks so...so happy. I can't imagine someone like that being raised here. Mom's her sister and she hardly ever smiles." Cal stood up straight, still staring at the photo of his aunt. "This is why I think she killed herself. She couldn't stand it here." He turned to Doran. "She probably took the only route she could to get out."

"I don't know, that seems pretty drastic," said Doran between sips.

"It's desperate," Cal corrected him. "But when you feel stuck in a place like this, I can see where you'd begin to feel that way."

The door creaked and Mona stepped in. Cal and Doran looked up from the picture.

Mona gasped, startled that they were home. "What are you doing?" she asked.

"What are you doing? Where's Rachel?" Cal countered back.

"She's still at the dance. Where've you been?"

"You left her there?" Cal asked.

"She's *with* your grandfather," Mona snapped back.

"You might as well of left her with a total stranger."

Mona walked toward them angrily, "Don't talk about him like that. What's he ever done to you?"

"Nothing!" Cal yelled, "Not a damn thing. He cared

45

so damn much about us, but he never did a damn thing." He reached for the picture of Jackie on the wall and pushed it out toward Mona. "Is that why she killed herself? He probably didn't do a damn thing for her, either."

Mona swung at the picture, knocking it out of Cal's hands. It fell to the floor, shattering the glass. She ran to it and began picking up the pieces. Cal sighed and bent down to help.

"Leave it alone," she screamed pushing him aside, "You have no idea what he did for her. She got everything she ever wanted. He loved her and she did nothing but hurt him." She drew back and examined her hand as a thin trail of blood appeared.

"Are you okay?" Cal asked.

"What do you care?" she screamed.

Cal shook his head, wondering why he even tried to talk to her. "So, tell me how," he said, going back to her comment.

"How what?" she answered, annoyed.

"How she hurt him?"

Mona stopped picking up the glass and turned to him defiantly. "She fought him. Nothing was ever good enough for her, not the house, her clothes—nothing."

Cal rolled his eyes.

"What's that supposed to mean?" she snapped.

"This place is a hell hole, Mom. Can't you see that? The roof leaks, the paint's chipping, and the screen door's hanging off its hinges. It's a mess."

Mona stood up calmly as tears filled her deep brown eyes, "This is my *home*," she told Cal. "You may think it's hell, but it's still my home." She stood looking at him, her bottom lip quivering. "At least the people here care about us. They want us here. You may hate it, but it'll always be home."

Cal got to his feet and swallowed hard. He stared at her quietly for a minute, watching her tears. "It isn't my home, and it never will be." He turned and walked down the hall to his room, a guilty knot stuck in his chest. As he closed the door, he heard Mona swear and what sounded like another picture crashed against the wall next to his door. Cal cringed and knew what he'd said was wrong.

He pulled his journal from under the bed and wrote about the events of the day. He poured out his expectations about the Bear Dance and how different it was from the way he'd pictured it, he wrote about the men at the auto parts store and how they'd called him Tonto, and the weird reaction to his last name—Burton. What was it that made them react that way? He cried again that night until his head throbbed, but he kept his sobs silent. He felt defeated and helpless, but he vowed never let anyone know that it'd brought him to tears.

The dusty morning air made it hurt to breathe as Cal walked across the reservation with Doran. They each dribbled a basketball as they headed to the tribal center where their grandfather told them they'd find a gym.

Cal was still uneasy about the argument with Mona. He wanted to talk to her, but instead he ignored his mother and couldn't make eye contact when his grandfather spoke to him. The crisp sting of an Eastern Utah autumn pinched at his face, making him wonder what the winter would bring.

"Look at that Camaro," said Doran, pointing off to an immaculate, shiny vehicle parked next to one of the small, diseased looking houses, "...and that truck. They must be brand new."

Cal huffed, "I don't understand it. Mom says they get money from the oil that comes off the reservation. So they all buy these killer cars and let their houses turn into slums."

Doran paused. "So what's the deal with Mom?" he asked cautiously, "It's like I don't even know who she is anymore. Why's she acting this way?"

"I don't know." Cal shrugged. "I can't believe she'd be like that around Rachel. She never drank back home."

"Who was that girl with Rachel yesterday?"

"I don't know, probably belongs to of one of Mom's wonderful drinking buddies."

"Well, at least maybe Rachel's found a friend. We've been here two days and all I've seen are those four Indian guys. Do you think they go to the same high school as us?"

"I guess we'll find out tomorrow," said Cal as he kicked a beer bottle out of the way.

"Did you ask Mom about those men in the parts store? What they meant about our name?"

"Yeah, she says the people in town have a problem with Utes because of all the money they make off oil. Isn't it obvious there's something to be jealous about?" Cal asked sarcastically, extending his hands to include the whole reservation.

"But those guys knew our name, Cal. You saw it. They turned weird when they heard we were Burtons."

Cal shrugged. Everything about the place was weird to him. He couldn't help thinking about the school and the familiar places he'd left. There were so many friends, and all those dreams that now were hanging idle as he tried to catch up to the problems that dominated his every thought. As he walked across the Fort, he thought about what he once imagined about the reservation. He always knew he was part Ute Indian, and had fantasized as a child about what his mother's home on the reservation was like. He visualized the beating of a single drum, as mighty painted warriors pranced and cried out in high pitched shouts at the night. There were feathers and teepees, and everything else that Cal saw on television. He'd been proud of his heritage, even though Mona tried to tell him it wasn't like what he saw in the movies; and now, it made him feel ashamed.

The tribal center was a large red brick building with blue and yellow bricks patterned around the top to resemble feathers in a headdress. The tile floors inside the hallway were chipped, and piles of equipment, files and orphaned office supplies lined the walls. Signs pointed to a library and a meeting hall. An older Indian man greeted them in a pleasant but monotone voice and directed them to the gym. It was large, with an amateurish painting of a buffalo skull and feathers covering the entire main wall. Cal felt a slight sense of comfort as the ball hit the gym floor with its familiar echo.

They shot free throws, practiced lay-ups, and then began a game of one on one. It felt good to sweat, to work out some of the frustrations they were both feeling. Just being back in a gym made Cal feel closer to his father and home. David had always told the boys that playing sports meant everything. It kept you healthy, it taught you discipline and determination, and it got you ahead in life, if you were willing to work hard enough. Cal had always put sports first; he lived and breathed it. And it'd always kept Cal and David close. After his accident, Cal had worried that David was disappointed he couldn't finish the season. But now he was just concerned that David might lose all interest in him, especially since he couldn't see Cal play anymore.

As Cal turned to make a shot, three of the Indian boys they'd seen the day before came into the gym, laughing and bouncing a ball. When they spotted Cal and Doran, they froze. Cal held the ball and Doran turned to face them. And for a brief moment, they all just stood there, staring silently.

A loud, peculiar laugh came from outside the gym and the smaller guy pushed his way through the group. He flipped his long sloppy hair back with his hand and looked over at Cal and Doran. "Hey, it's you," he said, with a slurred voice.

It's that "Hey, boy" kid, Cal thought. He looked at Doran as the others began to stir nervously.

The young man walked over to Cal, who was unsure what to do. "Hey, is this your ball? Is it?" he asked loudly.

"Yeah, it's my ball," Cal answered, wondering what to do next.

The boy looked up at Cal with small, lazy eyes. The bridge of his nose was flat and his mouth hung to the side.

"Are you gonna play with my brother Johnny? Are you?" he said, wiping his nose with his hand.

Cal looked over at the group, as if asking for guidance. "I don't know," he answered uneasily.

Johnny, who was tallest of the group, stepped forward. He was short, but he stood straight and seemed to tower over the others. His face was wide and expressionless, and his black hair hung down his back, tied back with a leather string.

"Eddie, go find your coat," he said sternly, addressing the smaller boy.

Eddie hesitated, looking back and forth between the two. "That's my brother," he said. "He'll punch your lights out if you're mean to me."

Cal smiled, realizing Eddie wasn't drunk or stoned, but mentally retarded, "Okay, Eddie," he said, reassuringly.

Eddie looked back at him suspiciously, "How'd you know my name?" he asked.

Cal began to answer, but Johnny took Eddie by the arm, "Go find your coat. Now."

As Eddie struggled, trying to free himself, Cal noticed numerous tiny scars covering Eddie's wrists. Johnny looked up and realized Cal was staring at the slash marks.

Eddie broke away and stomped from the gym, slamming the door behind him.

"Eddie's a retard," Johnny said, matter of factly.

"I..." Cal began to answer.

"And he's not my brother."

"Oh," said Cal, "I didn't realize. He said you were..."

"Well, he's not."

They all stood facing each other silently.

"Do you want to play a game?" Cal asked cautiously.

"Sure," answered Johnny, as the other two looked at him for direction. "This is my brother, Doran," Cal said. "We just moved here with our mother. She grew up here..."

Johnny smiled, "We know who you are. Everyone's been talking about Mona moving back. Everyone thinks she's nuts."

Cal looked at Johnny, confused. It angered him to hear his mother called names, but wondered, *Does Johnny really feel the same way about the conditions in the Fort?*

Johnny introduced himself, then pointed to one of the others who was as short as he was wide, "This is Puck," he said.

"Puck?" Doran asked.

"Yes," Johnny answered as Puck leaned forward to shake Doran's hand. "He looks like a hockey puck," Johnny explained as Puck stood smiling.

Puck had almost black skin and a brilliant white smile that beamed, and his eyes were framed with questioning brows. He firmly shook Cal's and Doran's hands, his warmth taking them by surprise.

Johnny shook his head and continued down the line, "And this is Fly."

Fly stood looking at the floor, his body shifting nervously. His clothes hung over his squatty frame, and his hair was short in front and on the sides, with one long braid that hung down his back to his waist. Acne scars covered his face, and his eyes never looked in one direction for very long. Cal and Doran looked at each other with a knowing glance, realizing he was the one being bounced around in the back of the truck.

"Why do they call you Fly?" asked Doran.

Johnny stepped in and answered, "When Fly was ten, he went to see the movie 'Peter Pan.' That afternoon, he got drunk and jumped off the roof of the tribal center. On the trip to the hospital, he kept yelling 'I can fly. I can fly.'"

Cal and Doran eyes widened in surprise as Puck chuckled.

Then Johnny bounced the ball and the noise made everyone jump, "So, are we going to play?" he asked.

"Sure," answered Cal, convinced things couldn't get any stranger. "How about Doran and I stand the three of you. We'll take Eddie when he finds his coat." Cal felt it only fair, since they obviously had them in height, and with both Cal and Doran playing on their high school team in Spokane, he knew that these three were little competition, even with an extra guy.

Cal learned a lot about his basketball abilities that day. He was used to playing against the lanky, tree sized athletes back home in the city. The Indians weren't tall, in fact they were shorter than anyone Cal played against, but they were quick and could shoot. Cal was caught off guard several times, and Johnny smiled when Cal cursed after having the ball easily stolen by Fly.

After several games, they took a break. Johnny left the gym to find Eddie, who still had not returned.

"Do you play on the Union High School team?" Cal asked Puck.

Puck laughed, "No, we try to stay away from that school as much as possible."

"What do you mean?"

"We don't need their crap."

Cal looked confused, "Whose crap?"

Johnny returned and, hearing Puck and Cal's last comments, answered, "The people in town. We avoid them."

"Well, I can understand that. We've already had our run in yesterday with your jackass Sheriff," Cal said. "But why give up basketball because of a few jerks? All the people in town aren't like that, are they?"

Johnny stood silently, studying Cal.

"What about school?" asked Doran, "How do you expect to get away from here if you don't go to school?"

"What are you talking about? Why would you think we want to leave? That's what they want us to do," Johnny answered. "If we move off the reservation, they can steal the rest of our land and we'll have nothing. We don't want to leave."

Cal sighed, "You don't want to leave. Why? There's nothing here."

"Maybe there's nothing here for *you*..." Johnny tried to continue.

"You're damn right," said Cal, "But I thought you said you were surprised my mom came back."

"I am."

"Why, if you think this place is so wonderful?"

Johnny looked at Cal apprehensively, "I thought because of your father."

"What about my father?" Cal asked.

Johnny looked at the floor as the others stirred nervously.

"What?" asked Cal, defensively. He thought a minute,

"Oh, I get it, because my father's white?" Cal shook his head in disgust, "You people are just as prejudiced as those idiots in the store."

"What are you talking about?" Johnny asked with frustration.

Cal looked back. "Let's go," he called to Doran, "We don't want to miss the morning pow-wow at our house." He looked over to Johnny. "That's where our mom and her other Ute friends gather around the kitchen table and get so drunk they puke. It's a beautiful ritual, one that makes me very proud."

He pushed his way through the heavy gym door and Doran followed behind. Outside, Cal took the ball and heaved it across the field.

"Can you believe those guys?" asked Doran.

Cal rolled his eyes, "It's like they're blind. I bet they've never been outside of this place...seen the real world. No wonder it's a dive. No one can see what this place is really like. I bet they've never been anywhere but this dump." He stopped and spread his arms and turned in a circle, "Look at this place. Why do they want this land? It's nothing but an excuse for being lazy."

Doran shrugged, "But what can we do? We're stuck here."

"There's plenty we can do. We're not like them, Doran. We may be half Indian," Cal said gesturing to his dark skin, "but in my head and my heart, I'm not, and neither are you."

Doran kicked a rusted can out of the way, "So what do we do until we're able to leave?"

"We start school tomorrow, which means we have at

least seven hours away from this place. We have to stay focused on getting ourselves and Rachel out of here."

"What about Mom?" Doran asked quietly.

"I don't know. She'll come around. She's still so shook up about the divorce that she isn't thinking right. She had no trouble leaving this place before; she'll realize soon enough that we shouldn't stay here."

Doran continued to keep up with Cal's feverish pace, "Would you feel differently about being here if you were full Indian?"

Cal looked at Doran strangely, "Why do you ask that?"

Doran shrugged, "It just seems that we don't fit in anywhere here because we're only half this or half that. We never had that problem in Spokane. Everyone thought it was cool that we were Indian.

"Half Indian," Cal corrected, "And that's because the people back home aren't prejudiced."

Doran thought for a moment, "But what about gays?"

"What about them?"

"Remember that big rally downtown? All those people were yelling horrible stuff at them."

"Yeah, but that was because of some political stuff. It's not the same."

Doran continued to think, then cautiously asked Cal, "Does it matter to you that Mom's who she is, or that Dad's who he is?"

"Of course not. What's with you?"

"Nothing. It's just that it doesn't matter to me, who they are, and I was checking how you felt about it."

"If it mattered, do you think I'd be hanging around this

place? If you think I feel any less about Mom because she's from here, you're wrong."

Doran nodded in agreement.

The red dust followed them back to their grandfather's house where Cal hesitated to go inside, not wanting to find the same scene he found yesterday. But the house was quiet as they walked in. At the kitchen table sat Rachel and Raymond. Several elaborate beaded necklaces were spread out on the table.

"Aren't they beautiful?" Rachel said, "They were our great-grandmother's. She made them herself, for her wedding."

"What's all that?" Cal asked Raymond, gesturing to a stack of old newspaper clippings.

"Those are stories about how our family fought against the Mormons to save the land," Rachel answered for him. "And that box has some very old clay pots. Some are over two hundred years old."

Cal shook his head slowly, "I don't know why you're filling her head with this stuff."

Raymond looked at him oddly.

Mona entered the kitchen and paused, hearing Cal's tone.

"You're trying to make her feel some sort of pride for this place, and I don't understand why."

"Cal." Mona tried to quiet him.

"Is there something wrong with me teaching Rachel some things about her ancestors?" Raymond asked quietly.

"It is, if it's all lies. If you're going to teach her anything, make sure you include a section about how the Utes feel about the white people, or even better how they hate half-breeds...you know, mongrels like the three of us."

"Cal, I've never said anything like that," Raymond said defensively.

"At least not where we can hear it. But everyone else is saying it, and at least they have the guts to say it to our faces. Is that why you never came out and visited us in Spokane?"

"Cal, that's enough!" Mona shouted.

"I never came out to visit because I was never invited. Besides, your father hates everything about who I am. He wanted no part of me or my culture." Frustrated, Raymond stood up.

"Well, that makes it very convenient. You say Dad hates you, but I've never heard him say that." Cal turned to Doran, "Have you ever heard Dad say anything like that?"

Doran lowered his head and shrugged.

"I have," Rachel piped up.

Cal swung around surprised, "You have? When?"

"Right before we left." She nervously glanced up at Mona, then turned back to Cal. "He told me the Fort does bad things to people. He said it ruined his life."

"Dad told you that?" asked Cal.

Rachel nodded.

"That's enough!" Mona yelled.

Cal ignored her. He barely heard what Rachel said, only concentrating on that fact that David took the time to talk to her at all. He hadn't talked to him, even though he was the oldest. Cal knew, just by the way Doran shrugged off Cal's question, that David talked to him, too. There was something going on that David didn't want him to know. He looked over to Mona, who started to clean off the counter. "What are you not telling me?"

"What are you talking about?" she asked.

"You're keeping something from me, both of you. Why would Dad talk to Rachel and Doran, and not to me?"

"Maybe he was sick of hearing your questions and your tirades," Mona said.

"My questions? He was never around to hear them. He took off and stayed away, but no one's ever told me why."

Mona stopped her cleaning. She turned, facing him with a tired, frustrated look. "We got a divorce. It happens all the time. It's not some big mystery that you can just hear the clues and solve. Look at the people we knew in Washington. Everyone was divorced. You're not that picked on, Cal. This isn't the end of the world."

Cal shook his head. "You don't care at all. You ruined my life, and you don't care one bit." Cal turned to leave the kitchen.

"It's going to be okay," Raymond said softly.

The statement made Cal stop and turn around. Then he saw Raymond gently hug Mona. She looked small and fragile in his arms, and Cal felt some comfort in his grandfather's actions.

Raymond looked over at Cal. "It really will be okay. The pain will subside and you'll be happy again. Let me help you."

"I wish you could help. I just..." Cal paused. "Nevermind."

Raymond released Mona and walked toward Cal. He held his hands out, "What is it, Cal?"

"I wish I understood more. I feel like there's something that's being kept from me."

Raymond nodded. "There is a lot that we can't explain. Some things we may never know the answers to. Sometimes that isn't all bad."

"I know. But I feel like my life's turned upside down. Everything I had and loved is gone."

"Sometimes it takes losing things and having change in your life for you to learn." Raymond looked back at Mona, who'd taken a seat at the table. "Life is supposed to be about experiencing new things and learning from them. You can't do that without challenges. Your kids will need your wisdom."

"My kids? That's a little far off," said Cal with a weak smile. But still, he felt the anxious chill in his stomach beginning to melt away.

Raymond smiled back. "Not that far. You can't have wisdom if you don't live a life of learning."

3

Union High School was small, with dark red bricks that blended in with the rest of the auburn land. It was the day Cal dreaded most. He'd spent most of the morning adjusting his clothes and combing his hair. He'd pulled on his lettermen's jacket. It was well worn, and the gold and blue were beginning to fade, but it was unmistakably the image he hoped to convey. Cal wanted the school to know he was an athlete. As he walked to his first class, the strength and confidence he'd always felt, sunk down to his knees and made them throb. He'd been with the same friends in the same neighborhood all his life. He'd loved his school in Spokane. He *was* a Lewis and Clark High School Tiger, playing both football and basketball. Many of the athletes there received large scholarships and went on to well-known colleges. Now he found himself walking the halls of a tiny high school, in a town most people never heard of. Worst of all, the divorce came right before basketball try-outs, which meant his chances for a scholarship were gone. His once bright future as a college athlete was dead, and any other aspirations he had were quickly dimming.

Most of the students in the halls at Union seemed normal enough. Some wore the western garb he'd pictured, and many of the girls wore their hair ratted high, with bangs teased so thin and tall, they practically stood straight up. He must have been staring at them with an obvious look of amazement, because several gave him a look back that was anything but friendly. He did get a few amiable smiles, but Cal couldn't smile back. He kept looking at everyone with pity, wondering if they knew what they were missing out on, in the world away from the Basin.

When Cal reached his first class, his face felt hot and his hands began to sweat. He opened the door and the entire class became painfully silent. Everyone sat up and took notice as Cal walked across the room. He handed the teacher, a small older lady with short auburn hair and large glasses, his admission slip. She smiled weakly and asked him to take a seat.

"We have a new student," the teacher announced with forced enthusiasm, "This is Cal Burton. Welcome to Union High." She lifted her glasses, trying to read from the small slip of paper. "Where are you from?"

Cal tried to smile as he answered, "Spokane, Washington."

"Oh really?" she asked surprised, "What brought you to Roosevelt?"

"My mom is from..." Cal paused, wondering if he should reveal the truth or give a face-saving lie, "here."

"Your mother is from Roosevelt?" The teacher asked slowly, trying to pull the words from Cal.

Cal cleared his throat. "No." He looked down at his

dark hands and arms resting on the desk. He then glanced over at the pale and freckled forearms of the girl sitting next to him. Cal looked back at his own arms and slowly slid them back and under the desk.

"Oh, are you living in Ballard?"

Cal shifted in his seat, "No, we live in Fort Duchesne."

The teacher tried to keep her expression in place, but she failed to keep it from slowly shifting into a pursed and condescending stare. Muffled giggles and whispers filled the room.

"Class!" the teacher yelled, "Let's get back to work. Cal, we're glad you decided to come to Union. Here's a book. If you need help catching up, see me after class."

Cal took the book, but couldn't help repeating in his mind her last statement, "If you need help catching up." What did she mean by that? He was an honor student.

It was barely after 8 a.m., and already Cal was exhausted. He wondered how Doran and Rachel were doing. The teacher's voice became an inaudible drone as Cal drifted off in thought. He couldn't believe that after the life he lived before coming to the Basin, he was now in this situation.

The people of the town either looked at him with sympathy or disgust. They didn't have to say a word; he saw it in their eyes. It made him furious. They didn't know him; they had no idea who he really was. They just assumed he was another Indian from the Fort. It embarrassed him to think about the pride he used to feel in his dark skin and black hair, his Indian blood, how the girls had loved it. The images of fierce warriors, their bodies sculpted and strong, were what he'd always pictured his ancestors to be. Not the unemployed alcoholics he saw around his kitchen table every night.

Cal heard desks moving and popped out of his daydream, realizing the class was already over.

"Don't worry, I don't think anyone is able to stay awake in her class," a soft voice said from behind.

He turned to find one of the only, truly beautiful things he'd seen since his move.

"I'm Katrina," she smiled. She had sweet eyes, and tumbles of naturally curly, dark red hair. Her heart-shaped face tilted to one side, "So, who do you have next?" she asked, trying to read off Cal's class schedule.

"Journalism with Henry," he answered.

"That's down the second hall," she pointed as they left the classroom together.

One of Katrina's friends, a taller girl with thin hair and the ratted bangs, slipped an arm through hers and gave Cal an odd look.

"This is Amy," Katrina said, smiling up at Cal.

"Hi Amy," answered Cal, not looking at her.

"Yeah, hi," Amy answered. She looked at Katrina urgently. "It's Mitch!" she whispered under her breath.

Katrina rolled her eyes as two guys approached from the side. Mitch, the more handsome of the two, slipped his hand around Katrina's waist, but she quickly pushed it away. He became annoyed, and looked over at Cal, who smiled to himself and looked off down the hall.

The boys were tall and dressed similarly, wearing solid color cotton shirts, jeans, and boots. Mitch wore an oversized belt buckle with a large silver bull hunched up and a cowboy riding it gloriously. Cal stared at it, wondering how anyone wore it in public.

"What are you staring at, Tonto?"

The name he was called and tone it was spoken in hit something familiar in Cal, and it dazed him for several seconds. "What did you call me?" he asked.

"You heard me."

Cal stopped moving and the group continued on. Katrina looked back sadly. Cal shook his head in disgust as Mitch threw an arm around her shoulders and guided her down the hall. Then Cal stood alone in the crowded hall, staring at nothing. He thought about the silver-haired man in the sporting goods store. He'd called Cal "Tonto," too.

"Cal!" he heard Doran call, "What are you doing?"

"Nothing," he mumbled, "How's your day been?"

"Kind of weird. I learned that you don't tell anyone you're from the Fort or they act like you've got some kind of disease."

Cal laughed. "You, too?"

"But, I did find out that basketball tryouts are next week and the practices have already started."

"I thought we missed them."

"No. I talked to a guy in my first class. He had a duffle bag with the team logo, so I asked him." All of Cal's senses took an incredible leap. If what Doran said was true, it could change everything. If he made the team, he knew he could attract some recruiters, and his dreams for a scholarship could still come true. Cal felt the urge to call his father and tell him the good news. He knew that it would make a difference; it would be his ticket back into his father's heart. Cal practically flew down the hall to his next class, and at lunch he quickly drove with Doran back to the house for his gym clothes. Mona was asleep on the couch, and they quietly gathered their things and left so as not to have to talk to her. The rest of the day dragged on, and Cal wasn't sure if they'd be allowed to try out. He stuffed an old player's roster in with his clothes, so if the coach wanted proof he'd been on the team back home, he had it.

The first thing Cal saw when he walked through the gym door was Silver Hair; same insolent stance, and same dark glasses. His badge hung from his belt for everyone to see.

First it surprised him, but then he saw Mitch and everything fit. Silver Hair was Mitch's father, explaining the crack about Tonto. Mitch was suited up and ready to play, as his father gave him tips from the side. Cal and Doran walked over to the coach. Coach Roos was tall and thin, and looked like he'd been quite a ball player in his youth. He wasn't a young man, but his hair was blond and thick, giving him a boyish look. He greeted them with little enthusiasm, until Cal showed him the team roster and encouraged him to call Coach Cather back home. As the two brothers talked with the coach, the boys who were warming up on the court stopped and stared.

In the locker room, as Cal and Doran changed clothes, Doran confided his uneasiness about the group.

"Sure, everyone's going to stare when two new guys come out onto the court. Who cares?" urged Cal.

"But they just looked at us like we were from Mars or something."

"I said, don't worry about it."

When they entered the gym again, the coach and Silver Hair were in a tense discussion. At the same time, Mitch and the others were convened in a discussion of their own. Mitch looked up from the group and glared at Cal.

The coach noticed the boys come in and quickly turned to them, "You ready?"

Cal nodded.

"Everyone, let's get started," he yelled, leaving Silver Hair and walking over to the bench.

Silver Hair walked toward Cal and Doran, and as he passed by, he mumbled, "The Indian league not good enough for you boys?"

Cal looked at Doran, his brow furrowed. Frustrated, he shouted back, just as Silver Hair was ready to open the gym door, "What are you saying? Aren't we allowed to play here? Or is it against the law?"

He stopped and turned back toward Cal, "You got a smart mouth boy. You'd better watch it," he snapped back.

The others in the gym were silent, intent on what was being said.

The coach clapped his hands loudly, signaling that practice had begun.

Mitch piped up and yelled over to the coach, "I guess they don't want to play."

"Enough!" the coach yelled back.

Silver Hair went through the door and allowed it to slam hard behind him. Then Cal took a deep breath, before turning around to face the others. Several of the guys grabbed basketballs and headed onto the court. Mitch stood with two of the others, making smart remarks about Cal and Doran.

The coach called everyone together and gave instructions. The practice started out awkwardly for Cal, but he pushed his frustrations with Silver Hair aside and concentrated on the game.

The others trying out were cold to Cal and Doran, and went out of their way to give them no encouragement or support. Cal felt that once they saw what he could bring to the team, all that would change. But even his best shots and steals were met with glares and rolled eyes.

At the end of the practice, Silver Hair came back into the gym. Doran cringed and looked over at Cal, who went for a lay-up. As he reached for the basket, Mitch rammed him hard in the side. Doran ran over to his brother, knowing Cal was hurt.

"What the hell was that?" Coach Roos called out as he ran over.

Cal held his side. Doran saw his eyes become fierce, the anger beginning to brew. Before Doran reached him, he blurted out, "Cal don't!"

Cal threw his body at Mitch and Coach Roos ran to hold Cal back, but not before Silver Hair got to Cal and pushed him hard to the ground

"You want to get violent, you do it somewhere else," Silver Hair growled.

"That son-of-a-bitch plowed into me on purpose."

"If you can't handle a little rough play, maybe you shouldn't be here."

Mitch stood behind his father and yelled at Cal, "Get the hell out of here! No one wants you here!"

"You're just pissed because you can't play ball in your stupid cowboy boots, you red-neck fool," Cal shouted back.

Doran nervously looked around the room, as some the other players took offense at Cal's outburst.

Coach Roos stood between them, "Practice is over. Franklin, you and Mitch go home. I'll call you and discuss this tonight."

Silver Hair turned his dark, shaded eyes at Cal, then walked out with his son.

When the gym cleared, Coach Roos walked over to Cal and Doran, who were sitting on the bleachers with their gear.

"You okay?" the coach asked Cal.

"That guy's got it in for us," Cal answered angrily. "I don't get it."

"Don't even try. Franklin Grayson acts like he owns this town, and he hates it when anyone talks back to him or challenges his power."

"But he hated us before I said even one word to him. He and his son both called me Tonto the first time they saw me." Even with the other boys off to the locker room and Silver Hair nowhere in sight, Cal cringed as he felt tears fill his eyes.

Coach Roos shook his head, "I'm sorry. I've found that's just the way some of the people are around here."

"Some? We've found it to be that way with just about everyone."

Coach Roos shrugged his shoulders, "It's not every-one. I wish I had the answers, but I don't. I've never coached any of the guys from the reservation. They've always stuck to the Indian basketball league. People don't like change around here."

Cal huffed, "But we're not *from* the reservation. And besides, there are some excellent players at the Fort, but I don't blame them for not wanting to be on this team and put up with this."

Coach Roos gave them little solace, but he did encourage them to play, and even with the frustrations of that first day of try-outs, Cal and Doran continued on, never missing a day of practice.

Everything Cal did that week was focused on making the team. He felt, somehow, that by bringing his skill to the squad, they'd want to treat him better. But the feeling bothered him; he'd never had to win friends before. Yet it wasn't really friendship he desired; it was respect. He needed it to play well. He knew there was no way he'd be able to shine without being part of the team, and he was reliant on them for the one thing he desired most. As he stood there in that large empty gym, Cal could feel his ticket to college quickly slipping away.

The chance he got to reveal who he really was came the next day in his journalism class. Cal sat steadily drifting off when the teacher, Mr. Henry, a tall, uncommonly thin man, wrote on the chalkboard in large letters, "My life." He put down the chalk and turned to the class. "I want each of you to write a profile story about yourself. Talk about your family and the experiences you've had that make you who you are today."

Unbelievable, Cal thought. It was his chance to let everyone in this school know that he wasn't your typical

Ute. It was his chance to tell them who he really was. He went through the rest of the day writing parts of his story during each class. As he wrote, the anger at the Fort welled up inside him and he had to stop to calm himself down. It was a unique and passionate tale that the teacher couldn't help but publish. And just getting the aggression out did him good. This project, along with the physical workout in basketball, made his life more bearable, and that was a start.

The practices seemed to go the same way every day. Mitch huddled together with his group and laughed loudly when Cal and Doran entered the gym. The strain of the practice took away some of the glares and snickers, but they always returned when everyone got into the locker room.

Cal found himself working harder than he ever did while trying out for his team back in Spokane. He sensed that some of the guys understood the benefits he and Doran could bring to the team, and they were actually decent to them. But most of the others followed Mitch's lead and acted aloof. Cal ignored them, convinced that once he made a difference during a game, the cold-shoulder act would end. Doran wasn't sold on that concept. He felt that all he did was run up and down the court. The ball was never thrown to him, and even when he did have it, no one was there to assist him. Any mistake he made was immediately greeted with groans and grumbles from the others.

When the day finally came that Coach Roos announced the team, Cal's stomach was tight. Making the team was everything to him. If he didn't have basketball in his life, what would he do?

He sat on the bench next to Doran as the Coach barked

out names. Cal knew he'd played his best, which was far better than anyone in that gym, yet he had the odd feeling that Coach Roos would crumble under pressure from Silver Hair and purposely cut him to make points.

When Cal heard his name called, he felt strangely deflated. He'd wanted it so badly, yet now that it was his, he wondered why. The coach called out Doran's name, too.

"Big whoop," Doran said leaning into Cal. "So I get to be laughed at and treated like crap for the next two months."

Cal shook his head, signaling that they'd talk about it later.

Later, they walked along on the crumbling pavement of the school parking lot toward their car, heads both hanging as though defeated. The exhaustion of proving themselves physically was bad enough, but the strain of being scrutinized for something they felt but didn't understand was overwhelming and wore them down.

Out of nowhere, a medium sized, brown and white dog scampered up on Cal's side. It startled him, but then made him smile. He bent down and patted its head. "Hey Buddy, where'd you come from?" It had short legs and no tail, and it resembled a furry pig. The dog panted and wiggled its backside, begging for more attention. Cal laughed and scratched its back, making its stubby tail bob furiously.

Doran squatted next to it. "I wonder whose it is."

The loud rev of a truck made them look up. It was Mitch. His friends were walking off to their own cars, and he sat in the shiny brown pickup, his arm draped casually on the open window, glaring at them. "Doogie!" he yelled.

The dog turned and sprinted toward the truck. Cal

stood up and watched as Mitch got out and pulled the tail-gate down, allowing the dog to leap into the back. Mitch leered at Cal and Doran as he walked back to the cab of the truck.

"Poor dog," Doran whispered, as the dog peered over at them and gave a goofy, panting smile.

"Doogie?" Cal said loudly, with a chuckle.

"Shut up, Jackass," Mitch grumbled. "Stay away from my dog."

"Gladly," Cal yelled.

The dog panted and paced in the bed of the truck. It went from one wheel well to the other, looking out and then back again. Mitch put the truck in gear with a grind and sped out of the parking lot.

"What the hell is it with him?" mumbled Cal.

"I wonder if Grandpa would let us get a dog," Doran said as they walked. "We couldn't have one back in Spokane because Dad had allergies. But now…"

"You don't give up, do you?"

Doran shrugged and gave Cal a simple smile that reminded him of the goofy grin on the dog. Cal just rolled his eyes and shook his head. His brother's unending optimism was something Cal didn't understand and it often frustrated him, but at that moment, it made Cal appreciate his brother and he was glad he wasn't stuck there alone.

In the car, Doran's happy demeanor faded as he contemplated the stress of being on the team. "Maybe we should have stuck to the Fort's team."

"Hell, no! Why settle for that? This crap with Mr. Redneck will end eventually."

"What do you think is going to happen? You make a couple of baskets at a game, and then everyone will like you?" Doran asked.

"No," Cal said quickly. He sat wondering how Doran had read his mind, and he felt foolish and transparent; it was what he hoped. Everyone always loved the star athlete. It *would* make a difference, and if they gave him the chance to shine, the team would benefit. Then they'd all see. At that point, Cal felt lucky to even make the team. He thought about Coach Roos and the risk he'd taken by choosing them.

Cal drove quietly through the dry emptiness of the Uintah Basin back to the Fort. He knew that it was a battle for the coach to put Cal and Doran on the team, and he realized then, that actually letting them play in a game would be a whole new war.

Autumn's cool breezes turned bitter cold by November. What green there was around the Basin shriveled and hid for the season. Thin trails of smoke wafted from every housetop, forming an ugly haze that spread across the sky and enveloped the sun.

Without basketball to keep him busy, Cal would have lost his mind; and even with it, he felt himself struggling to even want to get out of bed in the morning.

Doran all but gave up, but he'd made some friends and didn't seem to mind just sitting on the bench, socializing. At home, Cal found him doing small projects for their grandfather.

"Hey, look at this," he beamed as he swung the screen door closed.

Cal rolled his eyes. It always amazed him the way Doran found joy in such simple things. Though he never admitted it, Cal always envied Doran's optimism, but he wished that the same lofty hope would follow him onto the court. It never did; regardless of how Cal felt it would improve their standing at school, Doran seemed content with his small group of friends and his chores at home. Rachel, however, was different. She was more like Cal. He saw it in her and it worried him.

From across the dinner table Cal looked at Rachel; she just didn't seem the same anymore. At first, Cal thought she looked older, more mature. But then he realized it was more of a weathered appearance than one of growth. Doran stirred his corn in a circle and Rachel sat with one leg curled up under her, her ebony hair tumbled into her face as she leaned over her plate. With basketball and school monopolizing his time, Cal all but forgot about her and how she was coping with her new home.

"When did you get your ears pierced, Rachel?" Cal asked across the dinner table.

"About a week ago." She shrugged.

Cal turned with a disgusted face toward Mona. "I thought she wasn't supposed to have that done until she was sixteen."

Mona rolled her eyes. "Cal, it's just her ears pierced."

Cal looked back at Rachel. "Well, you shouldn't be wearing earrings that hang down so low. They look stupid. And are you wearing make-up?" The concern and care that

Cal was feeling came out in a way that made him sound like a tyrannical monster.

Rachel batted her black lashes, taunting Cal to explode.

"You're not allowed to wear that stuff. Now go take it off." If he didn't protect her, who would?

"Mom!" Rachel yelled.

"Cal, leave her alone," urged Mona.

"God, what's next? Are you going to start dating now? What happened to the rules that were set? And why are you all dressed up tonight?"

"I'm going to a dance."

"The hell you are. Dad would have never allowed this."

"Well, Dad's not here and you can't tell me what to do." Rachel pushed herself back from the table and ran to her room.

Cal turned on Mona. "She's fourteen. What the hell are you thinking?"

"Cal, it's a church dance."

"Where? What church?"

"The Mormon church. It's just down the highway. It's not a big deal."

"Fine. Then I'm going, too," Cal yelled for Rachel's benefit. He pulled on his lettermen's jacket and took a deep breath. "She's just a kid," he said softly.

Mona and Doran were silent.

Raymond spoke up. "You want to protect her. You're doing what an older brother should do."

"It's not doing any good."

Raymond smiled. "All you can do is show you care. They have to learn the rest on their own."

The drive to the church was long and silent. Cal convinced Rachel to let him drive her and April. When they arrived, he noticed Johnny, Puck and Fly in the parking lot, leaned up against a car.

"What are you guys up to?" asked Cal, walking toward the group.

"Nothing much," called Johnny back, "Why are you here?"

"I gave Rachel and her friend a ride. Aren't you going inside?"

The group shifted and shuffled.

"Are you waiting for someone?" Cal asked, trying to get eye contact with any of them. He looked into the truck and saw empty beer bottles lying on the floor.

Johnny stepped forward, "We're here to settle something."

"With who?" Cal asked.

Johnny shook his head, "Don't you realize why your sister and April are here?"

Cal looked at him oddly.

"April's seeing some guy from town, and Fly isn't going to stand for it."

Cal felt sick. "What the hell's going on here? April and Fly?" He looked at April, and then back at Fly. "I hope you're not serious. She's only fourteen." He grabbed Rachel by the arm and walked her back to the car. "You're not having any part of this," Cal snapped, as Rachel struggled to free herself from his grip.

"Cal what are you talking about?" she asked confused.

"You're not hanging around anyone who is dating someone my age."

Rachel stopped defiantly, "Cal. He's her brother."

"He is?" He looked back at Fly, who'd turned away. Johnny looked at him with a raised eyebrow, and Cal pulled at Rachel. "I don't care. I still don't want you in there. There's going to be a fight." As he neared the car, he heard a familiar voice call to him.

"Hi, Cal." It was Katrina, calling to him from the front of the church house. She wore a fuzzy white sweater pulled around her shoulders and her auburn hair blew in the wind. Cal saw her every day in class, but always avoided much more than a simple, "Hi."

Cal loosened his grip on Rachel. "Hey," he called back casually.

She walked toward him. "I didn't think you'd be here."

"This is my sister Rachel. I was just giving her a ride."

"Hello," said Katrina, smiling at Rachel.

"Yeah, hi," mumbled Rachel. She turned to Cal, hoping to seize the opportunity. "Thanks for the ride Cal; I guess we'll be going into the dance now."

Katrina smiled at Cal. "Aren't you coming in?"

Cal stammered, "Uh, I wasn't planning on it..."

"Oh..." answered Katrina sadly.

"But I guess I could for a little while," he said, releasing his grip on Rachel's arm. She scurried off quickly, and he watched as she disappeared into the darkness.

Cal walked over to the building with Katrina. "So where's your boyfriend tonight?" he asked.

"I don't know," she answered hesitating, "And he's not really my boyfriend."

"Will he be here tonight?" Cal answered, unconvinced.

"I hope not," she said with a smile.

Cal smiled back at her as they walked into the church. Cal searched for Rachel as they stood waiting to enter the gym. Katrina turned and looked into his eyes. He looked back at her, wondering if she'd have seemed so beautiful back in Spokane, or if the Basin's homeliness made her seem more attractive than she really was. At first she stood smiling at him, but then her smile faded and she looked away.

"What's wrong?" Cal asked, worried that she may have read his thoughts.

"Nothing," she said, glancing back quickly, "You just reminded me of something."

"What?"

"I don't know. It was like I'd met you before. Did you ever come to Roosevelt when you were younger?"

"No. Never."

Katrina shook her head. "I don't know. It's nothing, I guess. But it's strange. Your eyes remind me of someone I know."

"Who?"

"That's what's so strange. I'm not quite sure..."

The music vibrated the walls, and Cal's stomach twitched with the anxiety of entering a new place. Inside the gym, a large group was dancing and talking. Katrina put her hand through Cal's arm as they entered the noisy room. Several of Katrina's friends spotted her and bounced up to greet her. They gave Cal an unfriendly smile and tried to pull her away. He looked around the room for Rachel; he'd been so wrapped up in seeing Katrina, he'd forgotten about his sister. His head spun as he thought about Rachel and boys; she had no interest in them back home. A small pang of shame tugged at him as he thought about Fly and what he'd accused him of. But he hardly knew any of the guys from the Fort. How would he know Fly was April's brother?

Finally, he spotted Rachel. She stood along the gym wall, huddled with April, looking out onto the dance floor. He stood watching her as the music throbbed in his head. She looked curious and shy, but for the first time in months, he saw her smile. Cal took a deep breath and felt some comfort in seeing his sister happy.

"Do you want to dance?" Katrina called from behind, "You look like you're dying to get out there."

"Sure," he said, and smiled as he led her on to the floor.

She draped her arms around his neck and Cal pulled her close. Her long hair fell close to his face and it smelled like strawberries. For a minute, he let his mind drift off and he forgot where he was. Her body felt soft and warm as they swayed back and forth. He tried to talk to her a couple of times, but she avoided eye contact so he just held her close and talked through her curls.

The song faded to an end and Cal thought about how quickly it was over. As Katrina began to release her arms, she was suddenly ripped from his embrace. Cal was still so relaxed, he was caught off guard, making him an easy target. The blow knocked him off balance, but the dance floor was so tightly packed with people, it kept him from falling.

"Mitch! No!" Katrina yelled.

Cal gathered himself and charged Mitch. An older man in a suit and tie grabbed Cal from behind, but the force of Cal's speed and size was too much. Mitch was braced and ready for the hit as several other men in suits entered and tried to pull the two apart. Cal continued to punch at Mitch until he felt himself lifted from the floor. Mitch was also pulled back; he was breathing hard, his face was red with anger, and his hair covered with sweat. The two were led out into the hallway.

A tall thin man with glasses anxiously came between them, "We won't have that here. I don't care what your differences are, you will not fight in the house of the Lord," he looked over at Cal, "I think you and your group should leave."

Mitch huffed triumphantly and was led into what looked like a kitchen, where several older women began fussing over his scratches and bruises.

"Me and my group? I'm here with my sister," Cal yelled.

The group of men all looked behind him. Cal turned to see Johnny holding him up, and Puck and Fly like mismatched bookends on each side. They didn't speak, but did what the man said and began walking toward the door. Cal resisted Johnny's grip, "I'm not with them, and I can't leave without my sister. She's still in there."

The man tilted his head doubtfully and asked, "Who is she? We'll call her name over the P.A. system."

Cal cringed, thinking about how this would embarrass her. He refused to tell them, and again tried to shake himself from Johnny's hold.

The man looked toward Johnny who answered, "I think it's Rachel Littlebear."

"Bull!" Cal raged, "It's *Burton. Rachel Burton*." He began walking toward the door, but paused briefly at the group of men watching him leave, "I don't know why you're making me leave. He threw the first punch."

The men looked at him doubtfully, but one who stood casually leaning against the wall spoke up. "So, are you related to Mona Littlebear?" he asked.

Cal looked up surprised, "It's Mona *Burton*. I'm her son. Why?"

A tiny gasp came from the kitchen and the other men began to disassemble nervously.

Cal looked around, confused. He looked back at the man, who still stood leaning against the wall.

The man shifted his stance. Unlike the others, who were dressed in white shirts and ties, this man was in a plaid shirt and dirty jeans. He had a thin face and large brown eyes, and wore an elongated baseball hat.

Cal was curious, "Do you know my mother?"

"I did. It's a small place."

"Full of small minds," Cal shot back.

The man chuckled. "No wonder you're getting along so well with everyone. So, Mona and David are back."

"My parents are divorced." Cal flinched as he heard Rachel's name booming across the gym. "I guess that's my cue to leave."

Within seconds, Rachel stood red-eyed with her head down. She was obviously upset, but didn't resist when Cal took her arm to lead her to the car. April tagged along.

The cool air hit Cal like a slap as they walked outside. He pulled his jacket closed, but the chill seemed to penetrate his entire body. Once outside, Cal turned to Johnny, who stood waiting in the parking lot. "Why were you in there?" Cal asked.

"We saw Mitch and his group go in, so we knew there'd be trouble," Johnny answered in a soft voice.

"How'd you know that? You're never in school."

"We've lived here all our lives. We know how Mitch hates us and anyone from the reservation."

"But I'm not from the reservation."

Johnny looked down.

"I'm not," Cal urged.

Johnny glared up at him, "You don't have to say it like you're disgusted by the thought. We *did* help you."

"I don't need your help. I got kicked out of that dance because they thought I was with you."

Johnny shook his head slowly. "No. You got kicked out of that dance because you're an Indian and you're a threat."

"A threat of what? That I'm going to amount to nothing because I slough school and get drunk everyday? I may be half Indian, but I'm not like you," he looked back to the church house, "I'm not like them, either." The barking of a dog caught Cal's attention. It was Mitch's pig dog several rows over, still pacing the truck bed and barking at whatever moved. "I'm not like anyone in this hell hole."

Cal motioned for Rachel and April to get in the car and he sped off, leaving Johnny standing in the darkness.

4

The frigid sting of winter fell over the Basin, making the area even more barren and unfriendly than before. In the weeks that followed the dance, Cal kept to himself at school. Katrina tried to talk with him but he ignored her; eventually she gave up.

Cal worked even more diligently to complete his paper after the fight at the dance, slamming the Fort and making sure everyone was aware that he wanted no part of it. He wrote about his old life and how he longed to escape the Fort, just like his Aunt Jackie had tried and unfortunately failed to do so many years ago. He titled the story, "I Am Not from the Fort." He printed it out and put it neatly into a folder and handed it in at the beginning of class, feeling that he'd done some of his best work in it.

Near the end of the day, during his last class, a student peeked through the door and quietly motioned to the teacher. She went over and they whispered back and forth, and then the teacher turned to Cal and nodded. The student left and the teacher walked over to Cal's desk, then quietly motioned toward his books and backpack, saying, "Mr.

Henry wants to see you before you go to practice. You can take your things and leave now."

As Cal walked down the hall toward Mr. Henry's classroom, he began to wonder if his article was what Mr. Henry wanted to see him about. He probably was impressed with Cal's writing, and probably never experienced the horrors of the reservation. He might have been surprised that someone living there could write so well.

Mr. Henry was at his desk, reading through a stack of papers when Cal entered the room. He leaned back in his chair and motioned to Cal to sit in a chair next to his desk.

"Seems like you've made quite the splash since you got here," Mr. Henry said with his eyebrows raised. "You certainly enjoy stirring it up a bit."

Cal looked at him with caution, and then shook his head. "I'm not the one stirring things up."

Mr. Henry smiled. "Don't take it as a bad thing, Cal. I think stirring things up is what initiates change and makes people stronger." He pulled Cal's paper from the pile and handed it to him. "But this isn't making a difference. This is just ranting."

Cal looked at him, confused. "What do you mean?"

"You obviously have an agenda, but I don't understand what you're trying to accomplish. You're a good writer. Don't let bitterness and anger get in the way of a good story."

Cal didn't say anything but took a deep breath, annoyed.

"You have an amazing story to tell. And instead of doing that, you're being judgmental and ignorant of the very people that make your story so fascinating. If you're so passionate about setting yourself apart from the people of Fort Duchesne, you need to understand them—and yourself—a lot better."

"I don't want to understand them."

"Why? Just because you've run into some idiots who make you feel ashamed of them?"

Cal was getting agitated and wondered why he had to have this counseling session with a teacher he hardly knew. "So what are you saying? I have to do the paper over?" he asked, hoping he could just end the conversation and be on his way.

Mr. Henry sighed and said, "Yes, you do. But I think you're missing an amazing story."

Cal rolled his eyes, "There's nothing amazing out there."

"What about the aunt you mention? What happened to her and her child? Find out and write about what happened all those years ago. What made her take her life, as you claim? That makes an interesting paper, not a bunch of ranting and anger."

"What do you know about my aunt?" Cal asked.

"Not much, but I worked for a newspaper before I came here and I know a good story when I see it. I can't help but wonder why someone with so much boiling up inside doesn't want answers. Don't you wonder who she was and why she did what she did?"

Cal sat back against the chair. "Yes, I do wonder. But I probably won't ever know. Everyone acts like it's some big secret—even my own mother."

Mr. Henry lifted an eyebrow. "That makes it even *more* intriguing."

"You make it sound interesting. But for me, it's the hell that my life has turned into," said Cal, taking a deep breath with disgust.

"Everyone has a past, Cal. Your family's seems to be more interesting than most. I want you to tell the story. And not just for this class, but for the Murrow writing competition."

Cal looked at him skeptically. "What's that?"

"It's a scholarship for high school students taking journalism. Your story is perfect, but it'll take some research."

"What type of scholarship?" Cal asked, sitting up straight in the chair, more interested now.

"It's not a full ride, but it pays for most of your tuition. I don't want to get your hopes up, but there's a Native American component and…"

"Wait," Cal interrupted. "I don't want anything given to me just because I'm half Indian."

"Cal, you wouldn't be *given* anything. You have to *earn* it. I know that a lot of kids don't take advantage of it, and it's good money."

Cal sat back, "If I decide to do this, I'm entering the regular contests, not the one just for the Indians. Okay?"

Mr. Henry gave a frustrated sigh, but smiled. "Whatever you say, but don't waste this chance."

Cal nodded. "So what do I have to do?"

Mr. Henry looked through his files and pulled out the paperwork and instructions for the competition. He handed them to Cal, and then began to question him again about his story.

"You said your parents left right after your aunt died. You also said you have a cousin your mother never even told you about. Why? Where is that cousin now? Don't you think there may be a connection?"

Cal pondered what Mr. Henry said. "Do you think there's a connection?"

"Could be. If nothing else, it sure makes for a better story."

Cal stood up. "Okay, I'll do it. But I don't have time to write another paper by tomorrow for class."

"I don't expect you to. If you bring me another rough draft by next Monday, I won't take away any credit."

"Okay," said Cal. He stood up and started to leave, but then turned back. "Why didn't you just give me a bad grade and let it go?"

Mr. Henry smiled. "Because I know there's better in you. I was surprised when I saw that you were even at this school. Most of the Ute kids go to the school in Vernal; they don't bother with the high school here in town. It intrigued me. Then, when I read your paper, I was surprised. Most people are protective of their ancestors and their family, but it was obvious from your paper that you're ashamed of all of them. I have a hard time believing you're really that cold and uncaring, just because they don't have nice homes or don't live in perfect, picket-fence neighborhoods."

"It isn't just that." Cal felt his chest tighten and his eyes begin to burn; the pain of losing his father churned inside him, but he pushed the emotions back down where he buried everything—in that dark place where all his feelings and cares were locked up and hidden.

"Then what is it? How long have you lived there? About a month? I don't blame you for being angry with the people outside the Rez who treated you badly, but I think your own people deserve better."

"My people!" Cal scoffed.

"Why are you so defensive when it comes to them?"

"I'm not defensive." Cal tried to act as if Mr. Henry's challenge wasn't getting through to him, but it was. It gnawed hard at him, almost to the point of making him want to run out of the classroom.

"If you need help, just ask," Mr. Henry offered.

"I don't need anyone's help," Cal snapped.

Mr. Henry laughed, "Oh, no. You're not defensive at all." He shook his head and chuckled. "I was talking about help with your *story*, Cal."

"Oh," Cal said, feeling stupid that he once again let his temper get the best of him.

Mr. Henry began to gather the other papers into a pile. "You'll be fine if you just loosen up a little. You've got the rest of your life to become bitter and hard," he said, beaming a broad, assured smile. He was wiry and actually quite goofy looking, and Cal found him irritatingly perceptive. But he also provoked a strong desire to show Mr. Henry that he was right about the Fort; Cal wanted to prove to someone—anyone—that he should go home to Spokane. He'd do the research and prove to him that what he said in his first paper was true. And he knew it'd feel good.

Cal left Mr. Henry's room wanting to start on the paper right away. There was something intriguing about what his teacher had said. Maybe there was something about his aunt that explained why she killed herself. He didn't understand why he felt such a connection to her, but there was something about her life that didn't make sense. He just felt it.

His conversation with Mr. Henry kept playing in his head during practice that afternoon. Coach Roos gave Cal a lot of playing time, and it made him hopeful that he'd see that same amount in actual games. The exercise kept him focused, and it worked out his anger and frustration.

Then on the day of the first game, the cheerleaders made paper cutouts of basketball players, each bearing the number the player wore on his Union High team uniform. They taped these cutouts, along with an inspirational saying, onto each of the player's lockers.

But on Cal's locker, the basketball player was not the same as the rest. In place of the peachy-pink colored face there was red, and instead of words of encouragement, there was simply the word *Tonto*. Cal ripped it from his locker and threw it on the floor.

"What's the matter?" he heard a sarcastic voice braying from behind him, "Don't like the truth?"

Cal turned to find Mitch, surrounded by his posse.

Mitch curled his lip, "Come on, Tonto. Let's go—just you and me."

Cal looked over the group and an odd thought crossed his mind. Why would anyone wear jeans that tight? It looked uncomfortable and only made Mitch look thin and scrawny. "If it's just you and me, why do you need all your little body guards around you?" Cal asked.

"I don't," Mitch said, adjusting his weight and flipping back his stringy hair. "They just want to watch me kick your butt."

Coach Roos appeared around the corner and gave the group a look of exasperation. "Knock it off, you guys. Funnel all this energy into tomorrow's game."

Both Cal and Mitch looked away, and Coach Roos stepped between them. "I mean it, guys. This isn't a joke anymore. If I find you fighting again, both of you are off the team. And I don't care who starts it."

Cal looked at him in disbelief. "What about smart-ass comments or ramming me during practice? Are you saying I have to put up with it?"

"No. I don't even want you two talking to each other during practice."

"Fine!" said Cal. Then he reached into his locker, pulled out what he needed for his next class and began to walk off. He rounded the corner and almost ran head-on into Doran.

"Where'd you come from?" Cal asked, surprised.

"I was listening from the other side. Doesn't Coach Roos realize what that idiot is doing?"

Cal sighed as they walked slowly down the hall. "Sure he does. But I don't think he can do anything about it."

Doran thought for a moment. "Mitch is gonna keep picking at you. What're you going to do?"

"I'm gonna deal with it. I don't want to get thrown off the team. It's the only thing I've got out here that matters."

"What if he starts something? Are you just going to take it?"

"I don't know."

The isolation Cal felt turned his mind to his studies. He was surprised that with very little effort, he pulled mostly A's. His teachers were encouraging and seemed thrilled anytime he approached them with a question. At first the attention was welcome, but soon he began to feel patronized. The other students gave him disgusted looks, as if he tried to brown-nose. He soon stopped asking questions and answered in class with little more than a grunt or a mumble. It was only in Mr. Henry's class that he found any solace at all.

He titled his paper, "The Life and Death of Jackie Littlebear." He sat down with his grandfather after dinner the same day he'd talked with Mr. Henry. Cal told Raymond about the assignment and asked him to tell him all about the aunt he never knew. At first Raymond seemed uneasy. He looked at his dark, calloused hands and talked slowly, picking each word carefully. Cal was patient and asked questions to keep him talking.

"Do you miss her?" The question was innocent, but Cal flinched at how tactless it sounded. He began to rephrase it, but stopped when Raymond looked up at him with red eyes.

"I miss her every day," He said quietly.

That made Cal stumble. "Of course—that was a dumb question. I'm sorry…"

Raymond looked at him through teary eyes and put a reassuring hand on Cal's. "No, it's not a dumb question, Cal. It's been so long since I've really talked about her. It was all so painful at the time that I haven't wanted to talk about what happened, and ever since your grandmother died, there really hasn't been anyone *to* talk about her with—until now."

Cal just nodded. Raymond wiped his eyes and smiled. He looked at Cal with warm pride, and then, his voice still quiet, began to reveal his memories of his daughter and the type of person she was. He told Cal about her high-pitched giggle as a little girl, and her stubbornness that used to drive Cal's grandmother crazy.

The more Raymond talked, the more his emotions and love started to pour out. Cal was immersed in the passion that this old man felt for his lost daughter, and he found the paper almost writing itself. But it was missing something, and Cal knew that eventually he had to ask some hard questions about her death and why she took her own life. But for now, the rough draft only needed to be ten pages long; the rest would come later.

Almost every night, Cal found himself talking with Raymond about the past. At times, they laughed at the torments Jackie and Mona had put their parents through. And Cal found that many of the stories almost mirrored the antics of Cal and Doran. It was eerie, but somehow oddly comforting to hear. Cal enjoyed his time with Raymond, and clearly saw the love and care this old man felt for his children and his family. He wished he'd seen it sooner, and was now feeling guilty about the things he'd said after he first got to his grandfather's house.

Several days after he turned in his rough draft, Mr. Henry stood at the front of the class and, along with several students' papers, read a small part of Cal's story. At first the class seemed to squirm, especially upon hearing the title, but then they sat and listened attentively. After Mr. Henry stopped reading, some of the students turned back to Cal with looks of interest. They wanted to know more. Mr. Henry returned the rough draft with a large "A" in red at the top with a note scribbled next to it that read, "Now this is a story!" Cal smiled. It was the first really good feeling he'd felt at this school and it was welcome.

Unfortunately, out on the basketball court, where Cal always experienced pleasure and happiness, everything he did felt like hard work. But he kept at it, knowing things would change when he made a difference during the game. It had to.

Coach Roos' warning seemed to hit home with Mitch. He avoided Cal and kept his comments to himself for almost a week. The others on the team were friendly up to a point, but Cal wasn't sure which guys he could trust. He also didn't want to seem too eager and then get hurt. If someone passed him the ball, he gave them a nod, but they seemed uncomfortable having too much contact with him.

Doran was different; as usual, he spent most of his time trying to socialize and less of it working on his game. It drove Cal crazy, seeing him talking and laughing on the bench. That's where he'd stay if he didn't show more interest in learning the plays. One teammate in particular seemed to befriend Doran. Brent Johansen didn't stand out from the others physically; he was tall and thin, with blond hair and light eyes. But he had a constant smile, just like Doran.

"You spend too much time gabbing and not enough playing," Cal counseled Doran on one of their drives home."

Doran shrugged. "It's nice to finally have some friends."

"Are you sure that's what they are? I don't know if I'd trust them."

"I do," Doran said in his typical upbeat tone. "Brent's not from here. His dad came out to start a lumber store because of all the building that was going on in the area. It has something to do with a lot of people moving here because of the oil wells."

"Why don't they do some building in the Fort?" Cal asked in a huff. "That's where they need some help."

Doran just nodded and then stared out the window, deep in thought.

It was already the first game of the season and still the Coach hadn't chosen the starting team. Cal knew he deserved a position, but he also knew that Mitch was fighting hard for it. It was a tough call for Coach Roos.

During practice, Cal was invincible. His shots dropped into the net with ease and his confidence soared. Mitch did nothing but scowl, as if he hoped to curse Cal with his glare. Doran sat on the bench, his legs bouncing as he looked around anxiously. Mitch and two of his friends sat close by in a huddle. When Cal looked back again, he saw Doran standing by the group and Mitch peering up with an ugly glower. Doran turned and walked back to his seat, smiling. Cal continued to watch with interest as Doran sat laughing to himself.

Then Mitch walked over. He talked to Doran with a smug look on his face and when Doran stood up, Mitch pushed him back into his seat. Within seconds, they were locked together and rolling around on the gym floor.

Cal ran over to assist, but a large group already began pulling the two apart.

"That's it. I've had it. You're both off the team," growled Coach Roos.

Mitch angrily protested, "He started it!"

"I don't care. You were fighting and you were warned."

Doran kept silent, but glanced up at Cal with a smirk. This surprised Cal, and he furrowed his brows with a questioning look.

Coach Roos sat Mitch and Doran down and began lecturing them, but then threw his hands up in frustration and sent Doran and Mitch off to the principal's office with Mr. Sanders, the assistant coach. With that detail out of the way, he turned back to the rest of the team and began to select his starting players. Cal was still in shock over what Doran had done, and he couldn't help feeling a mixture of dread and excitement over being picked as the starting forward.

On the drive home, Cal asked Doran, "What the hell did you do that for?"

"Because I hate him."

"And that's worth getting kicked off the team?"

"Yeah, it is. I can't stand being on the team anyway. I don't like it the way you do. It's not like I'm ever going to see any playing time."

"But you've never fought with anyone in your life, not

even when Kenny Sonderberg popped you one at the park last year. What did Mitch say that set you off like that?"

"Nothing really," Doran hung his head and sighed.

"What?"

"Cal, Mitch was planning to sabotage you by having one of his friends pick a fight with you. It pissed me off, so I decided to beat him to it and get *him* kicked out instead."

Cal paused for a minute, then asked his brother for confirmation, "You did it on purpose to help me?"

Doran just smiled.

"Why?"

"I knew how much it meant to you. I didn't want him to ruin it for you."

Cal took a deep breath. "So what did you say?"

"I told him his father was a jackass."

Cal laughed, but then his faced turned serious. "That reminds me; we haven't seen old Silver Hair around much." He stopped for a second, and then a huge smile spread across his face. "Just think how pissed he's going to be when he hears Mitch was kicked off the team and I made the starting line-up!"

Doran grinned.

They both sat quietly thinking as they drove home. Cal had an even greater appreciation for his brother, and he sensed that Doran could feel it.

As they approached their grandfather's house, they saw an older truck parked in the driveway. It had a shorter bed and two large metal boxes backed up against the cab. A large propane tank was permanently strapped to the boxes, and it was smeared with sticky black oil. Doran looked at

Cal questioningly, but Cal just shrugged. They entered the house and Cal heard a voice that was odd but sounded familiar. Mona met them at the door, and with a smile led the boys into the kitchen. There sat the man who'd talked with Cal at the dance.

"Cal, Doran, this is Tim Avery. We knew each other back in high school."

"Hello, guys." Tim said, leaning comfortably back in the small vinyl chair. He was dressed in the same plaid shirt and jeans that made him stand out at the dance. His were working hands, stained black, just like his jeans. An odd-shaped hat sat next to him on the table. It looked like a baseball cap, but was hand sewn with alternating vivid colored fabric, and the brim was longer than usual.

Cal looked at Mona, then uttered an unenthusiastic "Hello."

Doran looked at Tim, then back at Mona. Then he turned, saying nothing, and walked back to his room.

Cal looked back at Mona, who stood watching Doran, confused.

"Do you remember who I am?" the man asked.

Cal smirked. "Yes. You saw me get thrown out of the dance the other night."

The man chuckled at Cal's defensive answer. "You're so much like your father, it's scary."

"You knew my Dad?" Cal asked, surprised.

"Yes. I went to high school with your mother. When I graduated, I went to work at the Plateau refinery; that's where I met David. We had a lot of fun together while he was here. We used to go hunting up near Flaming Gorge all the time."

"Dad used to hunt?"

"Sure. We mostly liked getting away from the job and relaxing, but we bagged a couple of pretty good-sized deer that year."

Cal became serious. He looked at Tim, with his weathered boots and broad shoulders. He stood out from the crowd at the dance, not just in his appearance, but also in his stance. Now he sat in their kitchen like it was his house and Cal was the guest.

"So why are you here?" Cal asked Tim. "Are you going to tell me I'm in trouble again for something I didn't start?"

"No. I'm here because I'm a friend of your parents'. I was also in the auto parts store that day, and I want you to feel free to use any of my tools to fix your car. I'll even help you."

"I don't get it. If you were at all these places, aren't you friends with that jackass Sheriff and those other people at the dance?"

Tim shrugged, "Don't let Franklin Grayson bug you. He's mostly talk..."

Mona looked at Tim with worry and surprise. "Franklin Grayson. What people?" she asked.

Cal looked at Mona. "The Sheriff calls me *Tonto*, and there were these people at the dance who got all weird when Tim asked me if you were my mother."

Tim shrugged. "Don't let those old biddies bother you, Cal. They remember your mom and Jackie from high school, and they're still jealous about how beautiful they were."

Even with that comforting comment from Tim, Mona looked concerned. "Who else was there, Tim?"

"Don Stevens, Kelly Hartley, Franklin Grayson. You know the group," Tim said.

Cal pulled out a chair and sat at the table. "What's the deal with Franklin Grayson? He and his son have had it in for me ever almost since the day I got here."

Mona hung her head and walked to the sink.

"What is it Mom?" Cal asked.

Mona began to say something, but Tim cut her off, "It was just stupid high school politics. You did tell him about Franklin and Jackie, didn't you?"

Mona's eyes got big and her mouth twitched.

"Franklin Grayson and my aunt?" Cal said loudly.

Mona urgently shushed Cal as Raymond walked into the kitchen. He looked at Tim and then a wide smile spread across his worn, leathery face. "How are you Tim? It's been years."

Tim smiled and said, "Nice to see you again, Mr. Littlebear. I've been okay."

Raymond walked over to Tim and put a hand on his back. "I read in the paper about your father. I'm very sorry. Dr. Avery was a good man."

Tim nodded. "Thank you."

Raymond pulled out a drawer and reached for a pad of paper and a pen. "I'll be at the lodge," he said as he walked from the kitchen and opened the front door. An icy breeze blew through the house as Raymond turned back to Mona. His face turned sad and pleading, but before he could say a word, Mona became agitated.

"Knock it off!" she yelled at him.

Both Cal and Tim looked at her, astonished.

Raymond held his gaze on her a moment, then calmly turned to Tim. "It was nice seeing you again, Tim," he said, ignoring her outburst.

The door closed and Cal immediately began to ask questions. "Knock *what* off?"

Mona became silent, so Cal looked over at Tim, who only shrugged. Getting nowhere on that question, Cal continued to pry about Franklin and Jackie. Tim, not knowing what Mona had told Cal, spoke cautiously. "It wasn't a big deal, Cal. Just high school stuff. I shouldn't have even said anything because it was nothing."

"Nothing? This guy has made my life miserable and I want to know why. I thought he hated the people from the Fort. He must have made an exception for Aunt Jackie." Cal looked at Mona, "What else aren't you telling me? Why won't you even talk about her?"

"Because it hurts too much," she said forcefully.

"That's bull. It was before I was born." He turned back to Tim, "She didn't even tell me I had a cousin."

"Why do you have to know everything?" an angry voice called from the doorway.

Cal looked back to find Rachel standing there, her hips squared and her hands clenched at her sides.

"What?" Cal asked.

"Are you trying to run Mom's life, too?" she asked.

"I'm not running your life Rachel. But you're sure as hell not going places where a bunch of guys are going to be when you're only fourteen."

"I turn 15 next month. And it's not just that; you won't let me wear the clothes I want. You won't let me wear make-up. You act like you're my father and I hate it," she shouted as tears soaked her eyelashes. Before Cal could answer her, Rachel turned and walked off toward her room.

Cal glared at Mona. "If you acted like a mother should, I wouldn't have to act like her father."

Mona ignored his comment and walked past him, following Rachel.

Cal took a seat at the table and hung his head in frustration. "I feel like my family's falling apart in front of me."

"It's not something a kid your age should have to worry about."

"If I don't, who will?"

Tim shrugged. "Sometimes no matter what you do, people do what they want. You can't control them. Your sister's testing her wings. Besides, those church dances are really harmless," he said, trying to comfort him. "My daughter Shelly was there the other night, and I don't mind her going," he said.

"Why are you here?" Cal asked, exhausted. "Did you just come here to stir things up?"

Tim shook his head. "No. I came here because I was surprised when I found out Mona was back. I thought she was one of the lucky ones."

"What's that supposed to mean?"

"It means someone lucky enough to escape this place. That's what my ex- thought she was doing when she married me."

Cal took a deep breath. Finally, here was someone who

thought the way he did. He smiled, "If you feel that way, then why are you still here?"

Tim shrugged, "My girls are here. I became a father so young, I didn't have the time to realize I was digging myself in. There's no way I could have left the Basin and gotten the same money I was making as a welder. I have two daughters; they were raised here and there's no way I can leave now." He stood and picked up his hat from the table. "I was serious about helping you with your car. The girls are both in high school, so they're busy with their friends and school stuff. That means I don't have much to do in the evenings."

"You never did answer my question, though." said Cal.

"About what?"

"Are you friends with Franklin Grayson and the rest of those people who hate me?"

Tim paused for a moment, his brows furrowed in thought, "No, we're definitely not friends. But it's a small town, and I have my welding business and my girls to think about, so I walk the walk for them. If you're wondering whether you can trust me, you can. I was a friend of your father's...and your mother's. I would have helped you out if I'd known who you were."

"But wouldn't that have turned all those people against you?"

"No. It wouldn't be the first time I stood up for some-one from the Fort. They understand that because of my daughter."

"Your daughter?"

"Yes. She's like you: Ute mother, white father. But she

just stays quiet. I wish she had your guts to stand up to people and be proud of who she is."

Proud, Cal thought. He wasn't proud. In fact, since he came to the Fort, his feelings about being a Ute quickly turned sour. Tim misread Cal's need to defend himself as pride, and his comment confused Cal to the point that all he muttered was a gruff, "Thank you."

As Cal lay awake in bed later that night, he tried to sort through his feelings about what had happened that evening, and everything that they'd talked about. His mother had changed and was a different person now that she was at the Fort. Cal felt his family crumbling around him, and he blamed her for not standing strong and being the parent to all of them that he thought she should be. He worried about Rachel, afraid that she'd either end up in trouble or hate him for trying to save her. He was well aware of what guys his age thought having been one and it scared him. With all these thoughts running through his mind, Cal's stomach twisted with emotions.

Finally, he thought about Katrina, her red curls, and her soft form in his arms. The feelings aroused him and he tried to push the thoughts from his mind. He fell asleep with a dull pounding echoing inside his head.

5

The paper cutout that was again taped to his locker the next morning was fully decked out in a headdress, loincloth, and red letters that spelled out *Tonto*. Yet it wasn't enough to take away Cal's excitement over the first game. With Mitch off the team, he felt that nothing would keep him from succeeding.

Each class seemed to drag on endlessly as he anxiously anticipated the game that night. He didn't see Mitch all morning and even at lunch, when Cal passed Katrina in the lounge, Mitch was nowhere in sight. Cal wanted so much to talk to Katrina as she smiled invitingly at him, but he knew that spelled trouble. She looked over at him like an abused puppy and he managed to smile back, but then he left the lunchroom quickly. He decided he'd talk to her after the game, after he made his impression on the school and Mitch was no longer reigning over him.

"So are you ready for tonight?" Doran asked as they pushed their way through the crowded hall.

"Yeah," Cal answered calmly.

"I bet Mitch is eating his heart out right now."

"Well, don't be patting yourself on the back too much," warned Cal, "I have a feeling you'd better watch your back from now on."

But Doran just shrugged.

During his last few classes, Cal's stomach ached with excitement. The challenge he faced dealt with so much more than winning a basketball game; it was actually more about being accepted. That feeling wasn't a comfortable one for Cal; he'd never had to work for friendship before—not at any point in his life until now.

Doran was just the opposite. He seemed to be getting along and making friends easily. When Cal pointed it out to his brother, Doran asked him a pointed question: "If you act like you hate everyone, do you think they are going to go out of their way to know you?"

Cal knew his brother was right, but his stubbornness kept him from letting his tough façade show anything but reserve. It'd never been an effort before, and he didn't want friends who didn't know who he really was. But still, he felt compelled to prove to them all that he wasn't who or what they thought; he wanted them to see that he wasn't just another Indian from the Fort.

When the second part of Cal's paper was finished, he left it on Mr. Henry's desk after lunch. Because he wanted to make sure the teacher got it, he went by his classroom after school to check. When he opened the door, he found Mitch alone in the room, reading something. When he heard the door open, he turned and found Cal standing there. Cal expected Mitch to be indignant, but instead his face showed the signs of fear and concern. Cal looked at what he was reading and realized it was his paper about Jackie.

"What are you doing with my paper?" Cal asked.

Mitch swallowed and looked down at the paper, then back at Cal. "Why are you doing this?" he asked, holding the paper toward Cal.

"Doing what?"

Mitch shook his head. "You're trying to ruin everything. I don't know why you want to do this. Why did you have to even come back here?"

"Come back here? I've never been here before we moved here." Cal said, then reached out and snatched the paper from Mitch.

Mitch tightened his lips and glared at Cal. "If you keep digging into the past like this, I swear I'll kill you."

Even with the hate Cal knew Mitch had inside him, this statement surprised him.

At that point, Mr. Henry walked in and asked, "What's going on in here?"

Mitch pushed past Cal and muttered, "Nothing."

"I caught him in here, reading my paper."

Mitch looked at him with a face that said more than Cal comprehended, then threw open the door and stalked out.

Then it all made sense to Cal. Mitch must know something about Jackie's death that he wanted kept secret. That meant Franklin knew it, too. It was so obvious to Cal that he almost hugged Mr. Henry. Cal knew then that it wasn't suicide that took Jackie's life; it was murder, and Franklin was the killer. That's why they were so upset about Mona moving back. They thought their secret was safe and that it left when Mona and David moved away. With Cal researching what had happened to Jackie, they knew that the truth would come out. All Cal had to do now was prove it and he could take them down. He handed the paper to Mr. Henry and headed home to get ready for the game.

As he drove, he thought about his father. When his old team entered the gym and took a lap around the floor before the game, Cal would look up into the stands to see where his dad was sitting. It was almost like he couldn't play until he'd made eye contact with his father and got that boost of confidence he needed to play his best. That smiling wink and nod played in his mind like a movie and the bittersweet memory tore at Cal's heart so much that he tried to push it from his mind. How could he play without his father being there to watch? The joy he'd always felt before a game was gone, and he wondered if he'd ever feel it again. Cal wondered if he could still enjoy or feel anything that used to make him happy anymore.

The days had started their slide into winter, and the sunlight was already slipping away from the valley as Cal continued on his drive. The juniper trees dotted the side of the highway, and their cloaked and crooked masses lit up as the headlights skimmed across them.

As he rounded a bend, he noticed a large, older model Oldsmobile parked on the side of the road. He studied it as he passed, and noticed an elderly woman seated at the wheel. With the sun dipping below the horizon, the faint light made it hard for him to see what color the car was, and could only tell that it was dark. It didn't sit well with Cal, leaving an old lady alone out there, but he knew he didn't have time to stop and figured she must be waiting for someone. But the worry tugged at Cal and it became worse the farther away he drove. The highway was so empty, and he knew there wasn't a store or house for miles in either direction. "I can't stop, or I'll be late for the game," he kept thinking. Then Cal shook his head in frustration and pulled the wheel, turned off the highway and went back around toward the old woman.

He pulled behind her and turned off his engine, keeping his lights on, then walked up alongside the car. As he approached the window, he noticed she was trying hard to keep her eyes focused forward, as if she was hoping he'd go away.

Cal tapped on the window.

She slowly turned to him. "Someone will be here soon," she said, nervously.

"Can I help you?" asked Cal.

The woman had tight gray curls and small eyeglasses. She wore a thick-knit green sweater and there was a large white purse on the seat next to her. She noticed Cal looking at it and she slowly tried to pull it closer to her.

"No. I'm fine," she called through the closed window. "There *is* someone coming."

Cal could see that she was scared, but wondered what her reaction would be if he'd been a white kid. The thought spurred Cal on. "You don't have to do anything, just tell me what's wrong. I know a lot about cars."

She looked up at him and made eye contact.

He smiled at her. "I can try to figure out what's wrong while you wait." Cal was guessing that there wasn't anyone on the way, and he could see by the look on her face that he was right.

She nodded. "I pulled over to get something from my purse, and then, when I tried to start the car again, it was dead."

"Turn the key and let me hear how it sounds," he said loudly, still having to talk through the closed window.

She tried to start the car and nothing happened, not even the clicking of an engine trying to start.

"Did you leave the lights on?"

She looked down at the switch and then back to him with a smile of chagrin.

He smiled back at her. "Okay. The battery's dead, but I have jumper cables. Pop the hood release and I'll go get them." Cal walked to his car and pulled the cables out of the trunk. Then he jumped in and pulled the car back out on the highway, then into position so both cars sat nose to nose. When he walked back to her car and opened the hood, he noticed that she was now leaning out of the window.

"This is awfully nice of you," she called to him.

Cal just smiled. He opened his own hood and positioned the cables where his father had taught him years ago. "When I give you the signal, start your engine."

She nodded.

Cal jumped into the truck and turned the key. He revved it several times, then leaned out and signaled to the woman to start her car. The lights blinked, and then came on full power. Cal felt good as he walked around and un-hooked the cables from both cars. He saw her smiling from the driver's seat, and then she motioned to him. Cal walked over, and when he reached the window, he noticed another set of headlights pulling up behind them. He put his hand up to shade his eyes, and saw a sheriff's car. He groaned.

The officer quickly walked up and gave him a skeptical look. He then turned to the woman. "Is everything okay, ma'am?"

The old woman looked at the officer and smiled. "Everything's fine. This nice young man helped me get my car started."

The officer looked at Cal again, but spoke to the woman. "I'll wait until you get back on the road."

"Don't bother," she asked. "I'm fine."

Cal sighed, "I need to get going."

As Cal turned back toward his car, the woman called out to him. "Wait."

The officer took the hint and reluctantly returned to his car. Cal stood there until the officer closed his door and was out of earshot.

"Here," the woman said, handing him a five-dollar bill through the window.

Cal smiled and said, "No, thank you."

"But you didn't have to stop."

"I know."

She studied his face. "What's your name, young man?"

"Cal Burton."

"Burton?" she asked, surprised.

Cal dreaded the fact that he'd told her his full name.

"That's not an Indian name," she said.

"I'm only half Indian," he said softly.

"Do you live at Fort Duchesne?"

He nodded, knowing what she must think about him.

She smiled. "I used to work there years ago. I was a nurse. I worked all over the Basin. I've been retired now for almost ten years, but I miss the people out there."

Cal tilted his head and felt an enormous sense of comfort and relief.

She patted his hand on the door jam. "I don't want to keep you, but if you ever need anything, please ask. My name is Nan Madsen, but everyone still calls me Nurse Nan. I live on Hudson Street in town."

Cal stood up as the officer's car drove off, deliberately kicking up gravel.

"Thanks again," she said.

Cal nodded, and then walked back to the car and waited until she pulled onto the highway. She waved kindly and he waved back.

As he drove the rest of the way back to the Fort, he realized that the short conversation with Nurse Nan was one of the few positive contacts he'd had with anyone since he moved there. It made Cal wonder about his own actions, and if what Doran had said might be true. Then he glanced down at the glowing clock in the dashboard. "Crap, I've got to get going," he huffed, realizing he had very little time to get ready for the game.

Rachel yelled something from the front door, but Cal wasn't listening. He sat in the car, staring at her chiseled face and long arms. Was she wearing a bra? When did that happen? The changes in her scared him.

He rolled down the window.

"Mom wants to know if this'll cost anything," she yelled.

"I don't know. Tell her to give you ten dollars."

Mona appeared in the doorway. She looked different; her hair was curled around her face, she was wearing a new sweater—and she was sober.

At first, Cal felt dismay that she was coming to his game, but then he felt good about having her support. For the first time since they'd arrived in the Basin, they were going somewhere as a family. Cal hoped that this was a sign of things to come.

When they dropped him off, Cal ran into the locker room. He was nervous and silent as he dressed with the others; it was his first time in the locker room without Doran or Mitch.

The run into the gym was exhilarating. It was only Union High, but it felt good to be back on the court, suited up and ready to play. Cal took in the noises around him as he went through the drills. The stomping of feet on the wooden bleachers, the buzz of the crowd filling the gym, the echo of the horn calling for the game to start—it was all a rush. The gym was much smaller than he was used to, but the crowd was deafening and that made it seem huge. Cal looked up into the stands where Mona, Doran, and Rachel sat talking. It looked odd, seeing them without his father, but Cal was still happy they were there.

He searched the stands for Katrina, which included two sections of bleachers, one on the floor and one on a separate balcony above. It was in that upper area where he spotted Franklin and Mitch, as they sat glaring, hovering over the gym like a dark cloud. Cal met their eyes and he felt his face begin to sweat. Then he turned away and tried to focus on the game.

Both teams huddled at their benches. The opponents were the Vikings from a town called Pleasant Grove. Cal surveyed their team and saw only one that looked like he really could handle the ball.

Coach Roos set up their strategy, then the horn signaled that it was time to play. The Vikings got the tip-off and they made their way down the court. When the forward passed, Cal saw his chance. He darted toward the ball, made the steal, and headed down the court. It was an easy lay-up and the two points were his. He exhaled and smiled; it was a familiar feeling, and yet something wasn't right. He looked up into the crowd and at Doran as he ran the length of the court. Doran was looking around at the crowd, confused by the reaction to Cal's lay-up. Cal brushed it off and went on playing; another pass, another easy steal. Cal saw the other coach cursing as he ran past and scored another two points. There it was again, that odd sound. What was it? Then he it hit him and he slowed his pace to a trot. It was silence. There were no yells. No cheers. No applause. He was making points for his team, but everyone in the crowd was hushed. Cal looked up to where Franklin and Mitch were sitting; Franklin sat rocking slowly, his evil dark mask unmistakable in the crowd.

Joey Kamdar took a pass from Cal, faked a toss, and scored. This time the crowd went crazy. Cal looked back into the stands at Doran, who stared at him like a deer in headlights. Cal thought maybe he was hearing things, so he decided he had to score again and find out what was going on. This time it was obvious. The crowd was roaring as Tom, a red headed kid, brought the ball down the court. He tried to pass it off to Joey, but a Viking swept through and stole it. That's when Cal saw his chance. Before the other player had time to gain control, Cal stepped in, recovered the ball, and scored. The crowd sounded like a wave being sucked back into the ocean. The Vikings stood dumfounded and looked into the crowd, confused. One yelled to his teammate, "What happened? Didn't that basket count?"

Coach Roos called Cal to the bench and said, "I'm sorry about this Cal. We'll discuss it on Monday."

Cal heard him, but instead of sitting on the bench with the rest of his team, he walked past his seat and into the locker room. He could feel Franklin and Mitch laughing at him as he succumbed to defeat. But he didn't care, he just wanted out.

He quickly dressed and left by the back door of the gym. He called Tim when he arrived home and asked him to go over and pick up Mona and the others. Tim asked him about the game, and Cal hung up on him, trying to avoid breaking into tears. He ripped the Union High jersey from his chest and threw it across the room, then sat on the edge of the bed. There in the quiet of the empty house, he at last let himself release all the pain in a flood of tears.

He hated what had happened, but even more, he hated

more what it was doing to him. He was reduced to sobs alone in his room, and it wasn't long before his anguish turned into fury.

Cal heard the door slam and the shuffle of his family slowly making their way into the house. Raymond was still at Bingo night at the Bottle Hollow tribal center, so Cal'd had a good two hours to think by himself before anyone else got home.

"You okay?" asked Tim, standing in the doorway of Cal's room. "Mona told me what happened."

"I don't get it," Cal said softly, "Not one cheer. It was dead silence. Franklin and Mitch got everyone to turn against me. What did I do? I know Mitch hates me, but why everyone else?"

Tim shrugged, "Cal, it has more to do with Franklin than you or anything else. It's impossible for me to try and explain it to you—."

"Why? I want to know what it's about. Can't you see this is driving me crazy?"

"It has to do with a lot of stuff that you have no control over, things that happened in the past."

"Like what happened to Jackie?"

Tim hung his head, "It's a lot of things."

"Tell me."

"I can't, Cal. It's not my place." He turned away and walked down the hall.

Cal scoffed and went into the bathroom, slamming the door behind him. He looked in the mirror, wondering how his life could have changed so drastically in just a matter of months. Even through the door, he could hear Tim talking with Mona in the kitchen. His voice was stern and commanding, but Cal only made out bits and pieces of their conversation. He heard Mona say "No!" very clearly and then Tim left. Cal came out of the bathroom and went to the kitchen, where Mona had already pulled out a beer.

"You brought us back here, knowing we'd be treated like this?"

"Cal, I didn't know that. Doran said you were flirting with this kid's girlfriend."

Doran came in quickly to defend himself. "I didn't say that, Mom. I said that Katrina was Mitch's girlfriend and that she liked Cal."

"Doran, get back in the living room," Cal shouted.

"Shh! It's your grandfather—he's coming in," Mona whispered.

"To hell with all of this," Cal said with a shrug, then grabbed a beer and headed toward the door.

"Cal, stop!" Mona called after him. But Cal had already made his way past Raymond to his car. He revved the engine once and pulled out of the driveway.

The windows were still iced over and he wiped them as he drove. As he rounded the turn, he heard a horn blow and was blinded by the flash of headlights. He quickly slammed on the brakes, hurling into the steering wheel. After the tires stopped screeching, Cal sat there for a moment, breathing hard, with the only sound coming from the radio. He took a deep breath and flung open the car door, and there sat Johnny, Fly, Puck and Eddie in a jacked-up truck. Johnny rolled down the window and Eddie screeched when he saw Cal.

"What the hell are you guys doing?" Cal asked.

"Trying to avoid having you hit us," Johnny answered.

Eddie tried to stand up and Fly almost sat on him to hold him down.

Cal came close to the window. Inside he saw a case of beer, so he asked, "Where are you going?"

"To the hollow," said Johnny, in the same rhythmic speech he'd only heard uttered by his mother, at least until moving here to the Fort.

"You can't come cause dare's no woom," Eddie hollered. "You have to dwive yours car."

Cal was too exhausted to be offended, so he just smiled as he turned to leave.

"Come with us," Johnny said.

Cal began to say no, but then he looked back toward the house and realized he had nowhere else to go. "I'll follow you," was all he said.

At night, the lake looked sullen and full of secrets, and its outline was barely visible, even with the brightness of the full moon. Along the edge of the water, there was a large boat ramp and the remnants of what used to be a picnic area and campgrounds. Cal saw a half dozen battered and abandoned buildings, and a parking lot with cracked asphalt and uneven cement barriers. Johnny stopped the truck near the water where someone had dragged one of the picnic tables and set up near a makeshift fire ring. The cold air was harsh, and Cal wished he'd worn a thicker coat. He pulled the ski gloves from under his seat and walked over to the rest of the group.

"What *is* this place?" he asked as the others carried a cooler from the bed of the truck.

"This is Bottle Hollow Lake," answered Puck.

"I know what the lake's called, but what about these buildings?"

Johnny sat the cooler on the table and rubbed the palms of his hands together, trying to warm them up. "This is where the old resort and museum were being built. That was the store," he said, pointing to one of the buildings that had an old gas pump out in front. He turned and motioned again towards the buildings. "That was where the museum was going to go, and that one was the hotel office."

"Hotel?" asked Cal.

"Yep. They had big plans for this place, but it never happened."

Cal surveyed the area as best he could in the dark, then asked, "Why not?"

"They couldn't seem to work together."

"Who?"

"The Indians and the whites. This is all Indian land, but we're a small tribe and we don't have the contractors and everyone else you'd need to build something big like this. They hired some of the people in town, but there were problems from the get-go and then everything just stopped. It's like everyone just walked away and tried to pretend like they'd never wanted it in the first place. It was a really long time ago," Johnny said as he stood watching the others begin to light a fire.

"It's too bad, because this could be really cool," said Cal, still looking around.

"I'm surprised your grandpa didn't tell you about it. He's the one who wanted the museum. He still has a bunch of the stuff in storage that was supposed to be put on display there. He was real involved, and when it all ended, he just seemed different somehow. I think he's still sad about it."

Cal looked at the museum with its triangular roof and teepee shape. He thought about the pride his grandpa must have felt, as well as the disappointment, and it made Cal realize how much he was beginning to care for Raymond.

"Heads up!" Puck called as he tossed a beer to Cal.

He caught the can but it began to slide from his gloved hands. He proceeded to lose it and re-catch it several times, sending Eddie into hysterical laughter. Realizing how he must have looked, Cal smiled to himself and called over to Eddie, "Don't be laughing at a guy trying to hold his beer or I'll have to throw you in this lake."

Eddie cried out in horror and ran away into the darkness.

Johnny turned on Cal, "What the hell is that supposed to mean."

Cal looked around, confused. "I was joking...I didn't mean—"

Johnny squinted at Cal. "Do you really think that's something to joke about?"

"Can't he swim? How would I know that?"

Johnny looked at Puck, who shrugged. He then turned back to Cal. "You know what happened at this lake."

Cal paused, and then answered skeptically, "No, I don't."

"No one told you?" he said.

Cal ran his fingers through his hair; he paused, took a deep breath and answered, "I have no idea what went on here. I'm beginning to think I don't know what's going on at all."

"Come over here and sit down," said Johnny. He motioned to Cal, then looked over into the dark where Eddie had run off. "Eddie, get back over here," he called.

Cal cautiously came forward.

"No one told you about your dad and Franklin Grayson."

Cal rolled his eyes in disgust. "I know that my aunt used to date that creep in high school, and that he hates my guts now, but what does that have to do with my dad?"

Puck and Fly came over and the foursome sat on two logs near the water's edge. Fly kept his distance from Cal and avoided eye contact. The two were silent, except for occasionally sipping from their beers. Eddie stayed close by and played with a stick in the dirt.

Cal became agitated and tried to change the subject. "What are all those marks on his arm?"

Johnny looked over at Eddie and then grinned at the others as he answered Cal. "Last week Eddie tried to kill himself by slitting his wrists."

"Really?" said Cal, shocked.

The group chuckled, and Cal looked at them with astonishment.

Johnny hushed them, and then continued in a calm drone, "He used one of those disposable razors, the double-edged kind. He barely broke the surface." Then he smiled, "There's no way he could have got deep enough to do any harm."

"God, why'd he try?" asked Cal.

"He gets out of control sometimes," Johnny answered, "I think he still remembers when his mom died."

"How'd his mom die?"

Johnny and the others sat back, giving Cal an odd stare. "You're not serious."

Cal huffed. "Serious about what?" he asked, frustrated.

Johnny shook his head in amazement. "You haven't heard about how Jackie died?"

"My aunt? Sure. She drowned." Cal looked at the others, who all sat waiting for something to finally register with Cal. "Jackie. You're saying that my aunt is Eddie's mom?"

Johnny looked confused. "No one told you?"

"No." Cal looked over at Eddie, who sloppily drew an uneven circle in the dark sand. The boy hummed to himself, unaware of Cal staring at him.

Cal looked back at Johnny with a somber face. "Eddie's my cousin? No."

"Yes."

Cal sat for a moment and studied Eddie as he sat humming to himself, not noticing what was being said about him. "So what are you to Eddie? Why does he live with you?" Cal asked Johnny.

Johnny gave Cal a sympathetic smile that showed the pain and confusion he'd seen in his life. He clasped his large brown hands in front of him. "Eddie's my nephew. My brother and Jackie were together for about a year."

"So when Jackie died, Eddie went to live with his father," Cal said.

"Kind of. I wouldn't call my brother much of a father. My grandparents have Eddie."

"But I thought he lived with you," Cal said.

"He does. I live with my grandparents, too. My parents died a long time ago."

"How?"

Johnny gave a sad but sarcastic smile. "Same way most out here do." He then held up the can of beer, then shook his head before taking a long chug.

Cal sat back and continued to look at Eddie, wondering why Mona hadn't said anything, yet realizing why she probably hadn't.

"They haven't told you much about this place at all."

"Obviously not," Cal said, exhausted, "Is there more?"

Johnny sadly looked up at the others, who stared back with somber faces, "You better have another beer."

Cal was frustrated. "Come on. Tell me what's going on."

"It's your father."

"My father?"

"Yes. He's the reason Franklin hates you so bad."

Cal lowered his eyebrows. "Why? What'd my father do to him?"

"Your father accused Franklin of murder."

"Murder? You mean Jackie."

Johnny nodded.

"My mom says she drowned."

"That's what the official ruling was...but back when it happened, supposedly it was a firestorm. Everyone was accusing everyone of killing her. She was pregnant, and Franklin said it was your dad's kid. But then the truth came out about Franklin dating Jackie, and that Franklin didn't want to have an Indian kid."

"So he killed her."

"That's what your dad said. Of course, Franklin said the kid wasn't his, and that your dad killed her because he was at the lake with her when she died. The people on the Fort said it was suicide, but the whites kind of believed Franklin because your dad wasn't from around here, and because Eddie said your dad was at the lake."

"Wait a minute. Back up. How is Eddie old enough to remember all this?"

"Eddie was there. He was four years old."

"He's that much older than us?"

"He's twenty-two now. That's how we get the beer."

Cal took a long slug of beer then stood up. He walked toward the truck and turned around slowly. "You're putting me on, aren't you?"

Johnny stood up. "No way, man. I wish we were. I really thought you knew all this."

"My god, no wonder my parents never talked about this place." He walked out toward the water's edge. "Is this the lake where they found her?"

Johnny nodded.

"And Eddie saw it. So why don't they just ask Eddie who did it?"

"They wouldn't believe him because he's a 'tard. And besides, all he says about it is that a monster got his mom."

Cal paced and drank. "No wonder everyone hates me out here. They think my dad's a murderer."

Johnny nodded.

"Do you think my dad did it?"

"No."

"Why?"

"Why would he? He wanted Mona, not Jackie. And besides, the Elders say he didn't."

"The who?"

"The old people who know our ways. You know, like your grandfather."

"My grandfather?" Cal asked.

Johnny looked at Cal strangely. "You don't even know your grandfather is an Elder?"

"Yeah...I guess my mom did mention it."

Johnny shook his head in disbelief. "He even came to our school and talked about it."

"Your school? I thought you said you didn't go to school."

Johnny stared at him and smiled. "I said we didn't go to Union High. You didn't stay around long enough to hear the rest of what I had to say."

Cal shrugged and Johnny continued, "We go to school in Vernal. We'll talk about this later. I think you've had too many beers and there's a lot you should learn, but most you'd forget by the morning."

Cal didn't argue, and took a long slug of his beer, hoping to push the tortured thoughts from his mind. How could this be? Cal tried to hold onto this feeling of distrust for Johnny and the others, but they faded quickly. The smoke from the fire Johnny built on the beach slowly dissipated into the black sky and for a moment Cal felt more at ease. As the beer kicked in, he grew less anxious. He'd just call his father in the morning and get everything cleared up.

6

Cal woke up, shivering in the dark. He strained to see who else was asleep on the shores of the black lake. From the glow of the moon, he made out four figures, all wrapped in blankets, lifeless mounds that looked like beached whales. He too was covered with a heavy cotton wrap. He tried to remember what had happened that night, but his head spun and all he wanted was to get home and out of the cold. The hot embers of the fire still flickered but gave off no light as he stumbled through the darkness to his car. The sound of the car door made one of the mounds on the shore stir.

The rev of the engine broke the early morning silence. Cal steered cautiously and pulled the car onto the small dark road. He tried to concentrate on where he was going, but the road kept waving and his eyes wouldn't focus. He blinked and shook his head as the car lurched several times before reaching the actual stop sign. The highway was barren, but he still crept slowly into his lane and continued to concentrate on his driving. He flipped on the heater, but it blew only cold air. His breath was visible and it began to form an icy film on the inside of the windshield, and he quickly tried to wipe it away.

The glare of headlights came blinding into his rearview mirror. "Just stay cool, drive slow, and they'll pass you," Cal whispered to himself. The car behind him stayed there for what seemed an hour. Then to Cal's horror, the sting of red and blue lights flashed over him.

Cal pulled to the side of the road and was surprised how quickly he seemed to sober up. He rolled down his window as the officer walked toward him. The cold air helped to clear his mind, but the glare of the cop's large flashlight didn't help the throbbing in his head.

"Where you headed?" asked the officer, obviously curious about Cal's Washington license plate. The cop was an older man with a good size belly and large mustache that covered his mouth. His eyes watered from the cold and his breath rose into the crisp night air.

"Fort Duchesne," answered Cal, "We just moved there about four months ago," Cal tried to talk clearly with enough politeness in his voice.

The officer stared into the car. "I need to see your license."

Cal reached into his back pocket and pulled out his wallet. He tried to keep his hand steady as he searched through the pictures of his once intact family and his glory days on the court. He found it and handed it to the officer.

"Have you been drinking tonight?"

Cal began to lie, but knew it was obvious. "A little. But that was quite awhile ago."

"Could you step outside of the car please?"

Cal did what the officer said and proceeded to take the various tests to determine his drunkenness. He understood the officer's questions, but couldn't control what his body was doing and it frustrated him.

"Did you do peyote tonight?"

"Peyote?"

"The drug."

"I don't do drugs. I hardly ever drink."

"Uh-huh," the officer answered as he scribbled in a small notebook.

"You're not going to arrest me, are you?"

The officer looked up amused. "You were driving twenty miles an hour in the fast lane of the highway. You've failed every test I gave you."

It was the first time Cal had ever been arrested. He was devastated and humiliated as he sat in the back of the officer's car.

"We'll call your parents when we get to the station and they can come and pick you up."

Cal didn't answer.

"So, where was this party that you felt it necessary to drive on the highway at two in the morning?"

"It was at some lake."

"Bottle Hollow. Why'd you pull onto the highway? The road leads directly to the Fort. You did say you lived there."

Cal shrugged. "Yes, unfortunately."

The cop chuckled.

They pulled into the station. It was a small yellowish brick building with large wrought iron lettering that spelled out "Law Enforcement Annex." Inside, Cal was led to a small tiled room, where he was fingerprinted and photographed. He was allowed to make a phone call, and instead of calling Mona, he dialed Tim's number. The phone rang half a dozen times until a scratchy, groggy voice answered. Cal apologized, and then explained where he was. Without hesitation, Tim agreed to pick him up.

Cal asked to use the bathroom and then he was led into a holding area. As the officer unlocked the barred door, Cal saw three others in the cell. All were Indian. Two he recognized from the Fort. They looked at him without expression as he found a seat on a wooden bench. Within minutes, he found himself drifting off to sleep.

The rattle of keys and the clamor of the cell door opening jarred Cal awake and had him wondering where he was. His head throbbed as the night before flooded his mind, and he looked up hoping to see Tim. Instead, he peered into the beastly shaded eyes of Franklin Grayson.

"Thought you'd pay me a visit?" he asked with an evil sneer. "You and I need to talk."

Cal was too ill and in too much pain to argue, so he simply turned away and laid his head back against the wall again.

"I said, get up and come with me," insisted Franklin.

"Go to hell," Cal answered calmly.

A guard pulled Cal to his feet, placed his arms behind him in handcuffs, and led him through a hallway and into a modest office. He sat Cal firmly in the smaller of two chairs. Franklin sat across from him and the guard backed out of the room, closing the door behind him. Cal avoided looking at Franklin, who leaned back insolently.

"So how is good old David doing?" asked Franklin, "Still keeping himself out of prison?"

Cal looked up. "Go to hell."

"Looks like father, like son. Maybe you'll grow up to be a murderer too. You're starting out real well."

"He didn't kill her," Cal sneered, getting to his feet. "You did."

Franklin, pleased with the reaction he got, stood up and threw Cal back into the chair, then grabbed his chin, forcing his head back. "So he's still singing that song is he?" he growled. "I couldn't have killed her. I wasn't even there. He was the one that wanted her, not me."

"My Dad didn't want Jackie. She was pregnant with your kid."

Franklin shrugged. "There's no proof of that. Those Indian bitches'll screw anyone if you get 'em drunk enough." Franklin released Cal's chin, but threw his arm across Cal's throat and held his gaze with a steady stare. "He finally couldn't live his little lie any more and he left Mona," he mumbled, "I'm surprised he stayed with her as long as he did."

Cal tried to free himself from Franklin's painful grip. "What are you talking about?"

Franklin tightened his pressure on Cal's neck. "Your father only married Mona to beat the rap. He didn't love her anymore than any of the other riggers did. You were the product of a drunken stupor. No one ever marries those bitches for anything else. Go back to where you belong and stop trying to stir crap up around here."

Cal struggled, but Franklin held him in place.

A knock came at the door. "I'm busy!" yelled Franklin over his shoulder.

"It's me—Tim," Tim shouted through the door.

Cal felt the grip loosen and his shoulders eased in relief.

Franklin cracked the door. "We'll be done in a moment."

"Tim!" called Cal.

Tim pushed the door open and saw Cal handcuffed.

"What are you doing, Franklin?" Tim said, pushing his way into the room. He lifted Cal out of the chair.

"He's interrogating me about Dad," answered Cal.

"This little turd better stay out of my jurisdiction or..."

"Or what?" Tim asked, squaring his shoulders and holding his stance.

Franklin took a deep breath and chuckled to himself, "I should have figured you'd be the one coming to his rescue, being the Indian lover that you are. Let me guess, you're doing Mona now. You might as well. Everyone else has."

Still handcuffed, Cal came at Franklin, knocking him back against the desk. The sound of keys and papers scattered onto the floor. Tim struggled to pull him off as an officer ran into the room. Unable to use his hands and arms, Cal still managed to head-butt Franklin's ribs and kneed at his legs as best he could before Tim and the officer pried him off Franklin.

Franklin's face was red and his glasses were cockeyed, letting Cal see his eyes. What he saw stung Cal into stopping for a moment and he felt as if needles had been shot into his spine.

"Get him the hell out of here!" Franklin snarled.

The officer led Cal from the room. He'd gathered Cal's belongings into a paper bag and told him, "I ought to arrest you for assaulting the sheriff, but I don't want to have to look at you for the rest of the night," he mumbled as he un-cuffed Cal and pointed him toward the door.

"Trust me, you'll have your chance to do that again someday," Cal muttered, still out of breath and with his head throbbing from anger. Then he followed Tim silently out to the truck.

"Stay out of his way, Cal. He'll only cause you trouble out here," Tim said as he started the engine.

Cal shook his head and felt frustration and helpless-ness take over his already weak and hung-over body. He tried to keep his emotions under control, but it was impos-sible and soon he was in tears.

Tim shook his head. "God, I can't even imagine deal-ing with what you're going through. I should have told you about the stuff that happened at the lake. I didn't realize no-body told you anything about it. I can't believe that Mona didn't think you'd find out."

"Do you think Dad did it?" asked Cal through the tears.

"No. But I'm about the only one, except the people from the Fort."

"Why don't they think he did it?"

"I'm not sure. Something about that retarded kid, Eddie. He said your Dad was dead on the shore when his mom was killed."

"Dead?"

"I think David was passed out. Eddie says the lake monster killed his mother. So I guess the Utes figure it was someone..."

"The lake monster? What's the lake monster?"

"Who knows? Remember, it's Eddie saying this."

"Yes, but didn't they investigate at all?"

"They did, but I don't remember a lot of the details. It was a long time ago."

Cal looked out the window at some cows in a field. The fence keeping them in was poorly made of barbed wire and dried out limbs of the scraggly basin trees. He followed the wire to each post, noticing that even though their shape changed drastically, each looked to be reaching, as if trying to free itself from the grip of the wire holding it in place. Cal felt himself become queasy and took a deep breath. "Franklin said my dad married my mom to beat the murder rap."

Tim wrinkled his brow as he stared out through the windshield of the overworked truck. "Really? He really said that?"

"Yeah. He said Dad wanted Jackie." He looked at Tim with sad, sullen eyes. "Did my dad love Jackie?"

"No. I really think your dad loved your mom. He followed her everywhere, and when he found out she was pregnant, they got married quickly. He never once tried to get out of it. I think Franklin's just trying to pull your chain by saying that. There was a strong rivalry between the two of them, mainly because David—your dad—wasn't from here."

Cal shook his head knowingly. "I can't wait to call

Dad. He's got to realize that we can't stay here anymore, not with all this happening."

Tim nodded slowly, thinking about what Cal said. He answered him carefully, "If David knew the problems you've been having....But I can't imagine how he'd ever have allowed you to come out here in the first place. Maybe you can't go back for some legal reason."

Cal looked Tim squarely in the eye. "I don't care. I can't stay here. I'd rather die."

They pulled into Tim's driveway. "I sent someone to pick up your car. They'll be here soon."

As they walked into Tim's house, Cal was surprised how clean it was. He took a seat on the sofa as Tim walked to the kitchen.

"Do you want something to drink?"

"No thanks," Cal answered, feeling the nausea rise in his stomach. Then Cal heard footsteps in the kitchen and a muffled voice he didn't recognize.

"Cal, this is Lacey," Tim said as he led his daughter into the living room.

Lacey was petite, with long black hair and dark, pretty features. She looked at him with a wry smile.

"Hi," Cal said, trying to be friendly, but still nursing his headache.

"So, are today's antics another attempt at winning the heart of the young white princess?" she asked.

Cal looked over at Tim, who stood quietly in the doorway.

"Huh?" Cal asked.

Lacey lifted a black silken eyebrow. When all she got was a confused gaze from Cal, she huffed and shook her head. "I'll be in my room," she said, ignoring Cal as she passed Tim on her way out.

Tim took a seat on the chair across from Cal.

"What was that all about?" Cal asked.

Tim shrugged. "I guess she thinks this morning's run-in with Franklin had something to do with what happened at the dance the other night."

"Was she there?"

"No!" Tim answered adamantly, "Lacey wouldn't go there for anything. Shelly and Lacey are very different. Lacey feels the Indian boys ignore the Ute girls. That's why she was getting on you about fighting over that girl."

"Ute girls? Isn't she *your* daughter, too?"

Tim nodded, "Yes, but she spends a lot of time with her grandparents who live on the Fort and she considers herself a Ute. Shelly's different. She lives with her mother in town; she's white, goes to Roosevelt Junior High, and is friends with the people in town. It's kind of hard, because they don't always get along."

"They have different mothers?"

"Yes. Lacey's mother died soon after she was born."

Cal looked at Tim with a furrowed brow.

"They found her dead in her car. Nobody's sure exactly what happened. She'd overdosed on something. I raised Lacey with the help of her grandparents. Then I met and married Shelly's mom a couple of years later, but we got divorced about five years ago."

"Where does Lacey go to school?" Cal asked, intrigued by the thought of someone else that was half Ute and half white, same as him.

"Uintah High in Vernal. She'll graduate this year."

Cal sat back as Tim stood and walked to the window.

"Here's Buck with your car," said Tim, as he walked to the door.

Cal began to get up from the sofa.

"Stay put," Tim urged as he walked outside.

Cal heard Tim talking and a man answering in a defensive tone. Cal slowly pulled himself upright and walked to the window. There he saw Tim pointing to Cal's car and the man walking past Tim to a waiting truck. He pulled away and Tim stood alone in the driveway, looking at the car.

Cal walked outside. "What's wrong?" he asked.

"Cal, don't," Tim called, trying to stop him. Then he gave up and motioned to the car in frustration.

As Cal got closer he noticed large scratches marring the car door. Dug deeply into the paint was the word *Tonto*. Cal shook his head and went to open the door.

"Leave it here. I'll fix it. You can borrow my Toyota for a couple days."

Cal tried to argue, but Tim insisted. As Cal turned back toward the house when Tim went to retrieve his keys, he noticed Lacey standing at the door. She looked at the car and gave Cal an empty stare.

Tim came back out and motioned for Cal to get in the truck. "You're tired and hung over. I'm driving you home. Lacey and I'll bring the car over later, when I drop her off."

Cal nodded, but he still kept his eyes fixed on Lacey. She, too, kept up her stare, as if challenging him to drop his gaze first. If Cal hadn't endured the previous night, he wouldn't have given in, but he soon conceded and walked to the truck, defeated.

7

The sun was peeking above the red rock bluffs just as Cal and Tim pulled into Raymond's driveway. Within seconds Mona was outside, her face tinged with worry.

Cal opened the truck door as she came toward him.

"Cal, are you all right? Where've you been?" she said reaching out to embrace him.

"Don't," Cal said, pushing her away, "I don't buy it anymore."

"You don't buy what anymore?"

"Your concern. If you cared about me at all, why'd you bring me here? You knew everything that'd happened and what it would do to me, and you didn't even care."

Mona looked at Tim with confusion. "Knew what?"

Cal rolled his eyes, slammed the door of the truck, and pushed his way past her to the house.

"He knows about Jackie and the mess with David and Franklin," Tim said softly.

"How? You told him? Would you want me telling Lacey stuff about the past?" Mona asked Tim as Cal swung the door closed behind him.

Inside, Doran stood waiting awkwardly in the hallway. He looked at Cal, trying to gauge what to say.

"Where's Rachel?" Cal asked.

"She's still at April's. She spent the night there last night."

"Good. Come with me. You need to hear this," Cal ordered as he walked to the kitchen and picked up the phone.

It always felt strange to dial his own number in Spokane, and when a woman's voice answered, Cal became numb. "Isn't this David Burton's?" he asked cautiously.

Doran looked at him oddly.

"Yes, it is. Hold on," the woman answered quickly.

Cal heard her call to his father, and he strained to hear something more as he waited for David to come to the phone.

"Hello," David said cheerfully.

"Dad," Cal said softly. The rage he felt just moments before turned to feelings of uncertainty and sadness.

"Cal."

"Yes. Who was that?"

David paused for a moment, then Cal heard him explain to the woman that it was his son on the phone, and that he needed to be alone to talk to him. Then he turned his attention back to the call. "Cal, I'm glad you called. I should have talked to you about Terri a long time ago."

"Terri. Terri who?"

"Terri Hunter," he answered.

"Sara Hunter's mom?" said Cal loudly.

Doran's eyes became wide. He wanted so badly to listen in, but instead he just stood across from Cal, taking in every word, mumble and facial expression.

"Yes, Terri is Sara's mother."

"You're not seriously dating her, are you?"

"Cal, I know you're probably upset because you weren't told, but..."

Cal blurted out a forced laugh. He felt exhaustion setting in, and the throbbing in his head began to pulsate downward through his entire body. "I'm actually finding out that you and Mom haven't been telling me a lot of things," he told David.

"What'd she tell you?"

"*She* didn't tell me anything. I'm finding out all these wonderful things from people I hardly know."

"Don't believe them. They're all a bunch of liars."

"Then get me out of here. It's like being in hell. The entire school treats me like crap."

"Cal, I know it's tough, but there isn't a lot I can do."

"Why?"

"Because your mother has custody, and right now there are a lot of things going on in my life that..."

"Like what?"

"Well...Cal, I didn't want to tell you like this, but...next month, Terri and I are getting married."

Cal felt his stomach heave, his back tingle, and the blood rush from his face. He tried to talk but he couldn't. He put the phone in his lap and stared at Doran as tears welled up in his eyes. "He's getting married," he told Doran quietly.

"What?" Doran said, "We haven't even been gone six months!" He reached out to grab the phone, but Cal held it away.

"Cal, are you still there?" David asked. "We need to talk."

"You're damn straight we need to talk," Cal said, wiping the tears from his face. "God, Dad! You have no clue what the hell you've done to me these past months, especially since we came here."

"It wasn't just me, Cal. Your mother—."

"Oh please! Don't give me that line. If you want to marry someone after only six months, then go ahead and be an idiot. I'm not talking about that Dad; I'm talking about all this bull with Franklin Grayson and Mom's sister, Jackie."

"What did he tell you, Cal? That guy's a liar."

"Funny, that's what he called you. But he added something; he also said you were a murderer." Cal wiped the tears that were now pouring out.

Doran stood up and looked at Cal with astonishment.

"He can say that all he wants," David tried to explain, "It's a lie and he knows it. I may have been there, but I never touched Jackie."

Cal shook his head in disgust. "God! Why did you keep this from me? Someone *died*. No one ever told me about this. I didn't even know I had a cousin here, until some guys from the Fort told me who he is."

Doran threw his hands in the air. "Our cousin is here? What are you talking about?"

Cal held up his hand to shush Doran.

David continued, "Your mother has a way of not wanting to talk about things. She has a knack for keeping things to herself that she has an obligation to tell other people— especially people whose lives those things can ruin."

"You could've told me about all this, too, you know."

"Not all of it, Cal. Not all of it," he mumbled.

Cal paused for a minute and tried to gather his thoughts. Doran took a seat on the floor, his head resting forward in his hands. He looked up at Cal when his brother stopped talking.

"Cal, you don't understand," David said.

Cal covered his mouth with his hand and struggled to keep from crying.

"What? What?" Doran asked, seeing Cal's eyes overflow.

Cal knew no matter what he said, his father's mind was on other things now, and it meant that he and the rest of the family would be forced to stay on the Fort permanently. There was no going back now. He couldn't bear the thought of spending even one more day at that detestable school, now that the long holiday weekend was almost ending. He was too tired and hurt to think about facing another day of Mitch Grayson's torments.

He pretended to be comforted by his father, and then hung up the phone.

"What's going on?" Doran asked, by now ready to explode.

Before Cal could answer, they both heard Mona shouting angrily from the front yard. They ran outside and found Johnny, Puck, Fly and Eddie. The wind slammed the door shut behind Cal, and Mona turned back at him, breathing hard. Tim had left by now, and everyone stood looking at Cal in silence.

"What's going on?" Cal asked Mona.

"I don't want these little creeps anywhere on my property," she screamed.

The boy stood silently, first looking at the ground, and then back at Cal.

"Why?" he asked calmly.

She walked toward him. "They're nothing but trouble, Cal. Stay away from them."

He paused for a moment, and then answered softly, "No."

"What did you say?"

"I said no. They're the only ones out here who treat me with any respect. *They* told me the truth. That's more than I can say for you right now, Mom."

"They told you lies," she shouted, as she stomped into the house.

Cal watched the door slam behind her, then turned to the group.

Johnny walked toward Cal cautiously. "God, you look awful."

Cal gave an exhausted chuckle. "Thanks a lot."

"What happened last night? Where'd you go?"

"I was freezing so I tried to drive home."

Fly chuckled, "We spent all night driving around looking for you. When we saw your car on the side of the highway, we thought you headed into the hills. Then we saw a tow truck come so we asked the driver what was going on. He told us it was a drunk's car."

"They arrested me," Cal said. "That idiot sheriff won't be happy until I'm behind bars. I can't stay here. He's probably on his way already to get me on something else," said Cal.

Johnny shrugged. "He can't come out here, and he can't do one damn thing to you."

"He's already tried to beat the hell out of me and his officers just stood by and watched."

"That's because you were in town. He can't do anything out here," Johnny said defiantly.

"He's the sheriff," said Cal. "He's the law."

"Not here on the Rez, he isn't," Fly said, walking toward Cal. "He has no power here. We're a sovereign nation."

Cal squinted against the sun. "What the hell does that mean?"

Johnny looked around at the group as though he were revealing a secret. "It means that as long as we're on our land, they can't touch us."

Cal scoffed. "That's crap. Are you saying you can go around doing whatever you want? What about murder?"

Johnny held up his hands in defense. "We have laws here, but it's the B.I.A. that enforces them."

"What's the B.I.A.?" Cal asked.

"It stands for the Bureau of Indian Affairs. We even have our own tribal court here. As long as we stay on the fort, it's our people who're in control."

Cal thought for moment and then looked intently at Johnny. "Then I should talk to the B.I.A. and tell them what this sheriff is doing to me. He can't get away with it."

Johnny just shook his head. "They won't help. They stay clear of the police in Roosevelt, just like the Roosevelt police stay clear of things out here. Like I said, as long as you're on the reservation, they can't touch you. Outside the

Rez…you're on your own." Johnny paused, then looked at Doran, who stood several steps back. "Do you guys want to come with us?" he asked the brothers.

"Where to?" asked Cal.

"We'll probably just drive up to Bitter Creek."

Cal laughed. "I don't think so. The last time I went for a drive with you guys, I ended up wasted."

Eddie squealed loudly and yelled from the truck, "Come with us, or you'll be here."

Cal paused, and then gave Eddie a haggard grin. "You're exactly right, Eddie." He looked back at Doran. "Are you coming?"

Doran shrugged.

"Come on." Cal motioned as he climbed wearily into the back of the pick up. "Unless you want to miss out on the fun."

Doran looked back at the house, but then reluctantly followed.

The brisk air felt good against Cal's face. Boston's "More than a Feeling" blasted on the radio and Cal closed his eyes. He reflected on the days when all he worried about was washing his car, getting to practice on time, and memorizing the words to that song. He felt himself drifting off to sleep, but the jolting of the truck kept him from relaxing completely and enjoying it. He tried not to focus on his father's impending marriage, but he couldn't help but think that his dreams of them all being back together as a family were quickly fading away.

As the truck turned onto a rugged dirt road, Cal looked over at Doran, who was huddled in the corner of the truck bed, trying to stay warm. The thought of telling him every-thing he'd found out from David was exhausting, but he knew he'd find out eventually. Then he thought about Rachel and what he should tell her, but he pushed that prob-lem aside for now. He was too tired to even begin worrying about that.

The drive to Bitter Creek was bumpy. But as Cal looked around at the land, he was surprised at the odd beauty he discovered. It was different; not green, like in Washington, yet alive; not growing, yet evolving from the elements that naturally sculpt and carve the earth. The blue sky bowed over them without a trace of clouds, and the lack of sleep began to make Cal delirious. He soon felt himself becoming numb to all of his pain and suffering.

A plume of dust encircled the truck as it pulled to a quick stop. Then Cal slowly stood up and looked around. The terrain was flat and rocky, and he walked to the edge of the cliff to peer out over the valley. He stood for several minutes surveying the vast area and was surprised to see how much life spread out for miles in every direction. To the south were fields with tidy green rows, boxed perfectly along unending dirt roads. To the west was the flat red dust he was used to seeing stretch out to the horizon; and to the east there were just trees. Real trees like the ones in the forests around Spokane, with dark green brushy branches and tall trunks pointing to the sky.

"Where are we?" Doran asked, looking around in awe. "I don't see any creek."

"It's down below," Johnny said, motioning toward the cliff's edge. He jumped out and pulled a shotgun from under his seat. "I used to have a gun rack, but Eddie accidentally unloaded the gun into the window, so now I keep it under the seat," he said smiling.

Doran looked at Cal, who raised his eyebrows and chuckled.

The others also drew guns from beneath the seat.

"You didn't tell me we were supposed to bring our guns," Cal said.

Johnny smiled. "It's fine. You can use ours."

They walked to the edge of the rocky surface to an overlook that dropped fifty feet. The barren land extended and seemed to be unending. At the bottom of the drop was a small creek lined with the scrubby trees that Cal was beginning to think could grow just about anywhere from the looks of them. Together the boys took a seat at the top of the hill.

"What are we hunting?" Cal asked.

"Deer, elk, whatever," Puck answered.

"What season is it?"

"For us, whatever we want it to be."

"Let me guess: sovereign nation?"

Johnny cut in, "On the reservation, we have the right to hunt whenever we need the food."

Cal looked at Johnny quizzically. "This is part of the reservation?" He looked out over the valley.

Johnny nodded.

"I thought the Fort was just where the houses are."

"No. The reservation goes on for miles. There's a lot more than just the town."

Doran spoke up. "If you are allowed to hunt year round, is there anything left?"

147

"We don't hunt all the time. And we only hunt what we're going to eat."

"You really eat deer and elk?" asked Doran.

"Of course. You've never had it?"

Doran shook his head and said no.

"Have you ever hunted before?" Puck asked with a grin.

Cal and Doran looked each other, then shook their heads slowly.

"Have you ever shot a rifle?" Johnny asked.

"No," answered Cal.

"I have," Doran answered quickly.

"When?" Cal asked sternly.

"When Rick's Dad took us target shooting."

"That was a police revolver." Cal laughed. "Everyone's shot a handgun."

Johnny looked at him oddly. "I haven't."

"You've never shot a handgun?" Cal asked, amazed.

"Why would I? I don't hunt humans." He turned back to the view, sitting silently, waiting for any signs of life down at the creek.

Cal continued to look at Johnny in amazement. It surprised Cal that anyone from the Fort had such strong sentiments about anything.

Suddenly a screech pierced the silence of the arid valley. Cal looked up to find an eagle—his eagle—soaring above them.

"Quanuch," Puck said tenderly as he stared up at the majestic bird.

"What's that?" asked Doran, looking tired.

"It's an eagle," said Puck with a smile.

"I *know* it's an eagle. I meant, what is Quan...whatever you said."

"Quanuch means eagle," Johnny answered. "The Quanuch, or eagle, is looked at as the sun god."

"Really? They still think that stuff?" Cal asked innocently.

"You ask that like it's stupid or something," Johnny said.

Cal looked over to him, wondering if he'd really upset Johnny. "I didn't mean it as an insult. It just surprised me. I thought everyone around here was Mormon."

"Everyone who's white, maybe. They converted some of our people, but many of them came back."

Cal never went to church regularly. Mona talked to Cal and Doran about the Mormons before they moved out to the Fort, but she never talked much about the religion of the Utes. She told them stories about the Indians, but Cal brushed them off as folk tales.

"Is that what everyone on the Fort believes?" Cal asked, hesitant.

"Most have been taught it. The Elders feel we're losing our traditions and beliefs. They're trying to get more people to teach their children the old ways."

"Last night you said my grandfather is an Elder. Is that something important with religion?"

Johnny looked at Cal oddly. "He hasn't told you anything about it?"

Cal shook his head. "I haven't really given him the chance to say much of anything lately." He paused and thought a minute. "I do remember a story he told us one night on the phone, though."

Doran perked up. "Yeah, I remember that. The story about the animals in the bag."

Puck laughed. "The creation story."

"Creation story?" Cal and Doran said in unison.

"Yes," Johnny said smiling. "We're told that Sinawaf, the creator, cut sticks and put them in a bag. This went on for a very long time. Coyote became very curious and wanted to see what was in the bag." He paused, enjoying the fact that he had a captive audience. "One day, when Sinawaf was away, Coyote couldn't stand it anymore and he opened the bag to see what was inside. Out came all types of people, scattering in every direction. When Sinawaf returned, he found only a few people left. He'd planned to distribute the people equally all over the land, but because of the unequal distribution Coyote caused, there were wars all over the land. You know who was left in the bag?"

Doran piped up, "Let me guess: The Utes."

"Very good, my man," said Fly handing him a beer, "You get the prize."

Doran took it and looked over at Cal, surprised.

Johnny continued, "That's almost right, anyway. It was Nuchu."

"*Nuchu*? What's that?" asked Cal.

"*Nuchu* is us. We are Nuchu. Ute is the name the white people call us."

"Really," asked Cal, skeptic. "I've never heard that word before."

"You've never been Nuchu." Johnny nodded at Cal.

"Why? Is it because I'm half white?" Cal asked, annoyed.

Johnny smiled and shook his head. "No. Being Nuchu is what's inside, not what people see." He then turned back to Doran and continued his story. "Because our people, Nuchu, were loyal and waited for the Creator, he made us the bravest and strongest in the land." He smiled to himself. "Is that how you remember it?"

Cal nodded. "Yes. But I never really thought about what it meant. Is the coyote thought of as an evil animal?"

"No. We don't believe any animal is evil. They're just acting out by nature."

"Is that why a lot of the Indians have last names that use animals, like my grandparents?"

"Yes. We don't use them much outside the Fort because it gives white people another reason to look down on us."

"Use the name they gave you back home," Doran said, smiling at Cal.

"What was that?" asked Johnny.

"It was nothing," Cal mumbled, upset that Doran even brought it up. "They gave me a nickname because of my eyes."

"What's wrong with your eyes?" asked Puck as he studied Cal's face.

"It's nothing. They thought my eyes looked different because they're so blue, and most dark people have dark eyes. They called me 'The Wolf.'"

Johnny's eyebrows lowered and Puck looked over at him with dismay evident on his face.

"Yohovich," Puck said under his breath.

"What?" Cal asked.

Johnny glared at Puck.

"Yoho what? What did he say?" Cal asked, pointing at Puck.

"It's nothing," said Johnny with a tired sigh. "*Yohovich* means you're here for a reason."

Puck looked at Johnny, then nodded at Cal.

Cal looked skeptically at the group. "There are people out here who act like I shouldn't be here at all. That stupid sheriff is an ass. He can't just harass me for the hell of it. And I can't stay on the reservation all the time. Does he bother *you* when you go into town?" Cal asked.

"I never really had many dealings with him," said Johnny.

Puck stood up straight. "My father knows him since they were young. He thinks Franklin killed Jackie and always told me to stay away from him."

Cal nodded. "Good advice. I've tried to stay clear of him, but for some reason he keeps finding ways of messing up my life."

"Maybe he thinks you'll dredge up all those old memories," said Puck.

"Why would I do that? I had nothing to do with what happened in the past around here."

Johnny scoffed. "No, but you have a lot to do with the old memories. You're the reason Mona left." He stood up after loading his gun and began walking down a thin path toward a crevice in the rocky hillside.

"Wait a minute. You can't just say stuff like that and walk off. Why am I the reason my mom left?"

"She was pregnant with you. Do you really think your Dad would've married her if she hadn't been?"

Cal looked at him with astonishment.

Johnny looked back at him and shook his head. "I'm not trying to be cruel, but white guys don't marry Indian girls unless they have to."

Cal was numb with the thought that what Franklin Grayson said was true. David never loved Mona. He only married her because she was pregnant with Cal. If the other things he said were also true, maybe his dad really wanted Jackie. What if he really did kill her? A sharp chill shot through his stomach and he took a quick deep breath. It wasn't true. He didn't care what Johnny said. His father was no murderer.

8

Cal missed school for a week. He contemplated whether to accept defeat and change to Uintah High School in Vernal or continue on at Union High and put up with the torments of Mitch and his stooges. Coach Roos called several times, trying to talk with Cal about what happened. But Cal knew his life as a high school basketball star was over, and he hoped he could lean on his past record at Lewis and Clark High to make his way onto a small college team somewhere far from the Basin...and the Fort.

Cal and Doran spent most of their free time with Johnny and the others. They were a different group than what Cal was used to. They grew on him, and he soon found himself looking forward to their hunting trips in the backcountry.

It was a gray and dusty morning as the group pulled into a gas station to put oil in Johnny's truck. Cal saw Katrina walking out of the small store. A young boy clung to her hand and looked up at her with an admiring smile. Cal hesitated, not knowing if he should call to her. She turned and noticed Cal sitting in the truck. She gave him a surprised but beaming smile and waved. He stepped down from the truck and met her half way in the parking lot.

"Who's that?" asked the little boy.

"This is my friend, Cal," answered Katrina. She smiled coyly at Cal, who stood staring at her. "Cal, this is my little brother Ben."

"Hi Ben," Cal said, taking his eyes off her for a moment to smile at the child.

"Be careful and go back to Dad in the car," Katrina said, pointing him in the direction of a large blue Cadillac.

Cal saw an older man sitting in the driver's seat studying Cal. Cal smiled at him and the man gave an uneasy smile back, then turned to the door as Ben pulled unsuccessfully at the handle.

"You haven't been to school for days. Are you all right?" Katrina asked.

"Yes. I'm okay."

"I feel so bad about what happened the night of the game—"

Cal couldn't stand pity and cut her off, "To hell with them all. I'm here to finish school, and then I'm getting as far away as I can from this place."

"Where do you want to go?"

"Washington State."

"Katrina!" a strong voice called from the Cadillac.

She turned back toward the car. "Okay, I'm coming," she said, then turned back to Cal and smiled. "It was nice seeing you."

"Let's go out tomorrow."

She looked at the ground.

"Katrina," the voice called again.

She turned to her father with an impatient glare, then looked back at Cal "I'm just not sure if..."

"Say yes," said Cal smiling. "Come on."

She shook her head. "It could cause trouble."

"I don't care," he said, knowing how it would grate on Mitch. "Say yes." Cal looked back at her father in the car. He took her by the wrist. "I'm not letting you go until you say it."

Katrina's eyes grew big with surprise, but she didn't struggle against his grip. She smiled and rolled her eyes. "Okay, but don't say I didn't warn you."

"You let me worry about that. I'll call you tomorrow."

She began to walk away, but turned back. "Call me tonight."

"Okay. I will."

She smiled and ducked into the car. Cal saw her being scolded by her father and he smiled as they drove off.

"You're nuts," Doran said as Cal climbed into the truck. "Why do you want to get involved with her?"

Johnny also looked at Cal with the same question in his eyes.

"Because two can play Mitch's little game of 'make life miserable'," Cal answered.

"Huh?" Doran asked, frustrated.

Johnny smiled. "You're just going to use her to get Mitch crazy."

Doran looked at Cal. "You're crazy. Why do you just want to piss him off? You have enough problems with that idiot already."

"He's not going to back off now. I'm not sitting around letting him get away with this stuff. If he wants to try and make my life hell, I'm going to make his even worse."

Johnny sat up straight. "I can't say I blame you, Cal, but Franklin Grayson is not the kind of person you want to piss off. People say he's done some pretty evil stuff."

"Like killing my aunt," Cal said.

Johnny shrugged. "I don't know. Eddie is really the only person who knows for sure. That's why he never comes to town. My mom and dad think Franklin might try something because of what he thinks Eddie knows."

Cal sat back with an evil grin, contemplating the feeling of having Franklin arrested for the murder of Jackie after all these years.

"I know what you're thinking and that's impossible. Don't be bringing up the past. You'll only get hurt. All of that's over. You'll hurt everyone if you start bringing that stuff up again. Besides, who's going to listen to some kid from the Fort?" Johnny said as he drove from the station and pulled onto the highway.

Cal sighed loudly. "Someone was killed. Maybe that's your problem, Johnny. Maybe that's everyone's problem on the Fort. You don't want to speak up or defend yourselves. You can't go through life keeping silent and backing down from people."

"We don't like to stir things up, especially with Mitch. Franklin Grayson is the law out there. He can cause real problems for people."

"Whatever," Cal said, brushing off what Johnny'd said. "I refuse to sit back and let those two idiots make my life miserable. I'm going to fight back..."

"Why?" Johnny asked.

Cal began to answer, but then he stopped. He let the question roll around in his mind. He had a hundred reasons why, but none of them was a good answer to Johnny's question. "Because they're jackasses and they go out of their way to make my life hell. If I sit back and do nothing, it'll be even worse."

Johnny shook his head. "You'll only make it worse by provoking them."

"Maybe Johnny's right," Doran said quietly. "I hate them, too, but he's the Sheriff and he can do stuff and then where do we turn?"

Cal tried to fake a convincing shrug of agreement. He knew how he felt and he was tired of trying to convince Johnny and Doran of his position.

They'd be at Bitter Creek soon, where Puck and Fly were waiting, and he didn't feel like arguing. He felt an unexplainable calmness in those hills. It was a comfort that only thoughts of his bedroom back home in Spokane evoked.

He'd never hunted until they moved to the Fort and, the thrill was new and exciting. The actual killing didn't interest him, and he rarely even carried a gun. But the feeling as they sat in wait, or stepped softly through the brush stalking their prey, was a rush. After the sun had set and they were getting ready to leave, Cal sat with the others on the red rock cliffs and stared out over the valley. From their vantage point, the sun performed a majestic mural of fiery reds and oranges. A lone tree at the bottom of the ridge with its twisted limbs was silhouetted, making it the star. Cal let his mind drift to the stories Johnny told of their ancestors and the Creator.

As he sat and thought about the animals, plants, and rocks actually feeling and thinking, Cal felt an odd sense of connection to the land, a land he found more and more difficult to hate. It was evident everyday that it wasn't the place he hated, but rather his situation. It wasn't the desolate Basin or the rundown streets of the Fort that caused him grief; it was the feeling of the unknown that filled him with a crushing sense of emptiness.

As the truck pulled into its familiar place, Cal spied Puck squatting in the middle of a sun-baked plateau, holding a magnifying glass over a bug. Fly leaned against a tree smoking a cigarette.

"What took you so long?" asked Puck with a grin as he pulled on his gloves.

"Cal was busy trying to steal Mitch Grayson's girlfriend," Johnny chided.

"She's not property. She doesn't belong to him," Cal said.

Doran walked quickly to a motorcycle parked near Fly. "Cool. Can I take it for a ride?"

Fly shrugged. "It's Puck's."

Doran looked at Puck for a response.

"Later," Puck called to him with a smile.

Fly ignored the conversation and looked out over the Basin as thin wisps of his black hair curled and twisted like the trails of smoke that flowed from his pursed lips. As he looked over the ridge into the valley, he noticed movement and strained to see what was walking along the base of the cliff. He ducked down out of sight and whispered loudly to the others. "Hey, get a load of this!" he said, motioning to the others to get down and take a look.

Cal slithered over, expecting to see a large deer or elk, but as he peered over the heat-baked ledge, he saw three figures walking along the azure blue stream. As he watched them for a minute, his curiosity turned to rage. "Oh God!" he whispered loudly, "It's Mitch!"

"No it isn't," said Doran. "Is it?"

Cal nodded slowly. He couldn't believe Mitch was there, in Cal's only place of refuge. He lay on the hot rock, watching Mitch and his friends pitch stones into the stream. "What are they doing up here?" he asked Johnny.

"Smoking, it looks like."

"Smoking? Why do they have to come up here to smoke?"

"Because it's against their religion. They're Mormons. They can't smoke or drink."

"Give me a break," said Cal.

"It's true," chuckled Puck. "If their parents knew, they'd beat the crap out of them."

"They can't smoke but they can ruin people's lives," said Cal.

"That's the Grayson's. Not all Mormons are like that."

"Why are they clear out here?" Doran asked.

Johnny paused as he watched Mitch and his friends continue upstream to just underneath the large promontory where he and the others lay in wait. He whispered softly, "They come here to destroy our sacred sites."

"They're the ones who paint over the writings. Why?" Doran whispered back.

"Because they don't give a damn," Johnny said.

"Let's stop them," Cal said, raising himself off the rock.

Johnny pulled him back into place. "Don't!"

"You're just going to let them destroy the writings? They were made thousands of years ago! I thought you said this was land that belongs to us."

A shadow passed over Cal's face and he looked up at the sky to see the large eagle soaring at a distance.

"Quanuch," said Doran, smiling as he peered up at the eagle.

"Very good," laughed Puck as he messed Doran's hair and turned back to watch the eagle swoop and soar above them.

"The eagle is our protector," explained Johnny. "If Quanuch gives you one of her feathers, you will be protected for life."

A shot rang out from the valley and the group flinched. Cal peered cautiously over the ridge to see Mitch reload and aim at the bird. "He's trying to kill the eagle!" He grabbed a rock and lobbed it over the edge.

They heard the group below react when the rock tumbled to the valley floor.

"Cal! What are you doing?" Johnny asked.

"Stopping them. Don't just sit there and do nothing."

"Don't. We can't control what they do. It'll cause bigger problems for everyone."

"Bull! Maybe you can lie here and watch, but I won't." He rolled over and grabbed Johnny's rifle. Loading it, he flinched again as another shot rang out from the valley. He looked up at the sky to see the bird still flying untouched. He wanted to yell out, "Fly away!" But the bird refused the chance to escape and kept circling above him.

"Cal, are you crazy?" asked Doran. "What are you going to do? Shoot them?"

"Hell no! But at least I'll give them a good scare." He looked up over the ridge, and as Mitch pulled the gun up into range again, Cal took aim somewhere out in the desolate valley and pulled the trigger. The shot echoed loudly and Mitch and the two others fell to the ground, then scrambled to some large rocks for cover.

"He won't kill an animal, but shooting at humans is okay," Johnny said to Doran as he motioned toward Cal.

"I didn't aim anywhere near them," said Cal, laughing.

"And besides, they're not human," mumbled Fly, his only words so far that day.

Cal looked back at him and smiled.

They heard a scuffle from below and a scared voice yelled out, "Who's there?"

Cal covered his mouth to keep from laughing.

"Watch this," whispered Puck. He pulled himself close to the ridge and then cupped his hands to his mouth and yelled, "I am the god of the eagle and I will crush your nuts with those rocks if you shoot at me ever again."

Even Johnny smiled as the others struggled to keep from laughing. He motioned to them to slide back to the truck. Cal took a final glance over the bluff to see the three huddled visibly behind an inadequate rock.

He slid back and crawled into the truck with the others. Once inside, they all roared. Cal looked up to the sky to see that the eagle was now a small black speck in the sky. He felt relief, but he also felt like he himself was the protector.

The engine of the truck turned over roughly and then died. Johnny tried again, but the truck only sputtered and heaved. Again he tried and tried, until finally all the truck did was make a dead, clicking sound. "I just put two quarts of oil in this thing," he yelled.

"Great. What are we going to do now?" Doran asked.

"We've got the motorcycle," Puck answered.

"That leaves three of us here," Cal said.

"We can bring back my truck," said Fly.

"That'll take over an hour. It'll be dark by then," said Doran, obviously nervous about staying behind.

"What else can we do?" Johnny answered. "Fly, take the motorcycle and go get your truck. Take Doran with you and hurry. We'll try to get the truck going."

"Maybe we should start walking back toward the highway," Cal said.

"It's not a good idea. When it gets dark, we'd risk getting lost and that's when the coyotes come out," Johnny said.

The wind started to pick up and Cal offered Doran his letterman jacket for the ride on the motorcycle. Doran pulled it on and put the helmet on, too. "Can I ride the motorcycle back?" he asked Fly with a childlike grin.

Fly gave Cal a look of frustration, then patted Doran on the helmet. "Yes, you can ride it back." Fly started the bike and the two headed off toward town.

Cal leaned against the truck, and several seconds later heard the same voice call from below the cliff, "Hello?"

Cal cupped his hands to reply, but Johnny hushed him, "Don't let them know we're still here. Maybe they'll leave."

Cal shrugged and kept quiet. He stood looking out over the horizon, feeling an odd bond with the sun and earth. The brilliant reds of sunset had already started their performance and it looked to be one of their finest.

Johnny slowly lifted the hood of the truck and jiggled hoses and wires, "I don't understand it. It's never done this before."

Puck pulled his jacket from the truck. "Murphy's law," he mumbled.

Cal scooted cautiously to the edge of the cliff and tried to look over. There were no signs of anyone behind the rocks, and he saw no one in the valley below. Then he noticed movement on the underside of the ledge and called back to Johnny, "They're trying to climb up here!"

He rolled back around and stuck his head out over the edge to see how far they'd climbed. A shot rang out, booming in Cal's ears. His heart jumped as he rolled back and ran for the truck. "Holy crap!" he shouted. "They're shooting at us!"

Johnny slammed down the hood and grabbed his gun. "This is just great. I knew you shouldn't have joked around by firing that shot. Grab the rifle from under the seat and get down."

Puck ran back with fear in his eyes. "What do I do?"

"Get your shotgun. There's a box of extra shells in the glove compartment," Johnny answered out of breath.

Puck grabbed his gear and then sat behind the tire and

tried to load the gun, his hands shaking visibly as shells spilled onto the ground.

The three sat behind the large wheels of the truck. The only movements visible were their chests heaving as they waited nervously, their guns cocked by their sides.

Several minutes passed in silence; then Puck whispered, "How long has it been since Doran and Fly left?"

Cal glanced quickly at his watch. "I don't know. Why?"

"I can hear something," said Puck, "It sounds like the motorcycle."

"I hear it, too," said Johnny.

They all looked off through the dimming sky to see a motorcycle coming toward them with a dark truck following behind.

"Is it them?" asked Puck.

"Yes, I think it is," Johnny said hopefully. "And there's a black truck. It's not Fly's. They must've found help."

As the bike got closer, a strange, sick feeling came over Cal. He knew that help was on the way, but he didn't feel relief; only fear. That feeling grew stronger until he felt his heart pounding uncontrollably in his chest.

When the bike came clearly into view, Doran smiled widely, the first time Cal had seen him happy in weeks. He was obviously feeling like the conquering hero. But then Cal turned back to the ridge and saw Mitch braced up over the cliff with his gun at the ready.

"Get down! He's got a gun!" Cal screamed as he waved his arms frantically at Doran and Fly.

Doran's eyebrows lowered at Cal in a questioning stare

as a loud crack shattered the cool, quiet night. Then Doran's arms flew back from the handlebars and into Fly, and the bike weaved slightly and spun to the ground, throwing off Doran and Fly.

Cal swung around from the truck and aimed the rifle. He shot twice as Mitch scurried from the ledge, then Cal heard Mitch scream. It wasn't a cry of pain, but one of terror. When he heard the sound of tumbling rocks, he knew that Mitch had fallen.

Cal ran from behind the truck to see Fly holding Doran's quivering body on his lap. A large Indian man came running from the big black truck and they quickly pulled Doran to cover behind the truck.

Cal yelled, "We've got to get him to the hospital!"

The man ripped Doran's shirt open, exposing a bloody hole at the base of Doran's neck. He tried to find a pulse and put his head down to Doran's mouth, listening for any sign of life. Then the man looked sadly at Cal. "He's bad. We need to hurry."

"Oh, god! This isn't happening!" Cal yelled. Then he hoisted Doran into his arms. But as he rushed to the truck, blood gushed from Doran's mouth, soaking Cal's shirt. He dropped his head onto Doran's chest and sobbed as he stood holding his brother's limp body.

"Help me!" Cal yelled. Johnny came to Cal and tried to help him lift Doran into the truck.

Then Johnny climbed in next to Cal, holding Doran's legs on his lap. The Indian man slid in behind the wheel as Fly climbed into the back.

"I promised my dad I'd take care of him," Cal sobbed

as they drove. "God, please no. Please don't take my brother. Please don't let this happen!"

The gurgling sounds coming from Doran's neck were an odd sense of comfort; at least Cal knew he was breathing.

Johnny, usually the calm one, turned anxious. "He'll be all right. He'll be all right," he kept saying.

Cal knew he was trying to convince himself rather than to comfort anyone else.

After a terrifying and blurred drive to town, the truck pulled into the ambulance entrance of the small Roosevelt hospital. Puck jumped out and ran into the emergency room screaming for help, and instantly a young doctor appeared, followed by two large men with a gurney who took Doran carefully from Cal, lay him down and raced him inside. Cal followed, trying desperately to see what was happening.

"He needs blood," the doctor shouted.

"Take mine." Cal called out to the doctor. "We have a rare blood type—AB negative."

The doctor turned back to him, annoyed. But seeing Cal's anguish, he tried to soften his tone as he explained, "We don't have time."

The gurney disappeared into a room and the door closed off his view of his brother. Cal stood numb and frozen in the hallway as the room began to hum with a high-pitch buzz and the walls began to weave. His knees began to shake and buckle, and then all he saw was black.

"Cal?" He heard a deep voice calling to him from somewhere far away. He blinked and opened his eyes, then squinted into the bright light. "Are you all right?" the voice asked him.

It was Raymond, and when Cal looked up into his grandfather's red, wet eyes, he tried to nod to show that he was okay.

"What about Doran?" Cal asked, trying to sit up as he suddenly remembered what brought him to the hospital.

But Raymond only lowered his head and put his hand up to cover his quivering mouth.

"What?" Cal asked. "What is it? Is he okay?" Cal asked as he sat up.

An older woman came to his side and looked to Raymond for direction.

"No!" Cal yelled. "Where is he?"

Raymond's sobs became uncontrollable now and as he reached out to Cal, his sinewy hands shook.

Cal pushed him aside and leaped up from the bed, then barged through the doors and into the emergency room's nurse's station. He took a sweeping gaze around at the cubicles, looking for any sign of his brother but saw no hint of Doran. He went to the waiting room where he saw Johnny, Puck and Fly, all sitting in a circle. Puck noticed Cal and stood up, his face etched with concern. Cal ignored him and looked the other way.

At the other end of the waiting room stood Silver Hair. His back was to Cal as he looked into the doorway of one of the exam rooms, a woman stood by his side. She was smiling and talking to a patient in that room, and as Cal walked toward them and looked past the sheriff, he saw that it was Mitch sitting on the exam table with a nurse wrapping a bandage around his leg. Seeing Mitch alive and well, with only minor injuries, made something inside Cal snap and he was flooded with rage.

Hearing Cal's footsteps, Silver Hair turned toward him and sneered, "I ought to arrest you right now, you son of a bitch."

With that, Cal walked over and flung Silver Hair aside.

The woman screamed as Silver Hair, not expecting the blow, toppled backward, his glasses flying off. He reached for them, giving Cal the time he needed to pounce on Mitch.

"I'll kill you!" Cal yelled.

"Help! Call Security—tell them to hurry!" the nurse screamed as Cal hit Mitch, knocking him from the exam table.

The chaotic sounds of metal equipment hitting the floor combined with the anxious voices flooding the room. Johnny, Fly and Puck tried to pull Cal off Mitch but he ignored them as he kept throwing punches at Mitch, who did little more than writhe and moan as Cal raged and thrashed. Finally, several strong blows to the side of Cal's head made him back down and he allowed himself to be heaved off Mitch. Then he turned around, trying to find Silver Hair, and noticed him being held back by one of the large men that had helped carry Doran in from the truck.

Cal's anger surged again and he lurched toward him. "He killed my brother. Your bastard son killed my brother!"

"He didn't kill him. *You* did. Mitch was just defending himself," Silver hair shouted back.

"Defending himself? You stupid piece of crap!" Cal

screamed as he lunged toward the sheriff again, struggling against the arms that held him back.

"Get him into that room," the doctor shouted to security. "Franklin, go help Mitch."

Cal struggled, only to find that Johnny, Puck and Fly were there, holding him back once more. The doctor followed the boys into a room, where Raymond and a nurse stood by looking solemn.

"Did we find the parents?" the doctor asked the nurse.

"Yes. We just located the boy's mother and she's on her way," she answered.

"What about *his* father?" he asked.

Cal shook free from his friends' grip and slumped into a chair. "My dad lives in Spokane," he muttered, defeated.

"What about Doran's dad?" asked the doctor.

Cal looked up at him, confused. "I just told you, he's in Spokane."

"You said *your* dad. What about Doran's?" the doctor asked.

Another nurse looked in and updated the doctor, saying "The mother is here."

"Thank you," the doctor said to her. "Keep him here," he ordered Johnny, Puck and Fly, who nodded as the security guard walked out.

The doctor left the room and Raymond followed him to the door. The old man stopped for a moment and tried to control his breathing. Then he wiped the tears from his devastated face and tried to hold back his sobs.

When a piercing scream came from outside the door, Raymond slumped against the wall. Cal, too, felt his emotions surface, realizing that his mother had just been told the news about Doran. The sound of her sorrow made everything at last hit Cal full force and he suddenly understood that a huge part of him was missing and gone forever. A vast emptiness and void was tearing him and as that crevasse became larger and deeper, the hollow pain it left behind made him want to vomit.

He turned to Raymond, saying, "Let's get her and go home."

Johnny looked at him, concerned.

"Don't worry. I'm not going to do anything else. Not now, anyway."

With that, Raymond pushed open the door. There Mona stood sobbing and ran to Raymond. Silver Hair was nowhere to be seen, and when Cal looked around the waiting area, there sat Rachel. "Oh god!" he thought. "What am I going to say to her?" She looked up at him somberly and began to cry, then ran to Cal, embracing him the way she did as a little girl.

"Why? Why'd they do this?" she cried through her tears.

Cal just held her, then tried to explain.

"They're not going to put you in jail, are they?" she sobbed.

"Me? Why would they put me in jail?" he asked, perplexed.

"Please don't leave me here alone. Please, Cal! I can't take it." she said whispered.

Cal walked her toward the door. "Rachel, I'm taking you home right now. And I'm not going anywhere."

"But that man…That man said our whole family should be locked up."

"What man?"

"He was with the lady, and his son has a broken leg. He was yelling and telling people that you did all this."

"Don't worry about him. And I didn't do anything." A stab of guilt struck his heart as he replayed the devastating scene at the lake in his mind. If he hadn't taken those warning shots at Mitch, would Doran still be alive? Cal walked Rachel outside, then turned back towards the door, wondering if he should wait for Mona and Raymond, or if it'd be better to just take his sister home. Then a horrible feeling struck him when he realized he'd never have to wonder where Doran was again. All his life, Cal had two people to look after, his brother and sister. When they went swimming, he'd always kept one eye on Rachel and the other on Doran. Even though they were both were good swimmers, he'd always watched over them. But now all that was changed forever.

The area's landscape seemed more desolate than ever. The manicured grass around the hospital was sterile and out of place, compared to the red rocks and dried brush of the Basin. Cal stood with Rachel, who still clung to him, when Raymond led Mona from the hospital.

"We'll meet you back home," his grandfather said softly to them.

Cal's instinct was to argue against the use of the word *home*, but instead he simply nodded and directed Rachel toward the parking lot. He wandered for a moment, trying to remember where he'd parked. But as Raymond pulled away, Cal's head cleared and he remembered that it was the man in the black truck who'd driven him to the hospital with Doran and the others, but he was too exhausted to run after his grandfather's car to stop him.

By this time, all he wanted was to sit down on the sidewalk and cry, but he knew he had to stay strong for Rachel. When he turned back toward the hospital to go look for a phone, Johnny, Puck and Fly emerged. "What're you guys still doing here?" Cal asked them.

"We didn't have a ride home, so we're waiting for Fly's mom. Why're you two still here?" Johnny asked.

"We kind of got left behind by accident. I forgot that I didn't drive here. Anyway, can we catch a ride with you?"

"Sure."

An awkward silence followed as the group stood there in the chill, staring out at the nothingness of the land. The sound of Rachel sniffling shook Cal from his trance and he pulled her to him to comfort her.

"It's going to be all right," he soothed, rubbing her arm.

"I can't believe he's gone," she sobbed.

Puck came over to her. "He's not gone, Rachel. He'll always be with you." He gently put his hand on her back.

The tender gesture surprised Cal, but he welcomed the added comfort for his sister.

But Rachel said, "What do you mean?" as she asked looking up at Puck.

"Puck—" Johnny cautioned, looking at Cal.

"No, it's okay," said Cal, nodding to Puck.

Puck smiled kindly and continued to rub Rachel's back with tenderness. "His spirit will always be here. It'll always be with you because he loves you."

Cal bit the inside of his cheek, trying to hold back the tears as Rachel sobbed into Cal's chest.

Puck looked up at Cal. "He's not gone," he said. "Nothing ever really dies."

Cal tried to speak, but instead just nodded and rested his head against Rachel's soft black hair.

A car pulled up then and a stocky Indian woman got out and ran to Rachel. In a quiet voice, she cuddled Rachel and took her into the car, looking up at Cal with pained and sympathetic eyes. Without Rachel to hold onto, Cal felt even more empty and alone.

As they drove back to the Fort, the wide expanse of the Basin made Cal feel lost in a void. He also felt that something was missing, as though he'd left Doran behind, and he wanted to go back and get his body. Should they have left him there? He thought again about what Puck had said and hoped that it was true. Would Doran's spirit live on? But how? And where?

The broken family stood forlornly in the wind on the long, dusty runway as a small plane took off with Doran's body. It was on its way to Salt Lake City, there to be loaded onto a large jet, and then home to Spokane. *That's where Doran wanted to be*, Cal thought. It was David's idea to have him come home, and Cal readily agreed. Doran had always wanted to go home, and it felt right to send him there.

But now, Cal wasn't sure where home was anymore. He used to know without doubt that it was the house on

Robin Road in Spokane, with its well-worn basketball rim, the large flowering trees lining the back yard, and the horrible green carpet in the family room. But he didn't feel the same way about it any longer. Without having his parents together, and especially without Doran, it'd never be home again for him. Now, it was just an ordinary house, one that held little meaning for him.

Even the city Cal grew up in no longer felt familiar and seemed so far away. His friends had all stopped calling him months ago, and he felt his burning need to go back there waning bit by bit each day. Part of him still longed to ask his father to let him move back, but he understood that most of it came from feeling so alone without Doran, rather than from truly wanting to return to Spokane.

Doran's funeral was planned through many screaming arguments over the phone. Mona wanted the funeral to be held at the Fort, especially if the burial was in Spokane. But David wanted everything to take place in Spokane. Cal somehow avoided any and all questions that sucked him into the middle of their fights. In the end, there was no funeral at all and as Doran's body was taken away, the only words that were said over it came from Rachel, there on the runway.

"Bye, Doran. I love you," she whispered through her sobs. Her black hair blew in her face as she stood in the wind, watching Doran leave the Fort forever.

Cal stood in silence as the small plane soared upward, and then turned toward the West. He kept his eyes on it until it was nothing more than a speck. Then Cal watched as the speck seemed to turn back and grow as it came closer and closer toward him. He shaded his eyes just as the wings fluttered down gracefully and he forced himself out of his daze to realize it was a bird crossing in front of the bright morning sun. As he stood huddled in an inadequate jacket, he wondered if it were his eagle as he searched the sky for Doran's plane. He searched the horizon but saw nothing but the bird.

"Cal," Raymond said.

He turned back to his grandfather, then was startled to find everyone else at the car. He wiped the tears from his eyes and said, "I'm sorry, I didn't realize—" Cal tried to gather his words.

"Quanuch," Raymond said, staring up at the bird.

"Yes, I know. Johnny told me," Cal said, walking past Raymond toward the car.

"The eagle is a protector," Raymond continued, trying to ignore Cal's back.

Cal turned to him, shaking his head, "Oh, yeah? Well, he sure did a hell of a job watching over Doran, didn't he! When are you going to grasp reality and admit that all this Indian stuff is a lot of bullshit?"

Raymond's face fell in despair and he sighed deeply, unable to look at his grandson.

Cal noticed how his words affected Raymond and felt a flood of regret and a sudden need to make amends. "I'm sorry—" he began.

"Doran has no anger. I know he doesn't blame you for what happened."

Now Cal felt the rage build inside him. "What's that supposed to mean?"

"I know you blame yourself. That's why you're so angry. You feel like you need to take care of everyone, and now you think you failed Doran. Cal, if you want to take out your anger on me, that's fine. In fact, you can blame the whole thing on me. After all, it *is* all my fault." Then Raymond turned and walked to the car.

"How?" Cal asked, following him. "How is it your fault?"

At that point, Mona came over to them and said, "Cal, what are you doing? Get in the car and let's go."

Cal ignored her and Raymond just stood there, his face weary and old.

"How is it *your* fault?" he demanded of Raymond again.

"I made Mona come back here," he answered quietly.

"Dad, stop." Mona yelled. "Cal, knock it off."

"You? Why?" Cal asked.

"I thought it was my only chance to be able to get to know you. I—"

"That's enough," Mona shouted.

Cal felt only shock at his grandfather's admission. He'd always thought Raymond had no interest in seeing his grandchildren. In fact, he was sure of it and argued his point. "If that's true, why didn't you ever come see us in Spokane?"

Raymond tried to answer but couldn't. He looked at Mona, who simply stormed off toward the car.

That's when Cal finally understood that Raymond was never invited to visit them. He must have felt as much like an alien being around David and the rest of their family as

Cal did coming to the reservation. Cal wanted to know more, but he knew it could wait. But still, he walked over to his grandfather and took him by the arm. "I guess we better go, Grandpa," Cal said, feeling the exhaustion of the day.

The drive home was quiet and dinner that evening went by like a blur for Cal. All he could think of was Doran; his constant optimism, his loyalty and the utter emptiness Cal felt now that he was gone.

Cal excused himself and went to bed early. He lay on his bed thinking, wondering how he could stop the pain and feel good again. He didn't see how he'd ever get over losing his brother. But then he thought about his mother. Was that why she seemed angry all the time? It'd been almost twenty years since she'd lost Jackie, but now Cal understood that some wounds might never heal.

As his eyes became heavy from the weight of life, he felt himself begin to float. His body was carried upward and soon he was soaring over the red rocks and scrubby hillsides of the Uintah Basin. He saw the town, with its tiny homes and the tribal center; he swooped down low as he came upon the glassy darkness of Bottle Hollow, and then he soared high above it all and found his way to the lookout point along the cliff at Bitter Creek. There he hovered, searching. Cal felt something missing and frantically scanned the area. Then he felt his ability to fly begin to fade; it happened slowly at first, but then it turned into freefall. The knot in his stomach rose up to his throat and his high-pitched scream, accompanied by banging on his door woke Cal from his dream, barely breathing and terrified. He came out of his room to see what the commotion was about.

"They're all out there!" Rachel told him, her voice quivering.

Cal looked at her, still half stunned by the dream and bleary eyed. "Who's out there?" he asked.

"I don't know. But they're all walking toward the house with torches. It's a big crowd."

Cal jumped out of bed and ran to the window to see what his sister was talking about.

Far down the street he could see a group marching slowly towards the house, surrounded by a fiery haze. He could see many parked cars behind them in the distance. The night was dark, but the torches the people held lit up the basin sky with a golden glow.

"Go get Grandpa. I'll be right there." He sent her away and pulled on his jeans and threw on his jacket. When he got to the front door, Raymond and Mona stood peering through the small side window, then turned back to Cal with looks of confusion and concern.

Cal pushed through them and opened the door.

"Cal, what are you doing?" Mona asked in a scared whisper.

Cal looked back. "I'm not backing down anymore. If they want a fight, I'll give it to them."

"Cal, no! There's too many of them," Raymond insisted.

Rachel started to cry in the corner. "Please don't get hurt. Please, Cal."

"Call Johnny," Cal told Raymond. "Tell him I need help."

As the group closed in, Cal took a deep breath, opened the screen door and stepped out onto the porch. He crossed his arms on his chest and stood in a stalwart stance under the dim porch light, watching the fiery shimmer against the cool black night as the crowd walked toward him. It was a large group of at least thirty people, and seeing them all made Cal feel even more isolated and alone. As they got closer, Cal noticed that the crowd included adults, teens, and even some young children. This in particular confused him and he wondered why these people brought children to a fight. The young men leading the group were ones he recognized from school. He was especially surprised to see them here—they were people that Doran had clearly liked and talked about enthusiastically. This made Cal even sadder, to think that Doran didn't know the truth about these guys who he'd considered friends.

When the group reached Raymond's front yard, Cal planted his feet and took a deep breath, ready for the inevitable fight. Then the crowd stopped and stood silent and Cal noticed two men in the back carrying something forward. He furrowed his brows as he scanned the group, studying their faces. And there, instead of anger or fury, he only saw forlorn expressions and sorrow. And what they carried weren't mob torches but candles. That's when Cal realized he was wrong about why these people had come.

Now Brent Johansen stepped forward and spoke to him, saying, "Cal, we're here because we wanted to honor Doran."

Cal gave him a skeptical squint and swallowed. "You do? But why?"

Brent looked down at the ground, gathered his thoughts and then went on. "Because he was a good person. I didn't know him very long, but I still considered him a friend."

Cal looked around at the others who were stirring and shifting uncomfortably now.

Then the screen door opened and Raymond came out to stand beside Cal.

At the same time, a man with a full head of grayish blond hair and kind eyes stepped forward next to Brent. "Cal, my name is Gordon Johansen. I'm Brent's father. I own the lumber yard in town, and Doran worked for me after school."

Cal tilted his head, clearly puzzled.

Gordon nodded. "He didn't tell you because he wanted it to be a surprise. It was Brent who introduced me to Doran. They were friends at school, and he told Brent about a project he wanted to do and wondered if he could work for me to get it done." Gordon looked down as his emotions overcame him. "Doran told me that his grandpa's house needed a new roof, and he said he'd work as many hours as he needed to help pay for it. I told him it could be several thousand dollars, but he said he didn't care. He said he wanted it done." He then turned to Raymond. "Sir, I have a group of men here who are going to donate their time. I'll donate the material and you'll have a new roof."

But Raymond just shook his head. "No," he said. "I don't want to take anything I don't pay for."

Gordon smiled and put his hand up. "But you won't be; it's not charity, sir. Doran earned it and we want to do this for him."

Now Raymond smiled sincerely. "That is very kind of you. Thank you."

Then Brent spoke up. "When we heard what happened to Doran, we felt horrible. And when we found out there wasn't going to be a funeral here, we decided to give him a memorial ourselves. I hope that's okay."

Now the two men at the back walked forward, carrying a large wood and iron bench that they sat on Raymond's lawn.

Brent went on. "We made this," he said, brushing his hand along the back of the bench. "You can't see it in the dark, but we carved his name into it. We hope you can put it in a place where you can go to sit and remember him."

Rachel quietly crept outside and clung to Cal. Cal looked down at her, then put his arm around her shoulders.

It was still sinking in that Doran had led a secret life. Cal was surprised, but he also wondered if he didn't realize what Doran was up to because he was too wrapped up in his own concerns. He sighed and tried to smile. "It's very nice, and thank you. But I still don't understand why you're all doing this. Mr. Johansen and Brent say they knew Doran, but what about the rest of you? I bet most of you haven't ever been out here before. Why come now?"

The crowd stirred and Raymond turned to Cal, stunned.

Gordon spoke up. "It's okay, Mr. Littlebear. Cal's right. We should have stood up before. There's no excuse. All we can say is that we're here now, and we want you to know your brother made a difference."

An older woman Cal recognized walked through the crowd and came forward, asking, "Do you remember me?"

Cal nodded. It was the woman whose car was stuck on the highway—Nurse Nan.

"I didn't know your brother at all, Cal. I came here for you. You didn't have to help me that day, but you did. You're a fine young man, and if your brother was anything like you, then I know he was good, too."

With that, Cal felt his armor melt and he stood there with his chest heaving and his eyes overflowing with tears.

Nurse Nan continued. "Our church group prepared a song and we'd like to offer a prayer—if that's okay and a respectable thing to do." She looked to Raymond for approval and he nodded.

Nan directed four young girls forward and to the front of the crowd. They looked at Cal shyly and fidgeted, then cleared their throats and looked to each other for the signal to start. Now the stillness of the quiet evening was filled with the soft chimes of the girls' voices. It was a slow and somber song, but one that sounded inspired from heaven.

His guard down completely, Cal just stood and let the tears fall. Rachel cried, too, but Cal could tell that she was comforted, and knowing this helped to buoy him up, too. Raymond smiled, but then he turned and went inside. This distracted Cal, and he stood wondering what Raymond was doing.

Then a loud engine roared from behind, and Johnny's truck rolled up with Puck and Fly beside him. They hurried out and rushed up defensively towards the crowd.

Cal jumped off the porch and ran to meet them, blocking their path. He put a hand up to Johnny's chest and said, "It's okay, man. They're not here to cause trouble."

Johnny was obviously fired up and looked at Cal skeptically. The he looked around and scowled at the group.

"It's okay, Johnny. They came to remember Doran. They brought us a bench they made, and they're going to help my grandpa."

Johnny was still tense. "Why?" he demanded.

Cal let his head drop and laughed sadly. "Because Doran made a difference. While I was busy fighting with people, he was out there making friends instead."

Johnny relaxed, but then became uneasy with dozens of eyes watching him.

Suddenly the screen door creaked and slammed. Cal turned towards the porch, where Raymond stood holding a small drum. All eyes turned to him and he spoke to the group. "Tonight we remember and celebrate my grandson." Then he lowered his head and paused with his eyes closed.

The rest of the group looked confused, but in wanting to support him, they also lowered their heads and closed their eyes. Cal watched transfixed as his grandfather slowly raised his hand and banged the drum with a slow series of beats. Then he sang out with a low, heart-wrenching wail.

Some of the people opened their eyes in surprise and they all stood mesmerized as the old man's obvious love for his stolen grandson rang out into the nighttime sky. Their awed faces were filled with respect and empathy.

Cal felt his emotions rise and then watched as Johnny went to Raymond and joined his song. Then he felt the presence of others emerging from the shadows. They walked with heads bowed as they, too, joined the group. Cal recognized people from the Fort, neighbors and others who felt compelled to express their sympathy, too. The warm glow of the candles in the black sky, along with the passion of Raymond's song, filled Cal with a comfort that overwhelmed him.

When he looked up at the porch, he saw that Rachel had retreated to a small stool; she looked down at him and they both smiled. It was only then he realized that Mona was nowhere in sight, and that he hadn't seen her since he'd gone outside when the crowd first appeared on the street.

He tried to explain away her absence in his mind, but the energy of the people and the song took him back to Doran and how much he'd have loved this memorial. The vigil comforted Cal, but it still didn't give him peace, and the kindness these people showed made him miss his brother even more.

9

In the days that followed Doran's death and the spontaneous memorial, Mona became almost robotic. She hardly looked up as she wandered through the house, and although Cal talked with David on the phone, he sensed a chill in his voice; Cal knew that his dad blamed him for Doran's death. As for Rachel, her moods swung between high-pitched giggles to heart-wrenching sobs. Through all of it, Cal's only source of solace was his grandfather.

"There are three worlds, Cal," Raymond explained one night as the two sat alone after dinner. "There is the human world, the one we live in; next is the natural world, which includes the plants, animals, and earth; and finally there is the spirit world. That is where Doran is now. He is not unhappy or scared or sad. It is a beautiful place full of warmth and love."

Cal nodded through his tears and he felt his heart rise up in his chest.

Raymond put a hand on Cal's shoulder. "I know you miss him. I also know you feel guilt and pain. We all do."

"But I'm the one who was supposed to watch out for

him," Cal said, his voice shaky as he tried to clear his throat. "I was supposed to take care of everyone!"

"Cal, no one can control someone else's actions. If you're responsible for Mitch taking aim, then I'm responsible for Doran being there in the first place."

Cal looked at him. "Why? Because you asked Mom to move us here?"

Raymond nodded slowly. "Yes. It was selfish on my part. I wanted you to see who you came from, and to know that you have people here."

"But why?"

"Why what?"

"Why did you want us to know? We always knew about the Fort—it wasn't a secret."

"Yes, but you need to know about your culture...your history."

Cal shrugged.

"Cal, I know you feel that there is nothing here for you, but someday you'll realize that being Indian can be a source of pride and that it will help you in your life. All I've ever wanted was to teach my children and my grandchildren about our ways." Raymond paused and took a slow deep breath. "I begged Mona to move back. I couldn't bear the thought of losing more of my grandchildren."

"More?"

"Yes. Eddie hardly knows who I am, even though he lives down the street. And then there was the baby Jackie was pregnant with when she died."

"Franklin Grayson's," Cal said knowingly.

"Yes. I believe the baby was his. I don't think Jackie

ever wanted to marry Franklin. I think it was an accident. She was already a very young mother, and she knew it'd be an even bigger mistake to marry him. Besides, she watched Mona try desperately to escape and saw the sorrow it brought her. Jackie was happy here. I feel that she, like Doran, was a contented soul who fell prey to the world around her." He stood up and cleared some of the dishes from the table. "Mona had little interest in any of the boys from the Fort. All she wanted was to get away from here. She thought that marrying a white boy would give her that freedom."

Cal's heart sunk when he heard yet another person validate what Franklin had said about his mother and father. He also saw the obvious comparison of himself to his mother. Even if Raymond wasn't trying to make the connection, it was clear to Cal that while Doran and Jackie were innocent victims of the people around them, he was more like his mother, wasting his energy and life trying to get away.

He thought for a moment, and then turned his attentions back to his grandfather. "Why didn't they arrest Franklin Grayson for Jackie's murder?"

"I'm not sure. I think his connection to the police had something to do with it."

"But that doesn't make sense. He's the sheriff now, but he wasn't back then."

Raymond lifted an eyebrow. "But his father was."

Cal moaned. "His father was the Sheriff? No wonder he was never charged. That's crap. He got away with it because his father was the sheriff—just like Mitch."

Raymond nodded sadly. "I was so upset when it all happened, I could hardly speak to anyone. Your great-grandmother had died of cancer just two months before, and I didn't think I could bear the thought of living anymore with so much grief. Mona took care of everything— the police and the funeral. And then I lost her, too."

Cal's heart ached, knowing well the pain of losing someone you love. "If the memories of this place hurt so bad, why don't *you* leave?"

"What good would that do? This is my home. Running away isn't going to erase what happened. Besides, I have many more good memories here that I don't ever want to forget. I also have responsibilities here. If we leave, we'll lose what is ours."

"Johnny said the same thing the other day," Cal said shaking his head. "He said they were just handed this land by the government."

Raymond took a deep breath. A look of hurt and sadness weathered his face right before Cal's eyes. "We weren't given anything, Cal. We were *robbed* of everything. Our people used to live all over this valley, from the town they call Provo through parts of Colorado and far to the South. It was beautiful, rich land that we farmed, and we lived the way we're told by the Creator. But when the white men found our beautiful valley, they wanted it for themselves. They pushed our people and our people pushed back. There were many battles; so many lives were lost. But the white man was too strong and he wore our people down. They chose the most desolate and undesirable part of our land and forced us to live on it. But they didn't take the time to really look. In the valleys and forests, what's left of our land is quite beautiful. And now our land produces precious petroleum and gas, so they want our land back. I could never leave and let them take the only thing I have."

"But what about the young people? Why don't they take up the fight? Why do *you* have to do it?"

"The young people don't understand the history, Cal. Many don't care or want to learn our traditions, and now I'm afraid they'll be lost forever."

"They won't be lost if you write them down. Aren't there books on this stuff?"

"There are. But most of them are written by other people; writers who are not *us*. If you don't live it and practice it, it's not the same and will be lost. Our traditions are good ones and they help us live a good life. But now all our young people think about is taking the easy way out and so the traditions are dying. We try to teach them and keep them going, but we are all getting very old. I'm sure I won't live much longer."

This talk of death upset Cal and he felt the tears again filling his eyes. "But *I* want to learn it, Grandpa. I want to feel good about who I am. But I have to know the truth, and sometimes I feel so helpless. I keep thinking this is all a dream—all of it, even moving back here. I can't believe that in all this time, I never knew any of this stuff. It's like I had this separate life going on behind my back the whole time."

"I should have been more involved in your life. Your grandmother and I were upset that Mona left, and if we'd done more to stay in touch, maybe none of this would have happened."

Cal smiled and wiped away his tears. "You just told me it was no one's fault, now you're trying to take all the blame. I love you Grandpa!"

Raymond took Cal in his arms and hugged him tight. His gravelly voice cracked and shivered as he spoke. "You haven't called me Grandpa since you were six years old over the phone. I didn't think you considered me worthy anymore."

A knock at the door intruded on them. It was late for anyone to be at the door, Cal thought, wiping away the last of his tears. He walked to the door and opened it slowly, and through the small crack he saw Katrina, shivering in her large coat that she pulled around her shoulders.

"Katrina," he said opening the door. He looked out toward the street, not expecting her to be alone.

"Can I come in?" she asked quietly.

"Sure," he said, trying to erase any lasting signs of emotion from his face. He motioned her inside and took another glance around outside.

"I'm alone," she said, noticing his caution.

They walked into the living room where Raymond stood awkwardly. Katrina took off her coat and draped it over a chair. Her peach colored skin and the icy sting that reddened her cheeks highlighted her emerald eyes and she noticed Cal and Raymond staring at her. She rubbed her hands together and said, "It's really getting cold out there."

"Yes," answered Cal and Raymond in unison.

She smiled. "You must be Cal's grandfather."

"Yes, I am," answered Raymond.

Cal cleared his throat. "I'm sorry! I should have introduced you. I'm just really surprised you're here," Cal said, stumbling over his words. Why was she there? His heart raced with excitement, and he realized that the act he put on about using her to get at Mitch was false. He stood there, nervously riveted by her every move.

"I need to do some things in the kitchen. It was nice meeting you," said Raymond as he left Cal and Katrina standing there alone in the living room.

When she knew Raymond was out of earshot, Katrina turned back to face Cal. "I came because I wanted you to know how sorry I am about your brother. I wanted to come by earlier but..."

"That's all right. I'm glad you're here now," Cal said, uncomfortable with her sympathy. He turned back to the clock. "It's almost eleven-thirty. Won't your parents wonder where you are?"

"No. They think I'm with Liz. But I probably should go. I just wanted to let you know how I felt." She turned and nervously headed toward the door.

"Wait!" Cal said, his senses jolted to the reality that she was leaving. "Don't go yet. Stay just a little while."

She smiled, "Okay."

Cal looked down into her eyes. She tried to look away, feeling anxious under his intense gaze. She closed her eyes coyly and her long black lashes brushed his cheeks when Cal reached around her waist and drew her close. His emotions were running high and he didn't care if she rejected him, but she raised her face to his and he kissed her. He paused for a moment, still expecting her to resist, but when she didn't, he kissed her again. Katrina tightened her arms around his neck and Cal picked her up and took her to the couch, where he sat down gently with her in his arms. He reached around to the lamp on the table and turned off the light.

"What if someone..."

"They're all asleep," Cal told her, as he searched for her mouth in the darkness.

"I can't stay too long," Katrina whispered.

Cal held her tight. "You can't leave. I won't let you."

Katrina laughed quietly as she reached for Cal's face. She caressed his cheeks as he kissed her neck.

Now Cal lay her on the couch and slowly moved her under him. In the paltry light that crept in from the night's full moon, he saw her looking up at him. "Are you okay with this?" he asked.

She smiled and nodded.

He kissed her again, stroking his hand along her waist and making his way gradually under her shirt.

But the turning of the doorknob startled Cal and he quickly sat upright.

"I thought you said everyone was asleep," whispered Katrina, as she hurriedly tucked in her shirt.

Cal saw the door open slowly and a figure padded cautiously into the room. Cal turned on the light and there stood Rachel.

Startled, she screamed; but then she stood there, looking defiant. "What are you doing?" she demanded.

"What am I doing?" Cal shouted. "What are *you* doing? It's almost midnight, Rachel!"

Then they heard stirring in the back bedroom, and soon

Mona came out, her eyes still shut, as she pulled her robe around her. "What's going on out here?" she mumbled angrily.

"I just caught Rachel sneaking in the house," explained Cal.

Mona looked over at him. She closed the robe tighter around her. "Who's this?" she asked, nodding at Katrina.

"This is Katrina," answered Cal. "Rachel, get in your room."

"Gladly!" she huffed and went off down the hallway. Mona looked at Cal agitated, then followed Rachel back to her room.

Cal shook his head in disgust. "I can't believe she's sneaking out of the house. She's probably meeting up with some guy!"

Katrina looked down at the floor and smiled. "It's amazing what we girls will do."

Cal looked up at her, confused. "Huh?"

Katrina shrugged. "I have to go." She kissed Cal quickly on the lips, and before he could gather his thoughts, she was outside and in her car.

He followed her out. "Why do you have to leave?" he asked, as he leaned into her car.

She giggled and lay her head back against the seat. She looked up and a smile spread wide across her face. "Maybe I should just stay all night. Then he'd really go crazy."

Cal smiled at the thought of her being with him all night, but then he stepped away from the car. "Who'd go crazy? Mitch?" he asked.

She laughed. "No. Who cares about what he thinks?!"

"Then who do you mean?"

"My Dad! He'd *die* if he knew I was out here."

Cal looked at his watch. "It won't be that late if you leave now."

"It wouldn't matter if it was two o'clock in the afternoon. He's forbidden me to ever come out here alone. If he knew I was seeing one of—" her concentration was broken and she looked at Cal awkwardly.

Cal studied her with furrowed brows. "One of what?"

Katrina paused and looked at him, embarrassed. "Oh, it's nothing. I just meant he'd get mad if he knew I was dating someone from the Fort." She looked down, knowing what she said was as terrible as what she was trying to avoid saying.

"You mean one of the Indians," Cal said softly. His voice trailed off as he realized what her true thoughts about him must be. A dull ache started in his chest and went down to his stomach. Then the hurt turned to anger. "Or were you going to call me some little slang name, like Tonto."

"No. Of course not. It's just—" she said, trying to recover.

"Don't. Don't even try," Cal interrupted. "I thought you were different, but obviously I was wrong. I used to think you were beautiful. But now I know better." Cal turned away and walked to the house.

"Cal, wait!" she called, "I *am* different."

He turned back and looked at her, then took several steps towards her, studying her face.

Katrina gave him a pleading, apologetic smile.

Cal nodded. "You're right. You *are* different. At least

the others don't lead me on or lie to me about how they feel."

Katrina tried to say more, but Cal held up his hand to silence her.

"You used me to get to your father. Like I'm some sort of criminal that you should be ashamed of." Cal scoffed. "I'm ashamed that I liked you. You're not worthy of anyone out here. Go back to Mitch. You two deserve each other." With that, Cal turned and walked up to the porch.

Katrina started to speak, but Cal just went inside and closed the door. Then he heard the car start up and leave.

He went to bed and lay there, not sure what to think, his emotions twirling in his head. Katrina was only interested in him because dating an Indian was somehow exciting and rebellious, and it would make her father mad. The guilt hit him hard now. How could he not see through her and want her so bad only days after he saw his own brother killed? He felt even more isolated and alone and lay in his bed, tormented with the questions in his mind. He tried to sleep, but the smell of Katrina's hair and the feeling of holding her in his arms made it impossible to relax.

Exhausted from trying to sleep, Cal got up and walked to the kitchen. He peered out the window where a light flickered in a house a few blocks away, making it stand out from the rest. Cal strained to see that it was Fly's house, and he watched as a figure paced back and forth in the window.

Cal pulled on his coat and quietly pushed open the front door. The bitter cold bit at his face as he walked toward the house. When he got closer, he realized it was Fly in the window. His long hair flipped as he turned with each pace and he was holding something. Cal continued to walk until he realized that Fly was pacing the floor of the small, run-down house with a baby tenderly cradled in his arms.

Cal stopped and watched him for several minutes, mesmerized, as Fly held and cuddled the small infant. Was it a little brother or sister? Cal wondered. Or could it be his? A chill shivered through Cal's body, breaking his trance, and he pulled his coat around his shoulders and turned back towards home.

His bed felt wonderfully warm as he crawled in, and within minutes he was asleep, dreaming about Fly's rhythmic pacing.

10

Cal's head was clear the next morning. Even with the disappointment over Katrina, he felt that at least she was consistent with the other people from town. Besides, there were other things he needed to do. His quest to learn what had happened to his aunt was only fueled by his growing affection and devotion to his grandfather.

He found an inner strength from that new connection, and understood that his past pride at being a Ute was becoming more real to him than what he'd felt before, which had been based on folklore and fiction. Now he felt the bond of blood with his family, but also the feeling of brotherhood with those he considered to be like family, especially Johnny, Fly and Puck.

After Doran was killed, Cal didn't expect the county police to be much help, but he did want Mitch arrested for Doran's murder. But when the B.I.A. relinquished the case because a non-Indian was involved, Cal was furious.

"How can you do this?" Cal shouted at the B.I.A. investigator when he told him they'd handed off the case to the county. "Mitch Grayson killed my brother right here on the reservation. You can't just let him get away with it."

The investigator, a stocky, clean-cut man with the same dark, weathered skin as Raymond, had a hard time looking Cal in the eye. He spoke slowly and with an air of disinterest that annoyed Cal even more. "It's no longer our case. I can't give you any other information about it."

"Did you even look into it at all?"

"We filed our report and gave a copy to the county police. Now it's in their hands."

Cal shook his head. "You're pathetic," he shouted, fuming as he stormed out of the office.

Even with the lack of help from the B.I.A., Cal still pushed the case, believing it was such a clear-cut case that even Franklin's yes-men would have to make an arrest. And yet, when the officers came in to investigate, and when Cal explained how Mitch had climbed the ridge and had taken aim at Doran, within a day, Mitch was back home without any charges, much to Cal's disbelief and frustration.

That night Cal sat slumped in a chair, the television droning on in front of him, when the story about Doran's killing came on the news. He listened intently and let out a disgusted laugh when the newscaster described the fatal shooting as an altercation between two teens in the Uintah Basin, one white and one Indian. The reporters continued, saying the police and prosecutor ruled the incident "self defense." The words rang in Cal's ears, even after two weeks.

The fact that no charges, fines, or even cross words were leveled at Mitch became an obsession and took over Cal's thoughts. On top of everything, Franklin's and

Mitch's smugness made him even angrier and he wanted more than ever to bring them down somehow. He knew that if he told his story outside the Basin, there'd be no way to hide the truth, so that night he called his English teacher, Mr. Henry, at home. Cal told him he was returning to school and still planned on writing his story. Mr. Henry was thrilled and agreed to meet with Cal the next day. Since there was no statute of limitations on murder, Cal was determined to see that both Franklin and Mitch paid for what they took from him—his aunt and his brother. An award-winning story, one showing real evidence, was the tool he needed to make it happen, and he was getting closer to finding all the facts to prove their guilt.

He wanted to see the court files on Jackie's death, knowing there had to be something in it that would help him. Just the thought that something could possibly be done to take down his enemies gave Cal the energy to face the day feeling somewhat rejuvenated.

The brisk morning sunshine spilled into the kitchen, and across the room, Raymond winked at Cal. Cal smiled back, grabbed a piece of toast, and with it hanging from his mouth, he threw on his coat. "Can I borrow your car for school today, Grandpa?" he asked, removing the toast to speak. Tim needed the car he lent to Cal, but promised to bring it back by that evening.

Mona looked up at him oddly.

"Sure," Raymond said.

"Are you going back to school?" Mona asked, surprised.

"I sure am. I only need three more classes to graduate,

and I'm not going to let anything keep me from getting out of here." Cal turned to Raymond and felt a twinge of guilt go through him.

"I have a meeting at the Tribal Center at noon." Raymond told Cal, "But I can walk, so don't worry about it."

Rachel threw her backpack over her shoulder. "Why do I have to take the bus if Cal doesn't?" she complained.

But before Mona could answer, Cal interjected, saying, "How about I drive you to school today?"

Rachel shrugged and hurried out the door to the car.

Cal turned to Mona. "Do you need anything from the store? I can pick it up later on the way home."

Mona shook her head and continued reading a small paperback book.

Then Rachel's high-pitched scream came from the front of the house, followed by her shouts. "Cal! Cal! Come outside, quick!"

His heart pounded as he ran outside to the driveway. What he found there made him stop short with a gasp. There sat his precious red Mustang, every dent, every blemish gone. He flushed with joy and he smiled broadly. The car glistened in the morning sunlight and Cal knew that Tim must have worked many long nights finishing it. He inspected every inch of the car, caressing it and admiring the quality of the work.

Rachel grinned for the first time in days. "It's just like it used to be."

Cal turned to go back into the house to tell his mother and grandfather, but Mona and Raymond had come outside to see what all the shouting was about.

"I guess I won't need these today," Cal said as he handed Raymond his keys.

Raymond beamed with joy for Cal. "It looks great. Tim did a wonderful job."

Mona said nothing as she turned and walked back towards the house.

"What's with you?" Cal called after her.

She turned back around. "Nothing's with me. Everything's just great," she answered. "You're great. Tim's great. Dad's great. Everything's totally great." Then she walked into the house.

Cal looked at Raymond, pleading for guidance with his eyes.

"She'll be all right," Raymond reassured him.

"I've never seen her like this. She acts like she's ten years old."

"This has been hard for her, Cal. She lost her son. But she'll be fine."

"It's been hard for all of us. But I'm getting to the point where I don't care how she acts anymore."

"Be patient with her. She needs you now more than ever. We all do."

What about me? Cal thought as he nodded and slid into the driver's seat. It felt good to have the car whole again, but all he really wanted was to show it to Doran. He thought about his brother as he drove toward town. Then he said, "Doran didn't like Tim. But I can't figure out why," Cal said to Rachel. He was thinking out loud, but he wanted to say something to her since they hadn't really talked in months. After the conflict when she'd snuck in so late, he wanted to warm things up again between them. "Every time I talked about how Tim helped me or I wanted to go see him, Doran got all quiet."

"Yeah, I know," she answered softly.

Cal looked at her, surprised. He hadn't expected an answer, and certainly not that one.

"You know? Why would you say that?"

Rachel shrugged and turned to the window.

"Rachel, what's wrong?"

She shrugged again, her eyebrows furrowed. "I heard Doran yelling at Mom one night about Tim. He thought she loved him or that she used to, or something like that."

"Tim? Doran thought Mom loved Tim? Are you sure it was Tim he was yelling about?"

"Yeah, I'm sure."

"Are you sure it wasn't someone named Franklin Grayson?"

Rachel shrugged. "No. I'm sure it was Tim that Doran said Mom was in love with."

This intrigued Cal, not because of the information, but because Doran rarely raised his voice. Whenever a conflict got started, he usually clammed up. It was rare that he ever lost control or drew attention to himself by complaining about something.

"How long have you known this, and what did Doran say?" Cal asked cautiously. He was worried that Rachel might get sad talking about Doran and retreat inside herself.

"It's been a while. I didn't hear everything. Mom kept telling Doran to shut up, and he kept saying 'Tim is the one, isn't he!' And then he told her to keep Tim away from us."

"Tim is the one?" Cal said to himself, "The one what?"

Rachel looked uneasy.

"What is it Rach?"

She turned to the window, unable to look at him. Her hands shook as she wiped tears from her cheeks.

"What is it, Rachel?" Cal asked softly, "It's okay. Please tell me what's wrong."

She continued to wipe her eyes. "Doran said that Dad wasn't really your dad," she said, her voice cracking.

Cal's eyebrows furrowed. "What? What exactly did he say?"

She cleared her throat and went on. "When Doran and Mom were fighting, he said something about Dad not being your real father."

A chill passed over Cal, making his shoulders tingle. "Are you sure? Why did he say that?"

Rachel squirmed in her seat, as if she knew that what she was saying would cause trouble. "You need to know, and I've already said too much to stop now. Doran said that's why Dad is so hurt. He said that Mom never loved Dad, and that she just used him to leave the Fort."

Cal felt that same sickening chill again, but this time it was overwhelming. "What else did you hear?"

"I heard Doran ask Mom, 'Is Tim the one?' And Mom said 'the one what?' Then Doran said 'Cal's father.' Then Mom told Doran to shut up. But then Doran said, 'It's bad enough knowing what you did, but do you have to let the bozo hang around to remind me of it?' But then Mom said, 'Doran, I swear, it isn't Tim.'"

Cal put on the brakes and the car lurched to a halt. A

truck swerved past them and the driver hung out the window, shaking his fist and swearing. Cal was breathing hard and he felt his heart pounding in his chest.

"Rachel, why didn't you tell me about this before?" he asked.

Seeing the fear in his face that it might be true, tears welled up again in Rachel's eyes. "I wasn't supposed to hear. I was going to talk to Doran about it, but I never got the chance."

It was several weeks since Doran had been killed, and now, more than ever, Cal wanted to talk to his brother again. Cal threw the car into gear and peeled out onto the highway.

"Where are you going?" Rachel whimpered.

"I'm going to Tim's."

Rachel hung her head and began to cry. "I'm sorry Cal. I shouldn't have told you."

"Bullshit! You're the only one so far in this family who's told me anything about what's going on."

Cal quickly pulled the car into Tim's small driveway and left skid marks trying to stop. Tim was around the back, working on the deck. He shaded his eyes and smiled at the sight of Cal in his newly repaired car.

"What's the hurry?" he asked cheerily.

Cal got out and slammed the door, then stood stone-faced, studying Tim.

Tim's smile faded to concern. "Cal, what's wrong?"

"I want to know the truth. Rachel overheard some stuff about someone else being my father and I want the truth."

Tim sighed deeply and looked at the ground. "Cal, I'm very sorry you had to find out like this."

Hearing those words, Cal felt his façade melt. Sorrow and dull pain vibrated from his heart and tears spilled down his face. He stood there for a minute, shaking his head. "You son of a bitch," he shouted at Tim, crying at the same time. "You, of all people, should have told me."

"Cal, it wasn't my place to say anything."

Cal hung his head and gave an exhausted laugh. Through his tears, he looked up and said, "Not your place? You were in the right place when you were doing it with my mother." With that, Cal swung wildly at Tim.

Rachel screamed from the car, "Cal, don't!"

"What?" Tim asked, ducking Cal's punch. "You think it's me?"

Cal swung again, nicking Tim's face.

"Whoa! Whoa!" Tim yelled as he wrestled Cal to the ground to control him. "Cal, I swear to you, it's not me. I'm not your father." He held him tight to keep Cal still.

Cal lay his head back against the dirt and stopped resisting. Then he said, "But that's what Rachel heard. That's why Doran hated you. Rachel heard him yelling at Mom about Dad not being my dad. So you're saying that's all a lie?"

Tim paused and took a deep breath. "This has all gone on long enough, and it's time you knew the truth." He looked over at Rachel crying in the car and waved her over. But she shook her head and hid her face in her hands.

"So it *is* true!"

Tim released Cal, who rolled up angrily to a sitting position, then panted and wiped the sweat from his brow. He felt like his whole life was over. If David wasn't his father, then Cal was no one. His feelings of pride, his image, and his identity were all stripped in those few minutes of learning the truth.

"Cal, Mona told me that when you were in the hospital, they discovered that David wasn't your father. It was something about your blood type and his not matching. I've asked her who your real father is, but she only says it was some other oil field worker. And I don't remember anyone else it could be. But one thing I can guarantee you; I'm not your father."

"Some other oil field worker?" Cal said to himself.

Tim shrugged. "It doesn't matter, Cal, because David loves you."

"Not anymore. And this explains everything—why he's been acting so weird."

"That's not true. He's just hurt because of what happened, but it's not your fault. He'll get over it."

Cal sat back and looked up at the sky. He thought about the man he knew as his father, and now it was totally clear why David had become so cold and distant. But why hadn't he told Cal?

"Can I call my Dad?" Cal asked Tim in a husky whisper.

"Of course."

Cal walked to his car and told Rachel to come inside with him. She refused and Cal gently knelt by the car. "Rachel, it's going to be all right. I just want to call Dad."

"Everyone's going to blame me," she cried. "I shouldn't have said anything."

"No one's going to blame you. You didn't do anything wrong."

She turned to him. "But I made you cry."

Cal gave an exhausted smile and shook his head. "No you didn't. What's happening to me made me cry. You told me the truth. You're the only bright spot I have right now, so please come inside with me. I need you to be with me when I call Dad."

Rachel sat up and gave him a tearful but strong nod.

Cal felt lifeless as he walked with Rachel up the cracked driveway and into Tim's small house. He looked around nervously, wondering if Lacey would emerge from the shadows and be a part of yet another nightmare in his life. Tim's dog, Nellie, met them at the door and excitedly jumped up onto Cal's legs. Cal gently swept her aside, and the dog, sensing something was wrong, turned to Tim for reassurance. Tim offered Cal and Rachel a drink of water, since he hadn't been to the store in a week and all he had in the fridge was beer.

Cal noticed the cans and wished he could have one, which made him think about that night at the lake. He wondered if Johnny and the others knew about this latest revelation. But if they did, they surely would have told him. He hadn't seen them much since Doran died. They came by the first couple of days, but Cal didn't want to go out. At the vigil for Doran, Johnny and the others stayed with him until only their small group remained on the porch. Puck and Fly had been silent but stood with him, and at one point during the singing, Puck had put his hand on Cal's shoulder. He was beginning to feel as though this group he'd once considered miscreants were now the closest thing to brothers that he had and he missed them.

"I don't know if I can do it," Cal told Tim as he sat on the side of the bed holding the phone. "What am I going to say? Hi, I hear you're not my real father. Do you know who is?"

11

The red of the Basin's earthy rim was a stark contrast to the morning's cloudless blue sky. Cal took a panoramic look around and realized that the cold was starting to fade. As he drove, he tried to plan what he was going to say to his mother. The reality that the life he'd known in Spokane was a lie still made his heart ache, and the evil and abrasive words he wanted to say to her only made the ache go deeper.

When he arrived at his grandfather's house, Eddie sat forlornly on the front steps. He looked up as Cal pulled into the driveway and gave a sad wave.

"Hey, Eddie!" Cal called as he stepped out of the car.

"Hi," he mumbled.

"What's the problem?" Cal asked. He had never seen Eddie look so down before.

"Mona's mad. She kicked me out."

Confused, Cal walked into the house and found Mona and Raymond quietly arguing in the living room. Mona was still in her bathrobe and had obviously been crying.

"What's going on?" Cal asked.

Mona turned to Cal and thrust out her hand, to show him the small pins from Doran's old Boy Scout uniform. "That little creep tried to steal Doran's things."

Cal furrowed his eyebrows. "You mean Eddie?"

"Yes. I found him in the back room, searching through my stuff."

Raymond shook his head. "He wasn't stealing these things. He thought they were his."

Mona huffed. "He doesn't even live here. He pulled this box from behind all that stuff in the closet after he snuck in here. He shouldn't be snooping around."

"But you don't understand," explained Raymond, "He knows that his mother's things are still in that backroom closet. He comes here every once in while to look at them. He didn't know that the stuff I put in there was Doran's."

Cal nodded in agreement and turned to Mona. "Mom, getting mad at Eddie isn't going to make you feel any better. If he really was stealing something, do you think he'd be sitting on the front step of our house, feeling bad that he got kicked out? He would have run off to hide."

Mona scoffed, "Who knows, when it comes to that kid."

"That kid just happens to be your nephew. Don't you care?" Cal asked.

Rolling her eyes, his mother walked away to her room.

Cal followed her. "I'm glad you're in here now, because you're not going to walk away from me on this one."

"I don't understand why you want to stick up for Eddie over your own brother."

Cal raised an eyebrow. "My own brother. It's funny

you should bring that up. Define that for me, Mom. Who exactly *is* my own brother?"

"What are you talking about?"

"Rachel overheard you and Doran fighting one night about Dad not being my real father."

"Oh that's a lot of bull!"

"Is it? I just tried to call Dad, and when I asked him that question, he yelled something about you promising not to tell anyone and then he hung up on me. He wouldn't have done that if there wasn't some truth to it."

"Your dad's a liar. He's trying to make this whole divorce thing my fault."

"Mom, at the hospital, the E.R. doctor who worked on Doran even questioned whether or not we were brothers. Tim said something about us having different blood types, and that Doran and I have different fathers."

Mona rolled her eyes and tried to push past him. "Cal, why are you doing this? None of it's true," she shouted.

Cal grabbed her arm and kept her from leaving. "It is true. I'm so tired of all the lies."

"Well, I'm so tired of you always trying to dig up problems. Why do you enjoy making my life hell?"

"I don't. *You're* the one who's made *my* life hell by bringing me here! My life was happy until you screwed everything up."

"I didn't screw everything up. If you hadn't gone around stirring up problems, maybe Doran would still be alive." Mona grabbed a small glass plate from her dresser and flung it at the wall, shattering it into dozens of little pieces.

Cal ducked, although it landed nowhere near him. "What are you doing? What do you mean by that? Are you blaming *me* for what happened?" he shouted.

"Don't you get it?" she screamed back.

"Get what? How can you say it's my fault?" he asked, guarded, and waiting for her to lob something else his way.

She stood and faced the window, her dark face now somber. She walked closer to it, staring out at some children digging in the dirt with sticks and a broken plastic cup.

"What!" he yelled.

She ignored him and watched the children for a moment. "I didn't want you to live like that," she muttered, motioning towards the children. "I lied so you could live somewhere better, Cal. I did it for you."

Cal sat on the bed and tried to rub the lines out of his furrowed forehead. "So it is true. I can't believe it," he said, feeling the twinge of sadness and regret surging through him. "Can you at least tell me who my real father is?"

Mona hesitated, then avoided the question entirely. "David always loved you, Cal. He still does."

"Mom!" Cal shouted in frustration. "How can he? You lied and told him you were pregnant with his kid. If you really wanted out of the Fort that bad, why'd you agree to come back now?"

Mona turned away from him.

"Who's my real father? I have a right to know."

"Your father is David. Nobody else matters."

Cal stood up and walked over to her. He stared down at her, as if he was hoping to see inside her for the answer he needed. "Mom, please tell me."

At that point, Raymond appeared in the doorway. "What's wrong?" he asked.

Cal looked up at him and then back down to Mona, who hung her head and covered her face.

"Did you know too?" Cal asked Raymond.

"Know what?"

"That my Dad isn't really my dad."

Raymond looked at Cal with astonishment, and then scratched the back of his neck. "That's not true. Who told you that?"

"It *is* true!"

Raymond stepped into the room. "Why do you think that, Cal?"

"Grandpa, I don't just think that. Our blood types don't match. Mom lied to Dad for all these years. That's why we're back at the Fort—because he found out I'm not really his son. I just called and asked him the same question, and he got all upset and hung up on me."

Raymond looked down sadly at Mona and shook his head. He looked back up at Cal, then put his hand to his chin to keep it from quivering.

"I'm not putting up with this interrogation anymore," Mona shouted, trying to pass Cal.

Cal threw her back onto the bed. "You're not going anywhere until you tell me!"

She looked at him with enraged eyes. "Let me go, Cal!" she shouted as she came at him.

Cal tried to hold her back and was surprised at her strength. She flailed at his chest as her tears flew and hit him in the face. Raymond pulled Cal back and pleaded with his grandson. "Let her go, Cal."

Then Cal felt his body go weak as Mona pushed her way past him and ran from the room.

"Why'd you make me let her go?" Cal asked. "I want answers!"

"Cal, are you sure that's what you want?"

"Yes. I want to know who my father is."

"Your father is David."

"I mean my real father. I don't want lies. No one told me anything about this whole place. They all lied and thought I'd never find out. Now I want to know everything. Everyone out here acts like things will just go away, but they won't. I'm sick of not knowing things that affect my life. Aren't you? Don't you want to know who killed Jackie? I do. I also want to know why I was never told about Eddie. *And* I want to know who my real father is."

"Cal, it takes a lot more than blood to make a father."

"I'm not looking to replace my dad. I just want everything out on the table. I think I deserve that. I won't stop until I dig up everything. Mom may have kept all this from me for seventeen years, but she's not hiding anything else from me anymore."

The sound of a car revved in the driveway and Cal heard Mona open and close the front door. He ran to the kitchen window and watched as she left with one of her friends. He stood watching the plume of dust as the car sped away. How could this happen? It can't be true. Maybe Raymond's right. Maybe I don't want to know. But it wasn't possible for Cal to stop wondering. No matter how it hurt or what he uncovered, it couldn't be any worse than what he'd already found out.

Doran's Boy Scout pins sat on the counter. He picked them up and looked at them. "What else have you saved?" he asked as his grandfather walked into the room.

"A lot," he answered. "It's all I have sometimes. When I lost Jackie, I kept everything that was hers. I couldn't throw anything away. I even have the paper napkin she used the day before she died. I did the same thing when Mona moved away. I never thought she'd come back."

"I can't believe all this is happening to me. It's like she's not the same person anymore. She lied all these years."

Raymond hung his head, not knowing what else to say.

Cal studied the pins in his hand, wondering what Doran would think about all this. But he already knew—Doran would have brushed it off like it was no big deal. *That must've been the Indian in him*, Cal thought. He never wanted to raise an issue or bring attention to himself. Cal never had that problem. He'd always stood up to people and thought he'd inherited that trait from David. But now all of that had changed, and Cal felt the need to connect with something. He felt as though a part of him was unraveled and exposed.

Cal hoped that if he knew what'd happened in the past, maybe everything would all fall into place together. And although he wasn't sure how, he knew there was something that connected him to Jackie and to everything that was making his life miserable. Since the first day they moved to the Fort, he knew instinctively something was being kept from him, and now it seemed like everything that went wrong in his life was somehow related.

Then phone rang and Raymond answered it, said, "Yes, he is," and handed the phone to Cal. It was Mr. Henry, wondering why Cal had missed their meeting.

"My life has taken an interesting turn," Cal explained. "Can we meet tomorrow? I promise I won't miss it. And I'll put together what I have so far so you can read it."

Mr. Henry agreed and Cal hung up. He turned back to Raymond, who sat at the table with a look of exhausted sorrow. He put a hand on his grandfather's shoulder. "What a turn your life has taken, too. Things were nice and quiet around here until we showed up."

Raymond looked up at him with a weak smile. "No, Cal. I'm glad you are here."

Cal nodded. "Can I look at the stuff in the boxes?" he asked. "I won't take anything, and I'll put it all back just the way you had it."

"Cal, you can do whatever you like." Raymond paused for a minute, then looked at him with concern. "But I'm worried about you. I don't think it's healthy to get too obsessed about all this. I know you're hurting, but—"

"Grandpa. This is my life. This isn't some minor thing. We're talking lies about my father—" Then he paused and shook his head, "And a whole bunch of other things that sat around hidden for almost twenty years. I don't understand why no one ever wanted to know what really happened. My Dad almost went to jail. You lost a daughter. Why haven't you ever wanted to get at the truth?"

"Well," said Raymond, thinking. He pulled out a chair and lowered his stocky frame onto it. His rough brown hands looked huge as they supported his weight, and Cal

217

wondered how a man so gentle had such immense hands. "I know it sounds naïve, but nothing I do now will ever bring Jackie back. Going out and trying to find out things will only bring back all the pain and I don't want to do that."

The phone rang and Cal grabbed it. Tim's worried voice was on the other end. "Is everything okay?" he asked.

"It's fine. Mom just left. She didn't tell me anything and just got mad."

"Where'd she go?"

"I don't know. To cool off somewhere, I guess."

"Are you going to be all right? You can stay over here if you need to."

"Thanks, Tim. But I'm fine. I'm tired from everything that's happened, but I'm fine." Cal hung up and walked over to the table. Before he could pull out a chair, there was a knock at the door.

"I'll get it," he told his grandfather.

It was Johnny and Fly.

"Hey," Cal said, trying to smile at his friends.

"What's going on? Mona just came to Fly's house and asked his mom to watch Rachel for a while."

"Really? Why?"

"I don't know. I thought maybe you knew. She seemed all crazy."

"Oh, God! What's she doing now?" he muttered to himself. Then he looked at Fly. "Tell your mom thanks, but I can watch Rachel."

"It sounded like Mona was going on a trip," said Johnny.

Cal motioned for them to come into the house. Raymond stood up, and both Johnny and Fly nodded to him respectfully.

"Do you know where Mom's going?" Cal asked Raymond, confused.

"No. Why?" he asked.

"Johnny and Fly said she was acting all crazy at Fly's house and said she was going somewhere and for Fly's mom to watch Rachel."

Raymond shrugged.

"To hell with her," Cal mumbled. "I'm tired of worrying. What are you guys doing today?" He hoped to drive to Bitter Creek so he could talk to them about what he'd found out about his father.

Fly looked at Johnny, wondering why Cal wasn't more concerned about his mother's actions.

"We're getting ready for the Sun Dance tonight," said Johnny.

Cal thought about the Bear Dance and how unexciting it was and how bored he'd been at that event. And yet his interest was kindled. "Tonight? Can I come?"

Johnny lifted an eyebrow surprised. "Sure. It begins at six. Come with us now. We're probably going to head into town to pick up some stuff."

Cal thought for a minute and realized he'd promised to get his story started for his meeting with Mr. Henry. "I can't," he said. "I've got to get some things done for school. But I'll meet you later."

"Okay. It's at the arena, up by the graveyard."

"Yes, I know."

After they left, Cal closed the door and walked back to

Raymond. "She's not going to do something stupid, is she?" he asked.

"I don't know. Mona worked her entire life to get away from the Fort. Now she's returned and the life she wanted to escape is being thrown back in her face."

Cal threw up his hands in frustration. "But she's not escaping anything. She never has; she's only running away. Every time she has a problem, she runs away instead of facing it. Even the drinking is just another way of running away from her problems. Grandpa, don't you think I have the right to know about all this stuff? She's the one who made these choices, not me."

"Yes, but she was so young, and she only wanted the best for you. You're blaming her for bringing you out here, and yet she did everything she knew how to do to keep you away from here."

Cal thought for a minute about what Raymond said. "She really must have wanted to get out of here, to live with all these lies. But I don't get it. She was born here; she didn't know what it was like anywhere else. What was it she was so desperate to get away from?"

Raymond's lip began to quiver. "I don't know. I only hope it wasn't me."

"You? What could you possibly have done?"

"When Jackie died, I let my grief take me away. I may have ignored Mona when we needed each other the most. I always felt like I pushed her away and that's why I lost her, too. I tried to be a good father. I loved them both so much, but I still lost them."

"Grandpa, it wasn't you. Mom was running from

something or someone, but I can guarantee it wasn't you." Cal walked to the cupboard and pulled out a bag of loose tea. He put the water on and turned back to Raymond. "I'm making you some tea. Then I'm going to take a nap and head over to the Sun Dance. Please wake me up if Mom calls, okay?"

Raymond looked up at Cal and nodded sadly.

Cal walked over to him. "Please don't think you caused any of this Without you, I'd be totally miserable."

"But you're miserable anyway," Raymond answered.

"I've lost my brother and my father. Some days it feels like I've lost everything," Cal said. "But I still have you and Rachel, and even with all her craziness, I love my Mom. So I'm not miserable. But I still need answers and I'm still in the dark."

Cal went to his room and pulled out a large yellow legal pad. He sorted through the papers he'd collected and began to list the evidence. He then began to write his story, or rather, her story. The more he wrote, the more a feeling of optimism and assurance came over him. It felt like he was keeping a promise, but he wasn't sure yet what that promise was.

12

Cal awoke to complete darkness as the consistent beating of a drum pounded away in the distance. He wondered what time it was. He hadn't meant to fall asleep, but he realized how tired he must have been after not sleeping for the last several days, especially in light of what he now knew about David. He hoped he hadn't missed the whole Sun Dance as he pulled himself to the bathroom and flinched at the bright light. He ran his fingers through his hair, then slowly brushed his teeth, trying to become alert. He went to get into his car, but then decided to walk to the ceremonial arena. It was probably only a mile away, which would give him some time to wake up. The air was still cool, so he pulled a blanket from the trunk of his car and began his walk. In the distance, the sound of a crowd cheering and thunderous applause broke the usually deafening silence of the Fort. It surprised him that there were actually people watching this event. He didn't remember seeing more than fifty people at the Bear Dance.

Cal was surprised to see hundreds of cars squeezed into every crevice of space around the normally deserted arena. He walked around and through the cars, searching for the entrance.

"Cal!" he heard a familiar voice call him from behind. He turned to find Coach Roos, walking with a tiny cherub of a girl holding onto his finger.

"Hi," Cal called back, wondering what Coach Roos was doing at the Fort.

"How've you been?" he asked smiling.

Cal shrugged. "Okay."

"I was so sorry to hear about Doran—"

Cal cut him off, too tired to deal with the emotions. "Thanks."

"Who's that?" the little girl asked. She looked to be two or three, with white-blond hair and blue eyes that were almost perfect circles. "Is he one of the Indians?"

Coach Roos gasped at her honesty, but Cal, although stunned by the question, had to smile.

"No, this is Cal," the coach explained to her. "He's a basketball player."

Cal was surprised by this answer, wondering if the Coach thought it an insult to be considered an Indian. He pictured Mitch and his gang in the gym, all pompous and gloating. Then he imagined Johnny, Puck and Fly as he knelt down and took the little girl's tiny hand in his. It looked so white against his dark skin. "What's her name?" he asked the coach.

"This is Amber," Coach Roos said, relieved that the subject had changed.

Still holding onto her little hand, Cal caught her eye and answered her softly, "Yes, Amber. I am an Indian."

She pulled her hand back and burrowed herself next to her father. She kept her eyes on him, but they'd turned cold.

Cal stood up and looked at Coach Roos. Stunned, he spoke softly and slowly, "She's obviously been told some wonderful things about the Indians." He shook his head walked toward the arena.

"She's only three, Cal," Coach Roos called back.

But Cal just kept walking without turning back. But he thought to himself, *That is what's scary. Teaching a three year old to be a racist.* He walked with intent, trying to brush off what'd just happened by thinking about something else, but then his thoughts turned to his father and then he felt even worse.

Cal kept coming back to the same question: *How could it be that he's not my dad?* The realizations he'd come to since moving to the Basin were overwhelming. It was like he'd landed in some sort of tornado that kept sucking up more and more debris about his life. And while he still hoped it might not be true about David, his father's reaction and his mother's anger were the kind of evidence that was hard to ignore.

When Cal reached the arena, he realized it would be close to impossible to find Johnny and the others because unlike the Bear Dance, this time the arena was packed with people. It looked more like a sporting event than a religious ceremony, and bright lights lit up the arena floor and crowds flooded the bleachers surrounding the field. The group that was performing was dressed in elaborately feathered costumes of great extravagance. Their quick, jerky movements made the bells on their costumes' arms and legs ring in time with the beating of the drums.

Cal didn't recognize the performers as being from the Fort and realized, after looking around, that there were many groups that must have come from other areas and other Forts. He considered going home, but instead stood there for a minute, watching the dance.

Then he thought he heard his name being called faintly from the bleachers. He looked around the arena and heard it again. He searched the crowd, then he caught the sight of waving arms and realized Rachel had spotted him somehow. As he waved back, he wondered what to say to her. They hadn't talked since Cal had learned the truth about his father, and he wondered how she was coping with everything.

He began walking toward her, and as he got closer, he tried to see who was sitting with her. At first he thought it was April. *But...my God*, he thought, *who IS that?* She looked to be around Cal's age and was obviously Indian, but he'd never seen her around the Fort. Her black hair glistened even in the darkness, and as he approached, she looked up and smiled at him. He smiled back at the pretty girl.

"Hi Cal!" Rachel said, no differently than she'd said it for the last fourteen years. "Did you know that Mom went to Salt Lake City for a couple of days?"

Cal nodded, still intently staring at the pretty stranger.

"Oh, and this is Jovan," Rachel continued, noticing Cal's interest.

She was even more beautiful close-up. Her skin was smooth and her eyes were dark and large. She looked up and gave Cal a warm, perfect smile.

"You don't live around here, do you?" asked Cal.

"Not right now. I live in Salt Lake," she answered, glancing back at Cal from the arena.

"Oh," Cal said, surprised. "Did you used to live here?"

"Yes. My parents are the Paniwicks."

Suddenly April appeared, holding a baby. It looked to be the same infant Fly was rocking the night Cal couldn't sleep. Jovan looked up and smiled as April squeezed into the seat next to her.

"Are you all cleaned up now?" Jovan cooed to the infant. "Here I'll take her," she said extending her long slender arms to the baby.

Cal's heart sank as he realized the baby must be hers. Maybe that's why he never saw the child until a couple of nights ago. Jovan must have moved away after becoming pregnant and marrying some oil field worker. But he wondered why he'd seen the baby at Fly's and April's house.

"So, you are related to April and Fly?" he said, realizing he didn't even know their last name.

She smiled and looked down at the baby, who gnawed on her long beaded necklace. Jovan smoothed the infant's thick wispy hair. "Well, because of this little girl, we're related."

April and Jovan smiled knowingly.

Cal watched them, completely confused. He felt a slap on his back and turned as Puck balanced himself on the bleacher steps.

"Hey, buddy! It's about time you woke up," he chided.

Johnny and Fly squeezed into the bench behind them.

"Hey, Jo!" Puck called to Jovan as she sat engrossed by

226

the dancers, "Let me guess. You came home because you missed me." He laughed as he elbowed Johnny.

She leaned her head back and gave him a wink and smile. "Of course, you've always been my true love," she teased back.

Fly rolled his eyes. "The whole family's trash," he mumbled.

"Oh, lighten up," Johnny said to Fly. "Jo's not so bad."

Cal listened intently and then realized she probably wasn't married and had moved away in shame to have the child. He motioned to Johnny to move to a higher bench. When they settled in, Cal leaned into him. "What's the story with Jovan?"

"Nothing. What's done is done."

"Why is she living somewhere else?"

"The school she's going to is the only one to offer that special program."

Cal looked at him confused, "Why'd she have to go to a special program? There are lots of girls who have their babies and stay right at the same school."

"Baby? What baby? Is Jo pregnant?" he asked, looking down at her.

"That baby?" Cal whispered, motioning to the infant in Jovan's arms.

Johnny drew back as if Cal had been lit on fire. "You are always so totally in the dark," he said, shaking his head.

"What?" Cal asked with dread.

Johnny took a deep breath. "That isn't Jovan's baby, Cal. It's April's."

Cal laughed. "Yeah, right. She's like, fourteen."

Johnny just stared at Cal. Then he said, "Actually, she's almost sixteen."

"I don't care how old she is. She's still a kid," Cal argued. "April's Rachel's best friend. She's not a mother."

"She certainly is. Her mother pretty much raises the kid, and the father is Jovan's older brother, Jim. He took off as soon as he found out she was pregnant. He comes back once in awhile, but Fly always finds him and beats the crap out of him."

Cal took a long hard look at April and the baby. He looked over to his little sister and felt the sickening pain of realizing that she, too, was capable, even at her age, of becoming a mother. "Why didn't you ever tell me?" he asked Johnny.

"I thought that one was a no-brainer. She's with your sister almost all the time."

Cal rubbed his forehead in frustration. It was a reaction he'd developed years ago, but he used it more in the last couple months than he'd had in his whole seventeen years before coming to the Fort. He watched as Jovan flipped a long silken strand of hair as she intently watched the performers.

"But what's the deal with this Jovan girl," Cal continued to question Johnny. "I thought you said she was away at school."

"She is. She's going to the University of Utah. She's taking a course to be a physical therapist."

"College," Cal said, surprised.

Johnny turned and gave him a sour look. "I thought that after everything that's happened to you, you'd finally shed that attitude."

"What do you mean?"

"You think only cocky little white kids go to college."

"No, I didn't mean it like that. I'm just surprised because I thought she was my age."

Johnny rolled his eyes, unconvinced.

"I don't know why you're so offended," Cal snapped. "You're the one who wants to stay here and not do anything."

"Why do I have to leave to live up to your idea of successful? Maybe my idea of success is staying here and learning from someone even more knowledgeable than any college professor."

"Really, who? The Budweiser delivery man?" Cal quipped.

"No," Johnny answered, annoyed. "Someone with a grandson who's still so hung up on image and status that when he finally learns the truth about himself, he'll probably rather kill himself than go on living with the fact that his father's a red-neck Basin boy."

Cal stood up, stunned. Then he looked down the bleacher steps, realizing their raised voices drew stares from some of the audience. Not caring what they'd heard, Cal swallowed hard and watched as Johnny stood up and faced him. "What did you hear?" Cal asked.

Johnny, realizing he'd said too much, just shook his head went quickly down the steps toward the arena floor. Cal tried to follow him and tripped, almost landing on Rachel.

"Cal, what's going on?" she shouted.

"Nothing," he growled, unhurt but embarrassed. He

looked up to see that Johnny was far down the steps and out of reach, especially once he joined the crowd. Cal pulled himself up and continued down the steps. When he reached the arena floor, he looked above the crowd for Johnny. His black hair blended with the masses and as Cal scanned the jostling crowd, he caught a sight that made his stomach turn with rage.

In a circle of about ten men, Franklin Grayson stood. He held a tall bottle of beer and used it as a tool for emphasis as he talked and laughed. His back was to Cal, but one of the other men saw him and motioned to Franklin to turn around. Cal dreaded another confrontation with the sheriff and turned in another direction to avoid going past them. He walked along the dirt path of the arena, the beating drum in sync with his heart. He felt the icy stare of Franklin Grayson piercing his back as he continued walking, searching for an escape.

Meanwhile, his head rang with what Johnny had said. Did Johnny know something that he hadn't yet told him? Could Johnny know who Cal's father is? But he hadn't said anything from the start, and he'd always been straight with Cal before.

As he continued to walk, Cal realized that the path he was on led him to the opposite side of the arena. The walk home would be even longer, but all he wanted was to find an exit and leave. He turned back to find Franklin watching him with a smirk. He was getting desperate for a way out, so he could disappear from sight. Finally, a small break in the fence gave Cal the escape he needed. He slid through the small opening and felt a rush of cool wind along with the feeling of relief wrap around him. He'd made it, but his escape route had put him in the back of the arena, as far away from the home as possible. Luckily the glow of the arena lights was enough for him to see what direction to take and he walked along with only the beating of the drums making up for his solitude. The path led around the back of the bleachers and backed up to a small wire fence. Cal walked beside it for a minute, then realized he was directly beside the edge of the small cemetery of the Fort. The arena lights and the brilliant basin sunset were the perfect combination to silhouette the few upright tombstones and he stopped and strained to read the inscriptions on the tiny grave markers. He found himself wanting to see the grave of the aunt he'd never known. He paused for a moment, wondering if she'd even been buried here in the Fort Duchesne cemetery. He continued reading the chiseled names and dates on the headstones; most of the grave markers were crude and handmade, but most were still legible. Tiring of trying to read in the dim light, he climbed over the fence and stepped carefully inside. The rows of graves were narrow, and small bunches of tiny handpicked flowers fluttered and rolled in the wind.

Cal walked up and down the rows in the dark, trying to make out the names on the headstones. He was surprised to see how many of the headstones marked the resting places of people who died so young; many were only in their teens and twenties. The failing light made it almost impossible to read and his eyes began to hurt from squinting, but at last he found what he was searching for; it wasn't Jackie, it was Cal's grandmother, Dorothy Littlebear. Cal knelt down and brushed the headstone free of the powdery Utah dirt. He'd never met his grandmother in person, just in brief phone calls. He was only five when she died, and he felt the urge to introduce himself.

As he knelt there, Cal felt as if he'd known her. And he was confident that if she were still alive today, she'd be a comfort to him, just as Raymond was. He stood up straight and looked around, certain that since his grandmother's grave was here, Jackie's had to be, too. He continued walking down the row and at last found Jackie's small marker, a metal plate that read, "Jaqualyne Littlebear." Cal again squatted down to get a better look. He pondered what it was that he'd expected to find there, as if he'd thought Jackie would somehow mystically contact him and reveal the truths about her death. Cal sighed and began to leave when he noticed the name of another Littlebear inscribed on the plaque below Jackie's. Cal knelt and brushed the dirt from the plate to find that the dusty inscription read, "Baby Ray Littlebear, July 4, 1977." It was Jackie's baby, buried with her!

"My god..." Cal whispered. "She was that far along, that her baby needed a plaque?" Franklin hadn't just killed Jackie, but Cal's baby cousin, too. Just the idea that Franklin Grayson was the father of his cousin made Cal sick. He began to wonder if the baby had a birth certificate somewhere. *Records*, Cal thought. There have to be records of something that proved Franklin had motive for killing his aunt. Surely with evidence linking Franklin as the father, they'd have proof that he was her killer.

Cal stood up and brushed the red dirt from his knees,

eager to find the truth and bring Franklin to justice. It seemed so simple: if he proved that Franklin was the father, he had the link he needed. And if the baby needed a burial, there'd be something on the records. Tomorrow he'd go to the courthouse. There'd be records of everything there. Why hadn't he thought of that before?

He walked quickly back to the cemetery fence, again stepping carefully through the narrow rows of graves. When he got to the gate, a light breeze washed across Cal's face and for an instant he turned back toward the two graves. Suddenly a deep feeling of dread weighed on his heart; he tried to shake it as he climbed back over the fence to begin his walk home. He noticed that the further he got from the cemetery, the less that heavy feeling tugged at him, and this realization forced him to push his tired body into a trot. He could still hear the beating of the drum, and when it stopped for a second, Cal froze; it was as if his heart paused along with it. The night was uneasily silent, and then the drum began again. Cal took a deep breath and got moving again, noticing his rapid pulse and trying to remember just why he was in such a hurry to get home.

When he arrived, the house was dark. He put the blanket back into the trunk of his car and pulled on the squeaking screen door. He swung it open and closed several times, paying attention to the sturdy hinge that Doran had fixed. It still squeaked, so Cal went inside to find a bar of soap. When he came back out, he propped open the door and turned on the porch light so he could see well enough to work on the hinge.

As he rubbed the soap into the metal grooves, Johnny

and Puck pulled up in the truck. Cal looked up, feeling discouraged. After what had happened between him and Johnny at the Sun Dance, he wasn't much in the mood to see him. But he greeted them with an unenthusiastic, "Hey."

"We wanted to make sure Grayson didn't get to you," Johnny said as he walked up the porch steps.

"No, he didn't."

"What're you doing?" asked Puck.

"Fixing the squeak in this door."

Puck giggled, "I have some loose floor tiles when you're finished, and some clothes that need ironing."

Cal looked up annoyed. "You finished?"

Puck just smiled.

"It's not like this place doesn't need some work. Look around. I don't see you trying to make a difference. Or you either," he snapped at Johnny.

"What did I do?" Johnny asked, defensively.

"That's exactly the point. None of you have jobs. All you do is wander around this place. Why don't you do something around here to make it look better?"

"And *you* worry too much about appearances," Johnny snapped back. "You treat people like crap, but then you worry about the paint chipping on a wall or a door that squeaks."

"I just think it's pathetic that we have to have the people from town come here and do the things that we should be doing ourselves."

Johnny rolled his eyes. "They fixed the roof, Cal. We can't do that ourselves."

"I know that. But we can do other stuff. What's your

excuse for that old fridge sitting in the front yard at your grandparents' house?"

"What? You want us to get rid of Old Frosty?" Puck asked, amused.

Cal gave a frustrated sigh. "See what I mean? No one cares."

"That's not true. I do. In fact, I'd love to see that thing gone. But why do you have to treat us like crap in the process?"

Headlights and a loud engine roared at the end of the street. The three boys looked up as it approached; it was Fly, who pulled up next to Johnny's truck.

"Where'd you go?" Puck asked as Fly stepped out of the truck.

"I had to run an errand."

Puck shrugged at his terse reply.

They heard a muffled thud come from the cab of Fly's truck, but in the dark, Cal couldn't make out what it was.

"I have something for you," he said to Cal flatly. He went to the cab, reached in and pulled something out. As he walked back to them, Cal noticed him pulling something along behind him. It was a dog—Mitch's dog.

"What are you doing with Mitch's dog?" Cal asked, confused.

Fly turned back and looked at it, then handed the rope to Cal. The dog looked curious and then went to Cal and started the same wiggling greeting as when they'd met that day at school. "He took something from you. Now you can take something from him."

Cal laughed. "I can't steal his dog. He'll eventually see it and have me arrested."

Fly looked at him and furrowed his brows in a serious stare. "Mitch saw me take it. The dog was right in the back of his truck at the Sun Dance. He knew I'd kick his ass if he tried to stop me."

"Don't do it," Johnny said, stepping in. "It won't make things right."

"Would you be saying that if it was your brother he killed?" Fly snapped back.

Cal held up his hands. "Wait. What are you talking about? Do what?"

Johnny shook out his arms and gave a labored sigh. "Fly doesn't want you to take the dog as a pet, he wants you to kill it. He wants you to get revenge that way."

Cal looked up at Fly, shocked.

"Show him how it feels to lose something," Fly urged. "Aren't you mad?" He then lunged at the dog and kicked it in the rump. The dog yipped and pulled at the rope, trying to get away.

"Don't!" Cal yelled. He held onto the rope and looked at the dog as it paced in fear.

Puck stood up and put his hands on his head. The entire group was uneasy, and Fly was even angrier. "I should've killed it myself. I can't believe you're going to let him get away with this. The damn cops won't do anything."

Johnny took a deep breath. "Killing his dog won't do anything, either."

Cal piped up. "It'd send a message."

Johnny turned to Cal, disappointed. The air seemed to hang silent and even the dog's panting was quiet as Johnny stared at him. "What message would it send?" he asked, quietly.

Fly nodded with a smile. "It'll send a message that you won't back down."

Cal shook his head. "No! You don't understand. It'd send a message alright, that I'm a heartless dog killer. Don't get me wrong here, Fly. I appreciate that you wanted to help me. But I could never do that, not ever. I'm not a killer."

Johnny agreed. "All it'd do is cause more problems. We've had enough of that already with the people from town. Things are finally starting to turn around. Let's not make it worse." Johnny pleaded.

"Make it worse," Cal said, cynically. He took a seat on the cold grass and let the dog crawl into his lap. He stroked Doogie's head. "Can it get much worse?"

"Yes, it can. But it can also get better," Puck said, joining the discussion.

Cal turned on him. "How would you know? It wasn't your brother that was killed."

Puck looked apologetic. "I know," he said. "But—"

"But, what?" Cal challenged.

Puck swallowed. Johnny started to defend him, but Puck put up his hand, then continued. "I know he was your brother," He choked out the words, his face full of pain. "But, Cal, when he died, I felt like I lost a brother, too."

Cal's put his face in his hands, feeling tired and very small.

"Well, you didn't lose a brother," Fly snapped at Puck. "It's not about *you*."

Johnny brayed. "It's not about you either, Fly. Do you really think I'm going to believe you did this whole thing for Cal? You didn't steal the dog for *Cal*. You did it for *you*."

"Bullshit," Fly said, as he looked at the others.

"That's what this is all about," Johnny went on. It's the same reason you do everything. You beat up people and act like a badass. That's all just for you. When're you going to realize that it isn't going to change anything?"

"Shut up, Johnny, or I'll kick your ass."

"Fine! Do it!" Johnny shouted. "Will it make you feel any better? Will it change the fact that April has a kid? It wasn't Mitch that got her pregnant, so why take it out on him? You're angry all the time because you hate your life. Has being mad all the time brought your dad back? Has it made any difference at all? Getting revenge on a poor innocent dog isn't going to change anything." Then he pointed to the dog. "Go ahead, Fly. Kill the dog! See if it brings Doran back."

Cal sat stunned, still holding onto the dog. He looked up at Fly with eyes full of pain and sighed.

Fly shook his head in disgust and walked back to his truck in the darkness. He revved it hard, then backed up and left in a hurry.

"Where's he going?" asked Cal.

Johnny shrugged. "I don't know." He looked out into the night. "I probably said too much."

Puck walked over to them. "He needed to hear it. Besides, he'll come around."

"I don't even care if he does. I'm tired of all this." Johnny turned to Cal. "For a second you scared me. I really thought you agreed with him."

Cal smiled. "Come on, Johnny. I thought you knew me better than that."

"Yeah, I do."

The three stood silent for a moment, and then Johnny looked at the dog. "So, what are you going to do?"

Cal lifted Doogie from his lap and pushed himself up. "I'm angry and I want revenge. I should just keep him. He's a pretty cool dog, but I'm going to take him back."

Puck gasped. "He'll have you arrested again. Just take it to the pound."

"No, this is something I've got to do." He looked at Johnny. "It's something Doran would want me to do. I'm not going to let anyone see me. I'll just drop the dog off and drive away."

"We'll come with you," said Johnny.

"I can't," said Puck, quickly. "My mom said I had to be home before midnight."

Johnny laughed. "Fine, then we'll drop you off on the way." He turned to Cal. "I'll drive."

"No way," said Cal. "I don't trust that piece of crap. You still haven't fixed that since—" he looked away, realizing that was the day Doran died. "I'll drive."

Johnny didn't argue.

Cal put the soap back in the house and swung the screen door back and forth a few times before heading to his car. He smiled in satisfaction at the smooth, now quiet swing.

"You're right. It *does* make a difference, you know," Johnny said as he took his seat on the passenger side.

"What does?" asked Cal.

"The little things, like the door and the roof. We *should* do more."

Cal nodded. He looked at the dog sitting in the back seat, as if he was ready for the trip. It made Cal smile. "I almost wish I could keep him."

They drove toward town and out to where Franklin and Mitch lived. With Johnny giving directions, Cal turned off the highway and through the back roads to a small neighborhood nestled along the hillside. The homes weren't big, but their yards were clean and landscaped. It made Cal think about his house in Spokane and how he used to complain about having to mow the lawn every Saturday. Now he wished he even had a yard to mow at the Fort.

"Pull over here," Johnny directed.

"Where is it?" Cal asked.

"Down there; it's the house with the light and the dog kennel on the side." He paused for a moment. Then the two boys looked at each other and laughed.

"I guess that's where the dog goes," said Cal, still amused.

"If you park here, then I can run the dog down without anyone seeing me."

"No way. I'm going," Cal insisted. "You take the driver's seat." He opened the door and then let the dog out. Doogie panted and started to pull Cal toward the house and Cal looked down at Mitch's home. There were no cars or trucks in sight and the house was dark except for the porch light. "I'll just run down there, put the dog in the kennel and run back. If someone shows up or comes around, just leave and I'll hide, then I'll meet you back where we turned off the highway. If I get caught, go get Tim."

Johnny nodded as he slid into the driver's seat. "Do me a favor and don't get caught, okay?"

With the dog leading the way, Cal walked toward the house. In the dark, he could see that it was white with dark shutters and dormers on the second story. A row of tall shrubs lined each side of the house, and there was a large broad-leafed tree in the front yard. The dog kennel had a cement floor with a chain linked fence surrounding it. A tin roof covered half the kennel and a wooden doghouse sat in the corner.

"Come on," Cal whispered to the dog as he tugged on the rope and picked up his pace to a trot. When they got to the house, he practically tiptoed across the lawn and over to the kennel. But when he reached for the latch on the gate, he saw a padlock. "Crap," he whispered. Then he looked up to where Johnny sat waiting in the car, as if he'd have the answer. In the dark, he couldn't even make out the car. Suddenly, headlights appeared at the far end of the street. "Crap," Cal said again, pulling the dog toward the house and creeping behind the tall wall of bushes. As the headlights came closer, he realized it was a truck, one that was slowing down at Mitch's house. It pulled into the driveway, then Cal heard the truck door open and then slam shut.

"Stupid son of a bitch," Mitch grumbled as he hurried up the walkway to the house.

A minute later, another set of headlights appeared at the end of the street and another truck made its way toward the house. Cal stayed hidden in the bushes and scratched the dog's ears to keep him from moving or making noise. It worked and the dog snuggled into his lap. Cal held his breath as he realized the other truck was Franklin's.

He heard Mitch open the front door of the house and

slam it shut, and from an open window above Cal's head, he heard footsteps walking quickly through the house. He heard Franklin turn off and get out of the truck, grumbling something as he walked up the steps to the house. Cal also heard the lighter steps of someone else following the sheriff. Once again the door of the house slammed.

"Mitch!" Franklin bellowed.

Cal stayed frozen in his brushy hideaway, quietly listening to the Grayson family drama unfolding.

"Don't you walk away from me, Boy. It's bad enough I gotta sit there and watch some damned Indian make a fool out of you, but then you disrespected me in front of everyone out there."

"Why do we have to go out there in the first place?" Mitch shouted back.

"What's the matter? Are you scared?" Franklin taunted. "No one intimidates *me*. I go out there because I can. I want them to see me out there. They don't scare me, and I'll never give them the satisfaction of thinking I can't do whatever I want, anywhere I want. I'm not like you. You might as well just bend over for them."

"Franklin, you shouldn't talk like that," a soft voice called from the other room. "They stole Mitch's dog."

"Shut up, Vivian," Franklin called back. "He deserved it. See, you gotta have your Momma stick up for ya. How pathetic!"

Cal cringed at what Franklin had said and was surprised that he didn't feel any satisfaction at Mitch's pain. He quietly crawled out of the shrubs and made his way to the kennel. With that fight going on inside the house, he figured he could tie the dog to the kennel without being heard and then quickly get back to the car.

He gave the dog enough rope to move around freely and tied the end through the mesh of the kennel's fence. He looked up, trying to see his car in the distance, and as he started to walk away, the dog began to bark. "Shhh." Cal said softly. He heard the conversation inside stop and realized that the dog had got the Graysons' attention. Cal heard the front door open and he dashed into the shrubs again with the dog yelping and pulling at the rope. He curled himself up tightly, then saw Mitch's boots walk by him.

"Doogie?" Mitch called out, surprised.

Cal could see through the bushes and watched as Mitch looked around in the dark. The dog continued to bark, and Cal knew he'd be sunk if Mitch untied him. Cal's heart raced as Mitch unthreaded the rope from the fence. With his other hand, he undid the padlock. The dog darted toward Cal, but Mitch pulled tight on the rope. Cal sat waiting for Mitch to notice him hiding in the bushes, but then a low rev came from up the street and Mitch looked up; it was Johnny, starting up the car. Then the porch light blinked on at the house where Cal's car was parked. Mitch pulled the dog into the kennel and then closed the gate. The dog barked and whined, but Mitch kept his attention on the car.

"What the hell?" Mitch whispered to himself as he watched Johnny slowly drive off. "What's he doing here?" He took a quick look at his dog, and then stood watching as the car drove away toward the highway. Mitch stood pondering for a moment, then walked back inside the house as the dog continued to bark at Cal, who was still hiding in the bushes.

"Who the hell was that?" asked Franklin.

"It was just someone returning Doogie."

"Who?"

Mitch didn't respond.

"Who the hell was it?" Franklin roared.

"I don't know. Just some kid from school."

The dog continued its feverish barking. But with Mitch back inside, Cal knew it was time to run for it. He decided to take the back way and avoid glare of the porch lights along the street. He wanted to run fast enough and hopefully far enough so that the darkness would blanket him from sight. Cal darted off and then realized that it was so dark that he couldn't see where he was stepping and worried that he'd trip and fall. He slowed his pace a bit and tried to watch where he stepped. As he came around the back of the house at the end of the street, he saw Johnny blink his headlights; Cal smiled and ran to the car. Now inside, he took a deep, victorious breath.

"We did it!" he exclaimed.

Johnny smiled broadly as he drove off, and sat quietly pondering what had happened as they rode silently but satisfied. "It's kind of funny."

"What is?"

Johnny gave a small laugh. "Think about it. We just risked getting arrested so we could return a dog to a person we hate."

Cal sighed.

"I'm not saying we shouldn't have done it. I just think it's weird that I feel so good about it," Johnny said, chuckling.

Cal nodded in agreement. He looked out the window and reflected on what had happened, along with what he'd heard through the window. After they'd driven for a while, Cal told Johnny what Franklin had said to Mitch.

Johnny listened, and when Cal was finished with the story, he raised his eyebrows, then said, "Sounds to me like Mitch is already in jail."

Cal shrugged and shook his head.

"Does it make you feel any differently about wanting him to pay for Doran's death?"

"Hell, no!"

Johnny put a hand up defensively. "I was just asking. After what you told me, it kind of sounded like you were changing your mind about revenge."

"I don't care what kind of crappy life he has. I can't just sit by; I want justice."

Johnny looked at him, frustrated. "Revenge and justice aren't the same things. I agree that we all need justice, but revenge is just anger. It never solves anything."

"I don't care. It'll make me feel better, seeing him suffer."

Johnny looked at Cal with a face that showed tired disappointment. "You're wrong. You'll never be happy until you can move on. And to do that, you need to forgive."

"What? Are you nuts? I'll never forgive him for killing my brother. Never!"

Johnny sat silently staring out at the dark road ahead of them. "Then you'll never be able to move on. Doran wouldn't have wanted you to spend your life trying to get revenge. You know that."

Cal scoffed.

"Why do you think you felt the way you did tonight? You felt good because you are starting to move on. But you can't do what you did without starting to forgive."

Cal shook his head. "Why do you care about what I do?"

"Because things need to change. You can see it as well as I can. I want good things to start happening and I think this is the only way it can. We all have so much pride sometimes. And it doesn't get us anywhere."

Cal laughed. "You sound like Doran." Then he took a deep, thought-filled breath.

Johnny nodded and continued to drive Cal's car down the desolate shadowed highway. They both sat thinking in the quiet night as the road stretched on toward the Fort.

When they reached Johnny's house, he pulled the car up to the front and both boys got out. They passed each other in front of the car as Cal went around to the driver's side. He sat behind the wheel and Johnny waved as he started to walk up to his door. But then he turned and walked back to the car and leaned in through the passenger side window.

"You did the right thing tonight."

Cal shook his head amused. Then he smiled and nodded. "I know."

13

Mr. Henry wasn't in his classroom and Cal didn't feel like walking the halls looking for him. Just the short amount of time he'd spent getting there garnered some peculiar stares from students he didn't even know, and he certainly wasn't in the mood to deal with Mitch. He tore a small piece of paper from his notebook pad and scribbled a message saying that he'd been there but needed to get to the records department at the courthouse before they closed. He put the note face down on Mr. Henry's chair and quickly left the building.

At the courthouse, Cal walked up to the glass window. Before he could even ask his question, the clerk pointed down the hall and muttered, "Criminal court is to your left." Annoyed, Cal resisted the powerful urge to push her smug little nose out the back of her face, then calmly said, "Thanks, but actually, I'm looking for the records department."

She glanced up from her writing and answered him in an annoyed tone. "It's also to your left."

Cal looked down the hall to his right and realized

everything was to his left. He turned away from the small circular hole in the glass and said, "Oh, sorry."

"What?" the woman asked.

Startled, Cal turned back to her and shook his head. "Nothing; I just said sorry."

She looked at him with skepticism, but then she took a deep breath. "Go down that hall, but instead of going to the window that says records, go to the next one and ask for Valerie. Tell her Linda sent you. She'll be able to help you and you won't have to stand in line. Then she smiled at him.

He gave her a grin. "Thanks, Linda."

She nodded back, and he went over to the window she suggested.

The women in the records department were much friendlier, but they too directed him down to criminal court when he first walked through the door. But when he asked for Valerie, an older woman wearing red-rimmed glasses greeted him like she knew him.

"I'm looking for any files for Burton, Littlebear, or Grayson," he explained.

She looked at him oddly and one of the other women overheard and went into a back room. After several minutes, she came out with a large folder and some files. "Which one do you want?" she asked. "There are two cases."

Cal sighed as the pain of losing Doran went through him again. "Both," he told her.

"You can look through them, but please keep them in order. The reading room is the first door on your right," Valerie told him.

Cal looked at the pile. The first two folders were the police reports from Doran's case. The rest, and there were at least a dozen, were from Jackie's murder. He flipped through the pages, glancing quickly at the bold type looking for names or anything that looked like it might be the link to Grayson that he needed. He felt like he'd been handed a ticket to a trip back in time and quickly wanted to absorb every ounce of the information in those files.

Then a man in a dusty dark suit walked into the office as Cal gathered the documents. His hair was sandy brown and shot with gray, and his face had soft but noble features. He was a gentle looking man in his early sixties, with a thick mustache and kind green eyes. The women in the office greeted him immediately with enthusiastic smiles, and the man was cordial to the clerks. Cal watched as Valerie took him aside and tried to talk with him about Cal without making it obvious, then the man turned around and grinned at Cal when he saw the pile of files. "Nothing better to read in our city library?" he asked.

Cal gave the man a forced smile and quickly slid past him into the small reading room. It was well lit and had a large table; and since he was the only one in the room, he spread out the documents into smaller piles.

Now the man appeared in the doorway. "Are you looking for something in particular?" he asked.

Cal shrugged, not wanting to waste time talking, but he answered him honestly. "I'm just looking at a file about my family. I think my aunt was murdered here."

"Here? We haven't had a murder here in years."

"It happened about eighteen years ago."

"Really? You said it was your aunt."

Cal nodded.

"Who was your aunt?"

"Jackie Littlebear," Cal said, becoming annoyed that the questions were keeping him from immediately diving into the documents.

The man stepped into the room and leaned over the table. "You mean the girl they found in Bottle Hollow?"

Cal looked up, surprised. "Yes. Why?"

The man adjusted his thin-framed glasses. "First of all, who are you? What's your name?"

"Cal Burton."

The man thought a moment, then said, "So you're the son of—" the man snapped his fingers as he struggled to remember the names, "the sister and the guy they found on the beach."

"Yes. How do you know all this?" Cal asked, surprised.

The man stood in a daze, looking at Cal as if he'd seen a ghost. "Cal, I'm Robert Brewster. I was the prosecuting attorney on that case."

"You were?"

Robert sighed. "I was pretty new to Roosevelt, and I remember it quite well. I'm in private practice now." He cocked his head sideways and started to look through the documents. "I thought your parents moved away after all that. Why're you back, and what are you trying to find?"

Cal hesitated, not sure if he should trust the man, knowing he was right in the heart of Franklin Grayson's territory, but he took a chance. "My parents are divorced and my mom moved us back here to the Fort. I didn't know about any of this stuff until we got here. I actually came looking for stuff about my brother's murder, but they handed me this stuff instead."

"Oh, God!" Robert said, studying Cal. "Burton...that was your brother, who was shot."

Cal nodded silently.

"I'm very sorry for your loss," Robert said gently. He looked at Cal quizzically. "Do you think that had something to do with Jackie's case?"

Cal began to answer, but then stopped and pondered what Robert had said. He thought about a possible connection. "I don't know. I never really thought about it before. I didn't even consider looking for files." He looked down at the pile. "And even if I had, I thought for sure the sheriff would have burned these to cover up her murder."

"Why do you say that?"

Cal shrugged, not feeling totally comfortable explaining his feelings about Silver Hair. He looked up at Robert and explained, "I think she was murdered."

"Oh, she was murdered all right," the lawyer said.

Cal sat back, interested, realizing he was going to get an earful.

Robert closed the door and took a chair across from Cal. "Do you mind?" he asked as he pulled some of the paperwork across the table. He picked out a document and smiled.

"What?" Cal asked.

"It's just that it's been so long, I'd forgotten a lot about this case. It seemed so open and shut at the time."

"Why? What happened?"

The man looked at his watch. "I only have about fifteen minutes before my next hearing, but I'll give you a thumbnail sketch of the case as I saw it. Okay?"

"Great!"

"I thought your father, David Burton, was the killer—" Robert raised his hands in defense, "—at first." He held out a mug shot photo of David, who looked very young and scared. A sharp pang of sadness hit Cal as he realized how alike David and Doran looked. "We even arrested him for it, but then we discovered that he'd been drugged and was unconscious at the time of the girl's death. The people who called the police said they'd heard a woman screaming, and they later told us they heard her scream David's name. When we found out that he couldn't have done it, we realized Jackie was most likely screaming for David's help."

"Drugged? With what?"

"Demerol. It's a prescription painkiller, and when the cops arrived, he was barely able to stand up."

"What about Franklin Grayson?" asked Cal.

The man smiled, "Yes. He seemed to be the likely suspect. He was dating Jackie at the time, and it was a volatile relationship with a lot of fighting. Supposedly, he beat her up several times. And she was pregnant. A lot of people thought he killed her so he wouldn't end up with a half-Indian kid."

The statement made Cal's heart ache, but he pushed his own problems aside and continued on with his questions. "So why wasn't he charged?"

"Because he didn't do it."

"How do you know that?"

"He wasn't there." Robert gave Cal a wry grin. "He was actually in bed with the gal Tim Avery ended up marrying."

"What?" Cal asked, as chills went down his back.

Robert shook his head and went on. "Yes. She came to his defense."

"Jesus," Cal said softly. His eyes widened in horror; Lacey was Grayson's daughter. Did she know? *That sure explained her surly attitude*, Cal reflected. "But that still doesn't mean he didn't lie about where he was. She probably lied to save him. And Franklin's dad was the sheriff, wasn't he? He probably covered up the whole thing."

"As much as I wish that were true, others saw Franklin with her earlier that night, and we had enough witnesses and testimony to clear him. Your father and mother also testified they didn't see him there. It was soon after that the death was ruled suspicious."

"Suspicious. What does that mean in legal terms?"

"It means the case was never really closed," Robert said as he slid the chair back to get up.

"But my Mom has always said that Aunt Jackie drowned. Did she, or do you think it was suicide?" asked Cal.

Robert let out a sarcastic laugh. "A lot of these rednecks want everyone to think that, and that's what everyone said. But that was no suicide, even though I couldn't convince anyone at the time. They all thought I was trying to get publicity off that case. It's a small town; we don't have people getting killed out here very often." He stood up and asked Cal, "How long are you going to be around? This hearing shouldn't take more than half an hour, and we can talk more when it's over if you're still here."

"I'll wait."

"Good. I'll come back and talk with you later, if you'd like."

"Sure. I need all the help I can get."

"Help with what?"

Cal furrowed his brows, surprised by the question. "Getting Franklin convicted."

Robert leaned back over the table and spoke softly, "Don't waste your time. He didn't do it..."

Cal rolled his eyes unconvinced.

"...And even if you had all the evidence in the world, there is no judge out here who's going convict Franklin Grayson for an 18-year-old murder of a Ute girl. My first words of advice are, don't go around telling anyone you're looking into this. You really don't need those kinds of problems and you'll have Franklin breathing down your throat if he even *hears* you're looking into this."

Cal scoffed. "He's already done more than breathe down my throat. He's pretty much ruined my life here and his son Mitch killed my brother."

Robert's face turned to despair. "Cal, trying to get at Franklin won't get you anywhere. People have been trying to take him down for years."

Cal shrugged. "But it was murder; I know Silver ... Franklin did it. Mitch got away with it, too. I'm tired of them getting away with it."

Robert took a deep breath and patted Cal firmly on the back, then smiled and waved to the women behind the counter as he left.

Cal dove into the documents. He had no idea what he was looking for, but had an urge to find something that made sense. Most of the papers were legal drafts, and Cal skimmed them until a word or phrase caught his eye. He read with interest the statement of the group on the other side of the beach the night of Jackie's death. They testified that they heard splashing and screaming most of the evening, but they knew when they heard Jackie's terrified screams much later in the night, that it wasn't fun and games anymore. Then Cal found the transcript of Raymond's testimony. As he read through it, a pang of sadness tore at his heart. He sensed the pain in his grandfather's words, and imagined him on the stand, feeling reticent and out of place, with tears of loss streaming down his face as he talked about the last time he saw his oldest daughter.

As he read, Cal saw Robert trying to lead Raymond into divulging a possible relationship between Jackie and David, but Raymond resisted. Cal wondered if Robert was a trusted resource. As he continued to read, he found Eddie's testimony. He smiled as he realized Eddie's speech and mentality weren't much different now or more mature than they were when he was four years old, the time of his mother's death. In the transcript, Eddie described a monster that killed Jackie; he talked about large teeth and how the creature drowned his mother in the lake. Cal realized then that he'd never asked Eddie about the murder as he gathered up the documents and went to the desk.

"Can I come back and look at these again another time," he asked the clerk.

"Sure. I can even make copies for you. But they'll cost five cents each."

"That's fine. When can I pick them up?"

The woman flipped through the stack of papers, counting them. "How about tomorrow?"

Cal thanked her, then dashed from the courthouse and sped home to find Eddie. He knew that Eddie would open up to him and reveal that Franklin was the real killer. Then, with Franklin humiliated and in prison, Cal finally would have justice, not to mention some revenge. That thought ran through him and made his heart beat quicker. The Mustang couldn't go fast enough as Cal's excitement continued to build.

He found Eddie at the playground across from the tribal center. He was playing with an old can next to the broken merry-go-round. He sprung up with excitement when Cal stopped the car. Eddie was covered in sand and he smiled at Cal with his half open eyes as Cal led him to a bench.

There Cal asked him about the monster that drowned his mom and Eddie immediately started in with an elaborate enactment of that night's events. He walked around, slowly dragging his feet and hunching his shoulders and made a scary face as he groaned and snarled. It was quite a performance, Cal thought, but he grew tired of watching Eddie play-act and soon realized much of what Eddie did was just a way to keep Cal's attention.

"Eddie, come here and sit down. I want to talk to you," Cal said.

He plopped himself down and studied Cal with sleepy eyes.

"Listen, Eddie; you told me about the monster that

killed your mom, but I want you to tell me everything that happened the night when your mom was killed at the lake."

Eddie took a deep breath and began to spew out a memorized string of events.

"Whoa!" Cal yelled, "Slow down." Cal realized then that Eddie had been asked so many times that it was easiest for him to keep a master version of his mother's murder in his mind.

"Was Jackie sleeping when the monster came?" Cal prompted.

"Yeah, okay," Eddie answered.

"Then what happened?"

Eddie began to take his deep breath again, but this time, Cal cut him off.

"Wait! All right, Buddy. Let's walk you through this one step at a time. Was the monster big?"

"Yes."

"Did the monster grab your mom and take her to the lake?"

Eddie thought for a moment, then said, "Yes."

"What did your mom say?"

"She yelled and cried. She say, 'David, help me!' She say, 'Why you doing this?' She cry and cry."

"Then what happened?" Cal asked, hopefully, seeing Eddie's surprising ability to concentrate and answer.

"Monster come out of the water and leave."

"Where'd it go?"

"It go far away. But it lose its teeth."

Cal looked at Eddie oddly. "Really. Where?"

"Grandpa find the teeth on the beach. I keep them."

257

"The teeth? Do you have them still?"

"Yes. I keep them."

Cal pulled Eddie to his feet and hurried him over to Eddie's house, where his grandmother sat out on the porch looking out at the rest of the Fort. She, like Raymond, was an Elder of the tribe, and she stared at the two, uninterested as they walked into the house. It was much like Raymond's home, cluttered and run-down, but with the same warm feeling of security.

Eddie's room looked like Cal's when he was nine years old. Racecars and action hero figures were neatly placed on his dresser, and Eddie fell to his knees to take a shoebox out from under his bed. Inside he showed Cal a picture of him and Jackie, along with a bracelet with her name in beads, and four small, round, white—.

"Teeth!" exclaimed Eddie as he held them out to Cal. "Monster teeth!"

Cal took the objects and examined them. They weren't teeth, but he'd seen them somewhere before. Suddenly it came to him. These were the Puka-shell necklaces that Mona and Jackie wore in the photograph at his grandfather's house.

He smiled at Eddie and handed back the shells, not telling him what they really were. Eddie put them carefully back in the box, replaced the cover and slid it back under the bed.

"Is that all you have from your mother?" Cal asked, disappointed he hadn't discovered more.

"Yes. Grandpa Ray keeps everything in his house. He says I might lose it, but that he'll give it to me when I grow up."

Cal wondered if that day would ever come; he left Eddie disappointed when he turned down his request to play a game, but Cal was eager to get home and look through the boxes in Mona's room. He was sure he'd find the answers he needed hidden there.

14

The boxes of Jackie's and other family things were stacked four high in the closet. Raymond was out, so Cal quickly pulled them out and onto the bed. Some were packed with clothes, but most were filled with papers, photos and trinkets. Cal had no idea what he was looking for, so he just started going through each box in the hope of finding something that made sense. The photos were fascinating; Jackie was a beautiful girl with an infectious smile, and from the photos, it looked like she was happy and always seemed to be touching or hugging someone. The pictures with Eddie clearly showed a mother who loved her child, despite his problems, and the photos of Jackie with Raymond depicted a daughter who adored her father. Raymond, too, looked young and happy, but it was one photo in particular that caught Cal's eye. It showed Jackie and Mona, arms around each other, in identical outfits. And around each of their necks hung a strand of Puka shells. *The murderer must have pulled at Jackie's and broken the strand*, Cal thought.

Cal heard the door creek open and Raymond poked his head in. "I was wondering who was home," he said.

Cal felt awkward having spilled the guts of Jackie's life out onto the bed. "I wanted to learn more about my aunt."

But Raymond smiled and said, "What would you like to know?"

"I'm not sure, Grandpa. I have this feeling that I need to know what really happened the night she died. Ever since I've been here, it seems something's been directing me toward finding out."

"That could very well be true. There are so many things I don't understand about her death. And I miss her still." He picked up the picture of Jackie and Mona and said, "Our daughters were everything to us, Cal. We gave them everything. Mona wanted to be just like Jackie, so we had to give her the same clothes and jewelry as her big sister. I remember the day they got those necklaces. Their Uncle Ron, my brother, was in the Navy. He was stationed in California and brought these necklaces back for the girls. They wore them all the time; we even buried Jackie in hers—she loved it so much."

"But, I thought—" Cal began to ask, confused. But the off-pitch chime of the doorbell diverted Raymond's attention and he left the room.

Cal sat for a minute, confused about the inconsistent facts about the necklaces. How could Jackie be buried with her necklace when Eddie had just showed him the broken pieces from that box in his room? Cal tried to come up with an explanation, but nothing he could think of made any sense. He'd ask his grandpa when he came back.

Cal thumbed through some papers, but then pushed them aside when he noticed a large, rigid envelope that stood out among the others. As Cal carefully opened the metal clasp, chills overtook him; it was Jackie's death certificate. As he began to read it, he realized that there were two papers in the envelope. He took off the top one to reveal a second certificate—this one for Baby Littlebear. *Since there was a death certificate, there must have been an autopsy on Jackie's unborn baby*, he thought. He made a mental note to make sure that the report was included in the batch of copies he was picking up at the records department in the morning.

Raymond came back into the room. "Find anything else?" he asked his grandson.

Cal hid the death certificates, knowing the pain they'd cause. "Grandpa, did you keep everything of Jackie's?" he asked.

"At first I did; I didn't want to lose any part of her. But over the years, I gave some things to Eddie."

"What all did you give him?"

"Oh, mostly pictures, and some toys. I think Eddie has come in and taken some things without my knowing, but it was his mother and I know he values them, so I'm not too concerned."

Cal smiled to himself realizing that Eddie probably kept some of the items hidden from Cal, thinking he might tell on him and get him in trouble. He held a photo of Jackie and Raymond. "She sure was pretty. And always smiling."

"She was. After losing her, it took me years before I smiled again. It hurt the relationship between Mona and me, but I was just so sad." Raymond sat and stared at the floor thinking.

"Are you all right, Grandpa?"

"Yes," he said as he took a deep breath and scratched his head. "Cal, that was Tom Wyasket at the door. We'll be going to the sweat lodge tonight, but I won't go if you want me to stay here with you."

Cal shrugged and said, "No. I'll be fine. What's a sweat lodge?"

"It is part of our tribal beliefs and rituals. We go there for spiritual growth."

"Can I go with you sometime?"

Raymond looked at him, surprised. "I'd love to take you. I'm so glad that you want to learn and experience these things."

"It's all because of you. You're the only reason I want to know, the only reason I'm proud of any of that. I actually feel some connection to this place, although I still feel somewhat like an outsider because I'm half white." Cal smiled sadly at Raymond. "You know, Grandpa, I really don't fit in anywhere. The people in town hate me because I'm considered a Ute, and the Indians don't accept me because I'm part white."

Raymond put his hand on Cal's arm. "It doesn't matter what any of them think. I feel that because you've seen and lived in other places, you'll appreciate your Ute family. You're my only hope, Cal; without you, I have no one to carry on our family traditions. Being Ute isn't just in your blood, it's in your spirit. And I believe the spirit brought you here to the Fort for a reason."

Cal raised his eyebrows and thought about it. Then he told his grandfather, "Yes. I'm sure of it."

Again the doorbell chimed its broken summons. Raymond got up and walked to the door, and Cal heard him talking to someone. Then footsteps came down the hall. After a light knock on the door, Johnny peeked in.

"Hey, Johnny," Cal said, surprised to see his friend.

Raymond looked in and said, "I'm leaving. I won't be back until late."

"Okay," Cal called after him.

After Raymond left, Johnny stood uncomfortably in the doorway.

"Why didn't you tell me you knew about David not being my father?" Cal asked.

Johnny shrugged. "I figured you already had enough bad news in your life."

"Who told you, Cal?"

"It was Rachel."

"Rachel? Why'd she tell you?"

"She didn't exactly tell me. Fly and I were trying to scare her and April one night when they were camping out in the back yard. As we were sneaking up on them, I heard Rachel telling April that your dad wasn't really your dad, and that he found out when you were in the hospital because of your blood type. She said that's why they got a divorce."

Cal nodded his head quietly. *My blood type*. He realized then why the problems had begun while he was in the hospital. "So, Johnny," he asked, "is there anything else you're not telling me?"

"Like what?"

"Like, do you know who my father is?"

Johnny looked at him oddly. "You don't know?"

"No. My mom took off for Salt Lake when I tried to get it out of her. No one else seems to know anything."

"No. I don't know," Johnny answered quickly.

Cal looked at him, unconvinced. "Are you sure? What've you heard?"

"Nothing," Johnny said more convincingly. Then he quickly changed the subject. "Let's go up to Bitter Creek. Fly and Puck are waiting out in the truck."

"I can't. I'm—" Cal looked back at the photos spread out over the bed, he then shook his head from exhaustion. "I might as well. I think I'm losing my mind."

"Why? What's up? What *is* all this stuff?" Johnny asked, picking up a photo.

"It's all my Aunt Jackie's things."

Johnny dropped the picture as if it were diseased.

"I'm on a quest," said Cal, putting on a jacket.

"A quest? For what?"

"I'm going to bring Grayson down. I know he killed Jackie and I'm going to prove it."

Johnny's face faded to disappointment. "You're on a dead end road. The whites will never let you prove it. They'll protect him, just like they did with Mitch."

"Not all of them. You've seen the difference already. Mr. Johansen said he'd fix our roof, and two days later they were all here working on it. Franklin doesn't control everyone. Besides, if I get enough evidence, I'll go above everyone around here. Just because the town is run by those good ol' boys, it doesn't mean Franklin Grayson or his son can get away with murder."

"When he finds out what you're doing, he'll murder *you*. I'm telling you, they don't care anymore. As far as they're concerned, we're all better off dead."

Cal turned to Johnny and looked him straight in the eye. "He thinks I know something. That's why he's been such a jerk ever since we moved here. That's why he and his stupid son devote their lives to running us out of town. I *know* he killed my Aunt, just like I know Mitch killed Doran. And I don't care if I die trying to prove it. He doesn't scare me anymore. He's going to keep trying to ruin my life, and I can't sit here and just let him do it."

The sound of an impatient horn came from the driveway.

"Let's go," Cal said. He began to straighten out the pictures but then stopped, realizing he had time to do that later. Raymond wouldn't be back until late, and Rachel was with April. The thought of them together sent shivers down his back, but he pushed the thought from his mind, unwilling to let another thing eat away at him.

Cal sat staring out over the Basin, remembering how beautiful that spot was before Doran was killed. Johnny sat beside him smoking peyote and looking up at the sky. "You sure you don't want any?" he asked Cal.

"No. I still want to look through that stuff and I'll need my head clear."

Johnny shook his head and rolled back onto the

plateau. He blew a thin stream of smoke into the air and stared out, looking as though he were solving the problems of the world alone in his head. "If there's anything you can learn about becoming Nuchu, it's being able to appreciate life. Bringing people back from the dead isn't gonna be pretty."

Cal rolled his eyes and ignored Johnny's lecture. He was enjoying the breeze and the buzz from the secondary peyote smoke all around him.

As they all sunned themselves on the rocks, a flock of large gull-shaped birds flew over. Johnny put his hands under his head, watching the group flutter by in a precise "V" formation.

In a voice that sounded more like a tribal elder than a teenager, Johnny spoke intensely. "Cal, do you know why one side of the "V" is longer than the other?"

Cal studied the birds and their pattern, pondering his question. He shook his head, saying, "No. Why is it?"

Johnny drew in a long, thoughtful breath and answered him. "Because there're more birds on that side."

Cal closed his eyes and groaned, knowing he'd been had.

Puck laughed hard and Fly sat up with a smile.

Johnny continued to lie there, watching the birds fly by. Then he said, still grinning, "Sometimes things are obvious and you work to make them more than what they are."

Cal lifted an eyebrow. "You think I'm making more of this than I should."

Puck and Fly walked away, not wanting to get into the middle of another discussion.

Johnny propped himself up on an elbow. "What will it change or solve?"

"I want to know the truth."

"You didn't answer my question."

Cal sighed. "If I don't find out what happened, I'll always wonder."

"What if you find out something that ruins your life?"

Cal scoffed, "Like it could get any worse?"

Johnny smiled sadly and looked down at the porous stone surface. "It can always get worse. But you don't have to let it."

"You act like you know something. Are you being straight with me?"

Johnny looked Cal in the eye. "There's a lot of pain around the stuff that happened with Jackie. I think you're going to make it all worse if you bring it up again, Cal. It's the past; let it stay there."

"I can't."

Johnny sighed, "Are you ever going to be happy? I mean, satisfied, or even content?"

Cal looked at him oddly. "What do you mean by that?"

Johnny shrugged. "I don't know. You always seem like you're looking for a way to be miserable. I know you're pissed about Doran; we all are. But digging up all this muck from the past for revenge, will it do any good?"

"It will if I can take Franklin Grayson down."

"I guess," Johnny muttered, not convinced.

"I don't get it with you guys. You never seem to get excited about anything. I'm miserable for a lot of real reasons, like because I'm not playing sports, not to mention that I've lost my father, my brother and my home."

Johnny shook his head and hurled a rock over the cliff edge. "Cal, I drive for an hour to go to school. I don't have a father or a mother, and my brother's in jail for killing two people when he was driving drunk. You're not the only one who's picked on or having a hard time. But digging up dirt isn't going to bring back your happiness."

Cal leaned back and looked at Johnny, amazed. "You never told me any of this about your brother. Is he Eddie's father?"

"Yeah. And why would I tell you? I don't think about it. Otherwise I'd go around drinking myself sick like the rest of them. That's what both my parents did; I'm lucky I didn't end up like Eddie."

"What do you mean?"

"Eddie's a retard because your Aunt Jackie drank night and day while she was pregnant. Look around at the kids on the Fort and you can see it; a lot of them have that same sleepy look. It's called fetal alcohol syndrome. And the problem is that most of the parents don't even live long enough to see the damage they've done. If Franklin Grayson hadn't killed her, Jackie would have done it to herself by drinking. And I'm not so sure that isn't what really happened to her anyway."

Cal sat and stared out over the Basin as its edges slowly began to glow with the fiery orange haze. Two oil rigs pumped in unison in the distance, their long necks dipping down toward the earth and then back up again, like long-necked birds pulling worms from the ground.

"You don't believe Franklin killed Jackie, do you?" Cal asked.

Johnny shrugged. "I don't know. It seems like she was headed in that direction already, why would he want to kill her? So she was pregnant. Franklin Grayson got other girls pregnant, too. He didn't kill any of them."

"Yeah, I heard that, about him and other girls."

"Supposedly Gina Jones is his daughter, and there's been talk that even one of your friend Tim's daughters is really Franklin's."

Cal's eyes widened in horror; it had to be Lacey, but then he said, "I thought Lacey's mother was found dead."

"She was. Alcohol, same as Jackie. Same as a lot of people on the Fort."

Cal thought about Tim and shook his head in sadness and disgust. "Do you know that for sure?"

Johnny rolled his eyes. "Do you really think Franklin killed every girl he got pregnant? Don't you think that's a little far fetched?"

Cal thought for a moment. "Don't you think it's kind of weird that both Jackie's and Lacey's mothers died after being pregnant with his kids?"

Johnny raised his hands in defense. "There's still no proof, Cal. Besides, what about Mitch? He's the same age Jackie's baby would have been. Franklin ended up marrying *his* mother."

"Yes, but Mitch's mother isn't an Indian. Franklin hates us. That's why he killed Jackie and maybe even Lacey's mother," Cal said.

Johnny began to laugh.

"What?" Cal asked, annoyed.

"You! That's the first time I ever heard you refer to yourself as one of us."

"Shut up. And hand me that pipe," Cal said, reaching for the peyote.

Johnny jerked the pipe away. "I thought you were continuing the big investigation tonight."

"It can wait."

15

Cal woke up on what used to be Doran's bed and he wasn't sure how he actually got there. The night before hung like a haze in his mind and he buried his head into the pillow, trying to find any trace of his brother's essence there. The pain of loss hit him hard and he lay there, unable to free himself from the grim reality that Doran was really gone.

The house was quiet, and as he padded down the hall, he found that he was alone. The remnants in Raymond's coffee cup signaled that he'd already left for the day. There were no signs that Mona was home, and Cal wondered if she'd ever planned to come back.

Cal tried to eat something, but had no appetite. He walked back to his room and shuffled the papers about Jackie, placing them in neat, uniform piles on the bed. He sat down and listed on the back of an envelope the items he hoped to find at the courthouse: an autopsy report, blood tests, and any evidence found at the scene. He set the paper down as a feeling of dread and exhaustion overtook him. Was the pain of his broken life taking its toll on his body, or was he just hung over after the late night and peyote at Bitter Creek? So much had happened in the last couple months, but it wasn't until that morning when he actually felt the real and utter loss, and the grief of all those events. Yet through his anguish, the one thing that stayed steady in his throbbing mind was the clear picture of his nemesis, Franklin Grayson, smugly staring him down at the Sun Dance.

The fire in Cal's belly began to burn and he clutched the list tightly as he headed out to the car. He flung open the door and there he found a leather covered box placed purposely on the seat. Cal looked around, wondering how it got there. It was the size of a shoebox and exquisitely tooled with delicate, curving lines and handsome gold seams. A large clasp and lock had been violently crushed to get it open and he cautiously picked it up and set it on the hood of the car. Cal carefully opened the box to find dozens of letters, all handwritten on notebook paper. He wondered how and why they ended up on the seat of his car as he took one off the top and unfolded it. Amidst the doodles of flowers and happy faces was the handwriting of a young girl. "Dear Juanita," the letter began. Juanita? I have letters to some girl named Juanita? Cal pondered that as he continued to read. The letter went on: "I love him so much. She'd die if she knew, but he sneaked in my window last night—" Cal stopped reading and turned the note over. It was signed, "Friends Forever, Mona."

"My God, they were written by Mom," Cal said aloud. "But who's Juanita?" He shoved the letter back in the box and placed it on the seat next to him. When he got the information from the courthouse, he'd sit down with it all and read through everything. He felt elated as he pondered the treasure he was given, and wondered who his benefactor was. It was his big break. If Mona wrote about her courtship with David, maybe there were clues about what happened to Jackie, too. And maybe the truth about his real father.

Cal sped to the courthouse and gravel flew as he pulled in quickly to the back parking lot. He debated whether or not to bring the letters in, fearful that if he took his eyes off them even for a second, they'd be gone. He grabbed the box and shoved it under his arm, then walked up the back steps. When he stepped inside, a group of people stood huddled outside one of the courtrooms. As he walked past, he heard Robert call his name.

"Where'd you head off to the other day?" Robert asked with a smile.

"I'm sorry I left you hanging. I found some stuff in the records that made me want to talk to Eddie and I totally forgot."

"No problem. But did you find what you were looking for?"

"Kind of; I'm back to pick up my copies, but I do have a list of some things I want to see."

"It looks like a pretty long list," he said, motioning to the box under Cal's arm.

Cal smiled. "No, not this. Actually, someone left it in my car. It's filled with a bunch of notes my mom wrote to one of her friends. And they were written right around the time Jackie was killed."

"How do you know?" Robert asked as he pulled Cal to a more secluded area in the hall.

"Because she talks about my dad."

Robert's face suddenly turned worried. "We need to get you out of sight."

"Why?" asked Cal.

"Because Grayson's coming out of that courthouse any minute and—"

Just then the door swung open and Franklin strode out in his usual pompous fashion. Two men followed him, both busily going through court papers.

Both Cal and Robert stood frozen, unsure of where to turn or what to do. When Franklin saw them, his face went from surprise to anger.

Cal looked at his face and saw something he'd never gotten a good look at before: Silver Hair's eyes. They were icy and evil, and Cal stood paralyzed as he watched them. Those eyes made him weak and turned his stomach sour.

"Come on, let's go," Robert said. He took Cal by the arm and began to lead him down the hall, but Cal struggled, feeling empowered by the ammunition he'd found and would soon disclose.

When they reached the records office, Robert again warned Cal about alerting Franklin to what he was doing.

"I don't care. I told you before. He doesn't scare me," Cal protested.

"Well, he should! Hurry up and get the stuff you need, then go." Robert looked out into the hall and said, "He's gone. I've got to get back to my clients, but call me later."

Cal nodded, then turned back to the records lady who looked at him confused. He told her what he came for and she began to search through several stacks of papers on a back table. She lifted a large stack and walked it over to him.

"This is everything, right?" he asked the lady as he paid for the copies.

She nodded and Cal smiled as he took the large pile and added it to the mass under his arm.

He strode out and as he rounded the corner, he felt his feet catch on something and began to go down. His instincts to catch himself released the box and the stack of papers, which fell all over the foyer floor. An older woman ran to help him and began gathering the papers together. Cal lay on his back stunned and turned back to see what it was that he'd stumbled over.

Franklin stood by on his cell phone, deep in a conversation, but then he leaned back casually and smiled widely at Cal sprawled out on the floor, his horizontal reflection clear in the dark glasses that Silver Hair was wearing once again.

Grayson looked down at the leather box and his face turned angry as he hung up the phone and stooped to pick it up. "Where'd you get this?"

Cal turned back to the lady, who had quickly collected his cache of papers with the exception of a few fugitive sheets. Thanking her, he turned back to Franklin, who stood examining another of the documents. The leather box was now tucked under his arm.

"You little thief! You broke into my house and took these."

Cal stood up and walked over to Franklin. Without hesitation, Cal swung, hitting Franklin unexpectedly, throwing him into the wall.

Angered and dazed, Franklin dropped the box and the papers. Cal snatched them up.

The woman stood upright with the few remaining papers, shocked at Cal's actions. She stepped back nervously as Franklin took a swing at Cal. Cal ducked and clutched the box and papers closer to him.

"What's wrong, Grayson? Bring back some bad memories? What were you trying to hide in that box?" Cal taunted. He looked around at the empty hallway. "Where's all your buddies? Or is it just you and me this time?"

Franklin steadied himself, and then angrily squared his stance. "Come on, you little half-breed punk. You wanna prove something with me? Now's your chance!"

Cal swung with his free arm and missed, but somehow caught Franklin on an upswing, connecting perfectly with his jaw and sending the sheriff stumbling back into the wall.

Now Cal saw his chance and turned back to the frightened woman. He quickly took the rest of the papers from her and thanked her as she looked on, bewildered. He turned back around as Franklin came at him, dodged the punch and tried to run to the side. Franklin swung again, this time hitting Cal's shoulder and turning him back. Cal grasped the shoebox and papers tight and lunged forward, hitting Franklin hard with his shoulder and head. The blow knocked Franklin back just enough for Cal to get a head start running for the door and he heard the stomp of Franklin's boots chasing after him on the tile floor. As he flung open the outside doors, he noticed a group of men standing in the parking lot.

"Grab him! I want him arrested for burglary and assault," Franklin shouted to the group, as he lunged from the building.

Cal tossed the box onto the passenger side floor of his car and put the rest of the pile on his seat. He was thrilled that he'd left the top down, making it easy for him to jump in. He didn't want the papers blowing out, so he sat right on top of them. He hurriedly pulled the keys from his pocket and turned the ignition. It hesitated a moment and Cal's stomach throbbed; he tried it again and the engine turned over. He threw it into first and peeled out of the lot, leaving Franklin and the others shielding themselves from the flying gravel.

Cal was beginning to breathe easy until he spotted a black truck gaining on him. He squinted into the rear view mirror and realized Franklin was following him. He needed help, but he knew he couldn't go back to the Fort for Johnny and the others—that'd only bring them trouble. Instead, he decided to try Tim. At least he had some say with them, and if he wasn't home, Cal could take the back road up to the hills and try to lose them on the path to Bitter Creek. Cal sped up to give himself some time to alert Tim that they were coming after him.

As he turned into Tim's neighborhood, he noticed Franklin falling back a bit. He continued to follow Cal, but it was obvious he was uncomfortable facing Tim.

Cal took advantage of the situation and continued driving as fast as he safely could. As he rounded the corner to Tim's house, he lay on the horn, hoping it got Tim's attention before he actually got there. It worked; before Cal even made it to the driveway, Tim was out front, looking puzzled. He stared at Cal as he pulled into the driveway, and then he noticed the black truck following at a distance. "What's going on?" Tim called to Cal.

"He tried to beat me up at the courthouse when I went to pick up some papers." Cal said, grabbing up the documents and the box as Tim quickly hustled him into the house. Tim led Cal back to his bedroom, where he watched what went on outside.

Franklin pulled into the driveway, blocking Cal's car. "Where is he, Tim? I'm arresting him for burglary and assaulting an officer," Franklin shouted as he got out of the truck. Another car pulled up beside him.

Tim walked toward him. "Funny, considering he's the one who's bleeding. And why the army? Does he have something you want?"

"Don't protect him, Tim. He broke into my house and stole things."

Cal walked to the phone. Seeing Franklin's backup made him want to call Johnny and the others for help. As he dialed Johnny's number he hoped desperately that he was home. He'd called over to Fly's house before, but was not confident he remembered the number; and he wasn't really sure where Puck actually lived.

"What's wrong? Is my father trying to save your butt again?"

Cal jumped and turned around to find Lacey standing in the doorway.

"What the hell do you know?" he answered back.

"I know you're still running scared." She walked to the box and began flipping through the letters.

"Running from what?" Cal asked her.

"From the truth," she said, holding out one of the letters toward him.

"Do you realize how weird you are? You mope around like you're half dead; I think you look for misery." Cal said.

"Me?" Lacey retorted. "You don't know the meaning of the word. But you will."

"Hello?" the voice on the other end of the phone said.

It was Johnny! Thank God, Cal thought. He turned away from Lacey. "Hey, I need your help," he said.

"Sure," Johnny said without hesitation.

Cal explained what had happened and explained what he needed him to do. They hung up and Cal turned back to Lacey, but she'd left the room. He went back to the window, where Franklin and Tim still talked.

He bundled the papers together even more tightly in case he had to make a run for it. He searched around Tim's room, wondering if he should try to hide it there or if he should risk trying to run with it all. He paced nervously around Tim's bedroom, as if his nervous energy could speed up Johnny and the others.

As the minutes dragged on, Cal found himself anxiously looking through Tim's things. His dresser was covered with papers and he picked up the pictures of Tim's daughters. As usual, Shelly had a smile and Lacey looked somber. But now he stared at the picture, unable to look away from her eyes. They were crystal blue, and even in the picture, they flashed a fury that made Cal's insides sick. He turned the picture over and found a clue that he didn't expect; it said, Lacey Juanita, age 15.

"Do you always snoop around in other people's personal stuff?" Lacey asked, appearing in the doorway again.

"Who's Juanita?" Cal asked, ignoring the sting in her voice.

Lacey smiled, but her expression then turned sour. "Juanita was my darling drunk of a mother."

"My mother and your mother were friends?"

"You didn't read the letters," she said, annoyed, and motioning to the box of papers.

Cal looked down at the box. "Did you give me these?"

"No. I have my own. We should both be real proud." She turned away and left the room.

Cal followed her with questions, but then he heard the screech of tires on asphalt and looked outside to see Johnny and the others pulling doughnuts in the road. It was Puck's jacked up Tornado and he backed it up and revved the car loudly. It peeled out and ran up and over the curb around to the back of Tim's house.

"They're coming to get him. Get in your cars," Franklin yelled.

It was working just as Cal had planned. He ran to the back and waved as Johnny pulled through the back yard and around the side. As they did, Fly popped up from the back seat and the three pulled back around to the front of the house and raced off down the street. Franklin and the others, thinking Cal had jumped into the car, followed in hot pursuit.

Tim tore back into the house, but when he saw Cal, he stopped, startled. "I thought you went with them."

Cal just smiled.

"Pretty smooth," Tim said, patting Cal on the shoulder. But then his face turned sullen. "What are you going to do? They'll catch up to you sooner or later."

"Yes, but Robert will be able to help me, now that I have the stuff I need." He looked back at Lacey, feeling she had to be the one who'd given him the letters. "Thank you," he said to her.

She gave him an odd look, but then nodded before turning away.

The sound of screeching tires in the distance made Cal jump. He realized it wouldn't be long before Franklin discovered that Cal wasn't in the truck and came looking for him.

"I have to go," Cal said.

"Where?" Tim asked.

"I don't know. Somewhere I can hide out for a while."

Cal peered carefully out the front door, then stepped outside and went to his car. He kept the papers and leather box close to him, once again sitting on the stack to keep it secure in the convertible.

Tim followed him out, the worry embedded in his brow and marked by the sun's afternoon shadow. "Cal, maybe you should turn yourself in. Nothing will come of this and then you can stop running. Doing it this way, you could get hurt."

"More than I've already been hurt? I don't think so, Tim. I'll be fine. In fact, I'll be great. I've got him now and he knows it. Johnny called Robert and he'll help me."

Tim began to argue but then stopped. He leaned down to the car and told Cal, "I'll be here all night if you need anything."

"Thanks," Cal said and pulled the car down and out of the driveway. He waved and headed north, up to the hills, to find the solitude and safety he needed. The road to Bitter Creek felt longer than ever, and the box on the seat beside him practically glowed with the information it contained. The answers were there—he knew it—and a sense of relief began to build in him as he imagined pulling together those last few vital clues.

Cal pulled up close to the edge of the cliff and put the car in park, then stepped out onto the ridge. The sun sat heavy in the west, and a light wind blew around him, kicking up the red powder of the Basin. He walked to the edge and peered over, remembering that horrible night he lost Doran. The chill of winter still had its grip on the valley, but the snow had disappeared. He walked to the place where Doran lay dying on the bluff; the faint trace of a bloody stain was still visible on the plateau. Even the harsh winds and icy climate of the Basin couldn't strip it away. Cal pulled his coat together, trying to keep out the cold, then walked back to the car where the heater was running on high. He put the papers on the passenger seat and looked at both the box and the stack, trying to decide where to start. He pulled one of the letters from the box and began to read, skimming through it until he came to a discussion of Jackie.

"I think I'm pregnant." The words jumped out at Cal. "If he knew, he'd die. I wish Jackie were dead. Then all of this would be fine."

Cal stopped reading and turned the letter over. Again, Mona's signature ended the letter. Cal couldn't believe the hate his mother felt for her own sister.

"Can Tim steal us some stuff from his Dad?" the letter continued. "I'll talk to you tomorrow and tell you what we need." Cal looked up from his reading, thinking he heard the sound of a truck in the distance. He put the letter back in the box and got out of the car to get a better look. He saw the dust trail and realized it was Johnny's truck. What were they doing, coming up here? He looked hard to see if Franklin's truck was following, but it looked like Johnny was alone. He stood watching as Johnny made the turn and pulled up onto the plateau.

"What's going on?" Cal asked as Johnny jumped out of the truck.

"Nothing much. I kind of figured you'd be up here."

"Where's Franklin?"

"He's still chasing the guys. I jumped out and ran into the Hill Top Bar, then ducked out the back. Dirty Dan gave me a ride home." He walked over to Cal's car and saw the papers and box. "So, can I help?"

Cal walked over to him. "I don't know. It's all kind of..." For the first time, he felt the things that happened all those years ago were a part of him, and he was uncomfortable with the feeling of someone else peeling away the shell and exposing his intimate secrets, even if it was Johnny.

"I just want to help you," Johnny said. "We don't have much time before Franklin figures out where we are. After what happened up here with Mitch and Doran, he'll remember that this is our place."

Cal nodded. "Okay. But please don't ever tell anyone what you see in these letters."

"Never."

He handed Johnny the box of letters. "These are letters that my mom wrote to Tim's wife. I'm looking for anything that speaks about Jackie and Franklin. She writes a bunch of gushy stuff about her and my dad, but just ignore that."

Johnny nodded as he took the box and sat in the shade of a scraggly tree. Cal took the stack of papers and joined him. He found a large rock and used it as a paperweight and began flipping through the papers, trying to find any evidence of an autopsy. But he found nothing; most of the papers were legal documents from the hearings.

"God, she sure sounds like she hated Jackie," Johnny muttered as he turned a letter over, then turned it back again, "This doesn't make any sense."

"What's that?" asked Cal.

"She says here that she met this guy from Spokane who works on the rigs."

"Yeah. That's my Dad."

"Yeah, but in an earlier letter, she already said she was pregnant."

"We all know I'm not his; besides, the letters aren't in any order. I dropped the box."

Johnny looked up at Cal. "But she says all this in the same letter."

"Give me that," Cal said as he snatched the letter from Johnny's hands. "Does it say anything about who my real father is? The first letter I read, some guy was crawling in her window and she *thought* she might be pregnant." He continued to skim but found nothing. He grabbed another letter from the pile. "Nothing! She never even mentions his name. What does this say?" he asked Johnny, pointing to a word on the paper.

Johnny looked at it for a minute, then said, "I don't know."

"Ya-jo-wich. Isn't that an Indian word or something? Do you think my real dad was an Indian, too?" he asked.

Johnny just shook his head and pretended to continue reading.

Cal kept repeating the word, trying different pronunciations. "Yojovick. Yohowich. Yohovich." He paused and looked off into the distance, as though something had struck a chord.

"Let's look through this stuff," Johnny said, pointing to a stack of papers, trying to distract Cal.

Cal shrugged, putting the letter back in the box.

They continued searching through the stacks of the copies of Jackie's records. Cal instructed Johnny to look for anything that looked medical. "Here it is!" Cal exclaimed. "It's her autopsy report." He handed Johnny the pile underneath. "Keep this separate so we can go through it later." Cal studied the report hard. "It says here she drowned, but there were signs of struggle. This is good. It shows she didn't just drown."

Johnny leafed through the other papers, and then pulled one out. "What's this?"

Cal glanced up quickly.

"It looks like another autopsy report. Did they do two?"

Cal took the paper. "Yes, this is it."

"What is it?" Johnny asked.

"This is the autopsy report for the baby!"

"The baby?" asked Johnny. "How? It was never born."

"Yes, but they did an autopsy on it because of the investigation. This could prove that Franklin was the father."

"How?"

"By the blood type. See, Jackie's is A negative. It says so right here. But there's nothing about the baby. It should be right here." Cal looked at the paper closely. "It's like the baby never existed," he said, turning the paper over as if he might find something else. "But something isn't right about this. Look." He passed the paper to Johnny.

Johnny studied it a moment, and then shrugged. "What am I looking for?"

"The writing ends, and then there's something that was erased. See those white marks?" Cal said, pointing to the space.

Johnny looked at it again.

"Something was there and someone erased it."

Johnny looked at Cal unconvinced. "Why? Why would they do that?"

Cal rolled his eyes in frustration. "Because if it shows the baby was Franklin's, then it shows motive. It proves that he had a reason to kill Jackie. He didn't want an Indian kid, and with her dead and the report erased, no one could prove that the baby she carried was his. He got rid of the evidence."

"But who would do that? They could be arrested for tampering with official records."

"Not if you're the sheriff. I'm going to have Franklin's father arrested, too. I know he's the one who covered it up."

Johnny chuckled. "Now you really are trying to bring people back from the dead."

"What do you mean?" Cal asked.

"Franklin's father died years ago."

Cal huffed. "Well, Franklin's gonna wish he was dead when I'm done. I just wish I knew how to get those original autopsy reports. I know the information will all be there. Do you think the hospital still has records?"

Johnny thought for a moment. He started to speak, but then stopped.

"What?" Cal asked.

Johnny gave a long and labored sigh. "What about the B.I.A?"

Cal shook his head. "They didn't help me with Doran's case, so why should I turn to them now? Besides Jackie's case was closed years ago. There's no way they'd start a new investigation now."

"I'm not talking about starting a new investigation; I'm talking about the old evidence. The drowning was at Bottle Hollow, so it happened on the reservation. The first police to arrive were from the B.I.A."

Cal's eyes widened. "Just like with Doran's case."

"Yes. Even if they turned Jackie's case over to the county cops, they'd probably still have some of the files."

Cal pointed at Johnny. "If someone erased all the information about the baby, it wouldn't be someone on the Fort. It'd be someone loyal to Franklin—like his father. If the B.I.A. still has those files, they'll be the originals. They'll show everything." He looked at his watch and said, "We need to hurry. I need that file."

The boys sped back to the Fort and walked up to the small tribal courthouse. It was an older brick building with crumbling cement stairs and a rusted handrail. As they stepped inside the small foyer, Johnny nudged Cal toward a sign directing them to court records. The area was tiny compared to the records department at the County Courthouse in Roosevelt. A large Indian woman who almost filled the window looked up at them without a word or a smile.

Cal cleared his throat. "I need to look at some records," he said softly.

She lowered her brow and frowned. "We don't give out files."

"I don't want to take them. I just need a copy."

The woman looked at Johnny, and then back at Cal. "We don't give any records out."

Cal huffed. "At all? You mean no one can ever look at any of these records? What's the point of having a records department?"

Johnny, seeing the woman's temper rising, stepped toward Cal to try and calm him.

The woman stood up. "The only people allowed to look at the files are the police, the judges and the tribal council members, and you aren't any of those." She slid the glass pane shut and sat down.

Cal turned to Johnny. "That's a lot of crap. Now what?"

Johnny smiled widely and Cal threw up his hands in disbelief. "What's so funny? This is the only chance I have, and now the B.I.A. won't help me one bit."

Johnny shook his head and sighed as they walked out of the courthouse and back to Johnny's truck. "You have what you need but you can't see past your own quick temper."

"What are you talking about? I have nothing without those files."

"You idiot, you didn't even listen to her. She said the tribal council could get the files."

Cal stopped and looked at Johnny. "We aren't on the tribal council."

"I know," said Johnny, still grinning. "But your grandpa is."

The drive to the house was quick and they both trotted up to the door and into the house. Raymond sat at the table and a large metal pot was bubbling on the stove. "I'm making chili," he said, as they came into the kitchen.

Cal looked at the pot and then at his grandfather. "Grandpa, I need your help."

Raymond nodded.

"I need some files at the tribal courthouse and they said only tribal council members can get them."

Raymond tilted his head. "What files do you want to see?"

"I need the files from when Jackie was killed."

"Why? I gave you all the information I had stored here at home."

"I know, but there is something I need that'll prove

Franklin killed Jackie. It's an autopsy report. I have this one the County gave me," Cal explained, showing the paper to Raymond. "But right here, where the baby's information should be, it's blank and it looks like someone erased it."

Raymond looked at the paper and bit his bottom lip. He paused and put the paper on the table. "Who would erase it?"

"Someone trying to protect Franklin. I bet it was Franklin's father; he had access and a reason. Grandpa, I know Franklin killed Jackie and I can prove it with those files."

Raymond shook his head. "It happened so long ago, Cal. The case was closed. Nothing is going to change what happened."

"That's because there was no evidence. They erased the proof. That's why Franklin wasn't convicted. If I can show Jackie was pregnant with Franklin's baby, then there'd be evidence. Don't you see? Then we can finally let Jackie rest; we'll be able to make it right. Please help me."

Raymond nodded. "You stay here and I'll go get the file."

"No, Grandpa, I need to come with you."

Raymond put his hand up. "I don't want you linked to all this. I don't want them to know why I'm getting them. I'll get the files and bring them back here."

Cal reluctantly agreed, and Raymond took a jacket from the closet, then left the house.

Cal looked at Johnny, who stirred uncomfortably. "I am glad you're here. I don't think I could handle this crap on my own."

Johnny just nodded without a word.

It'd been less than an hour when Raymond returned and handed Cal an envelope full of papers.

Cal opened it and immediately spread the papers on the kitchen table. He pushed them around, looking for the one report he needed.

The phone rang and Raymond answered it. His voice was low and he didn't say much, except "Thank you." He hung up and turned to Cal, worried. "That was the B.I.A. County officers are there right now, trying to get a warrant for your arrest."

Cal looked at Johnny. "Let's go."

Raymond grabbed Cal's arm. "They can't hurt you here. They have no jurisdiction."

"Eventually, they'll find a way. I need time, and as soon as I get what I need, I won't have to keep running." He gathered all the papers and fled the house.

Johnny drove as Cal scavenged through the files. He pulled one out and held it up. "I found it! It's the autopsy report." He looked at Johnny. "And it has the missing information. I *knew* it was erased." He read it intently as they drove up the dusty hills toward the plateau. As he studied it, his head began to spin. The words leapt from the page and screamed a horror Cal couldn't imagine. As Johnny pulled the truck up to the cliff, Cal rolled out of the seat feeling like he'd been punched. He stumbled to the terrace and his breathing became harder as his eyes began to tear.

"I can't believe it. It's not true." Cal moaned.

Johnny went to him. "What is it, Cal? What's not true?" Johnny asked, trying to read over his shoulder.

"It's the blood type. It shows it right here. See, Jackie's is A negative, same as Mom's. The baby's is right here," he looked down at the paper and pointed to the typed in box. A nauseating shiver went through him and the muscles in his neck locked up, making his breathing ragged.

"What is it?" Johnny asked.

But Cal just kept staring at the paper in silence.

"What? What did you find?" Johnny pressed.

Cal's hands shook as he talked, "The baby's blood type—AB negative—it's the same as mine."

16

"I still don't think that proves anything," Johnny said as he walked to where Cal stood at the edge of the cliff. "So, the baby had the same blood type as you. You don't really think Franklin Grayson's your father, do you?"

"Leave me alone," said Cal as he stood silently facing the sprawling mesa. *But it couldn't be anything else*, he thought. The blood type was too rare, and Mona's letters to Juanita were beginning to make sense. It was Franklin who'd crawled into her window at night; the thought sickened him. "Why're you acting like you don't know?" Cal asked, turning back to face Johnny.

"What do you mean?"

"You've known for a while, haven't you? That's why you kept trying to convince me to stop looking into everything. What does that word mean that they called Franklin in my Mom's letter?"

"What word?"

"Knock it off!" Cal shouted. You know what word. *Yohovich*. Tell me. I know you're hiding something." He stomped off toward the car to find the box.

294

Johnny walked up to him. "Now where are you going?"

Cal tried to ignore him and stepped away from Johnny, but his foot caught a rock and he stumbled. Johnny grabbed Cal's shoulder to keep him from falling all the way to the ground. That's when the emotions inside Cal snapped and he lunged toward Johnny, taking him by surprise and knocking him down. Then he grabbed Johnny by the neck, and through clenched teeth, he screamed, "Tell me! Tell me what the goddamn word means."

Johnny struggled as they rolled on the solid surface, kicking up the auburn dust. But Cal was tired and it didn't take long for Johnny to overpower him and push him off. Then he pulled himself to his feet and flipped his black hair away from his face and turned back to Cal.

"*Yohovich*, you stupid fool," Johnny yelled,"It means wolf. *It means wolf*." He walked off toward the truck, shaking his head in frustration.

Cal remained on he ground, lying on the heated slab and looking into the dawn-tinted sky. The letters, the evidence, the name, "Wolf"; it all tied back to Franklin. Cal had Franklin's eyes; they were ice blue, making the pupil seem even more black and piercing. He wished he could claw out his own eyes—they were the reason he'd been nicknamed The Wolf back in Spokane, the same reason they called Franklin *Yohovich*. And now those dreadful eyes linked Cal and Franklin forever.

All he wanted now was to tell Doran what he'd learned, and once again the lonely ache of his loss hit him again hard. He lay there depleted on the warm plateau as the evening's cool breezes crept in. "You knew all this time," he said to Johnny. "What are you trying to hide?"

Johnny slowly shook his head. "No, Cal. I suspected it, but I couldn't know for sure."

"Why didn't you say something? You knew I was running in circles, trying to get answers."

"I didn't say anything because it doesn't matter. You are who you want to be. It has nothing to do with blood type."

Cal rolled onto his side. Up in the tall tree he spotted a large, dark form. The daylight was fading and the silhouette wasn't clear, but as he shifted his position, he saw that it was the eagle—his eagle. The bird sat reigning over its valley and it was also watching Cal. It seemed like the eagle was always there when things got tough, but it always remained strong and regal, even when it was being shot at. It had seemed so out of place at first, but now it looked to be completely at home.

"Oh, my God!" Johnny shouted from the distance.

"What's the matter?" asked Cal, propping himself up on one elbow.

"It's Franklin. Damn! They're already half way up here."

Cal leaped to his feet. "How'd they get around Bison Bridge without us hearing them?"

"It could be that's when you were wrestling me to the ground."

Cal ignored him, grabbed the papers from underneath the rock and ran with them to the car. He paused as he turned back to the eagle still perched in the tree.

"What are you doing?" Johnny yelled.

Cal turned back around. "I'm not going."

"What?" Johnny yelled, "Get the hell in the car and drive. Even though they're on the reservation, they can still hurt you. Get over to the B.I.A. for protection."

Cal grabbed the box of letters and papers, then walked over to Johnny and told him, "I need your help." He gave his friend the box of letters and said, "Take these and hide them somewhere. Then hurry up and go to Robert and tell him I need help."

Johnny nodded his agreement.

"When you're done with that, please go to my school and take this folder to Mr. Henry. Tell him it's just the rough draft, but the facts are there and I have a lot more."

"We'll go the back way. It's longer, but we can lose them. You can't stay here, Cal. He'll kill you."

"I don't care anymore; I've done nothing wrong and I'm tired of running. If I run from him now, that's all I'll ever be able to do. I'll be just like my mom and never be able to come back." He looked at Johnny with pleading eyes. "Please take the stuff and go. This way there's a chance the truth will come out. Tell Robert I'll probably be at the jail."

"What about your Grandpa? Should I call him too?"

Cal closed his eyes when he thought about the pain this would bring to Raymond. He wished he could protect him, but he knew the truth would come out eventually. "Yes, call him too."

"I should at least stay to make sure he doesn't hurt you."

"No. If you stay they'll just arrest us both and that won't do me any good. This way there's a chance the evidence will finally come out. Please, get going."

Johnny agreed and took the box and the folder full of records. He quickly climbed into his truck and gave Cal a supportive nod. Then he drove off, leaving Cal alone to face Franklin.

Cal went back to the eagle and stood watching him perched on his sovereign throne. He heard the sound of a truck driving up onto the cliff, but he stayed facing away until he heard Franklin's voice.

"Put your hands on your head and turn around," Franklin shouted.

Cal slowly turned around to see Franklin and another officer poised in a defensive stance with their guns drawn. There was a flapping of wings and the rustle of leaves from behind Cal as the eagle took flight. Startled, Franklin aimed for the shadow in the branches and fired.

"No!" Cal screamed. He turned and hid his face, not wanting to see if the bird was dead. He slowly pulled his hands away and looked over the ridge to the mesa floor, but the bird was nowhere in sight.

"Turn back around!" Franklin yelled to Cal.

Cal did as he said, but then looked up at the sky. The eagle soared in a large circle high above his head and Cal's chest heaved in relief. The eagle meant so much to him, and it wasn't until he saw it almost destroyed that he realized the emotional strength he'd invested in it. He felt that somehow the eagle kept Doran's spirit alive, and that it soared with the eagle that day when his brother died.

Cal looked up as Franklin and the officer raced over to him. He didn't resist as they threw him to the ground and handcuffed him. They searched his pockets and then pulled him to his feet. The officer walked Cal to the car as Franklin followed silently behind.

The ride to the jail was quick, and Cal now sat silent and despondent on the wooden bench inside the cell.

When Robert arrived, he was out of breath and his face was red and sweaty. "Cal," he said. "What's going on?" he looked worried.

"I want to talk to you, but we need to be alone first," Cal said, motioning to two other men playing cards in the next cell.

Robert nodded and left the room, then came back with a guard who unlocked the door and led Cal in handcuffs to a small room with a cheap table.

"Sit down," Robert said, motioning to Cal as the guard left the room.

Cal took a deep breath and sat on the edge of the chair. Robert saw his anguish and quickly walked around the desk and sat down, leaning forward towards the boy.

"What's wrong?" Robert asked. "You look horrible. Are you hurt?"

"No," Cal answered, exhausted. Then he thought about Robert's question and he smiled wearily. "Actually, I'm very hurt," he said quietly.

"What did Franklin do to you?" Robert asked in his best attorney form.

Cal shook his head and tried to wipe the exhaustion from his face. "It's not what you think. Did you bring the papers?"

"Yes," Robert said as he leaned down and popped open his brief case. He lay the papers and leather box on the table.

"Did you read them?" Cal asked.

"I didn't have a lot of time, but isn't most of this stuff just the court documents from the old murder case?"

"Yes."

Robert just shrugged helplessly.

"I know who killed Jackie," Cal said.

Robert shook his head and leaned back. "Cal we've gone over this before—"

But Cal cut him off. "No. I really know who killed Jackie. It's all right there," he said pointing to the stack.

Robert cocked his head sideways. "I already told you, there's no evidence against Franklin."

"It's not Franklin," Cal said, lowering his head. "It's my mother."

Robert flinched back when he heard Cal's words. "Mona? Cal, come on. You're not serious."

"Yes, I am. She was there and I know she did it."

"Cal, we already looked at her when it first happened, but there was no evidence—nothing."

"What do you mean, nothing? Did you even look at the evidence?"

"What evidence, Cal? There was nothing. And most importantly, there was no motive."

Cal put his face in his hands and wiped away the tears

that began to fill his eyes. "There was motive—it was *me!* I was the damn motive!"

Robert stood up and walked around to the other chair next to Cal. "You were the motive? Cal, you weren't even alive. What are you talking about?" he asked.

Cal looked up at him with sad red eyes. "My mom killed Jackie because she wanted Franklin for herself. Jackie was pregnant with Franklin's baby, but so was my Mom—with me."

Robert looked at Cal, stunned. "Franklin's your—? How do you know?"

Cal grabbed at the papers on the table and shoved a copy of the autopsy report at Robert. Jackie's baby had the same rare blood type I do."

"That means nothing. Lots of people have the same blood type."

"Not this blood type. We have AB negative; it's rare. She used Demerol to drug my dad so he wouldn't wake up. And Mom's friend Juanita helped her by stealing the drug from Tim's father's drugstore. It's all in these letters Mom wrote. Tim's daughter found them."

"Are you sure?"

"Yes. Even the necklace points to her."

"How?"

"The pieces were from Mom's necklace. My Grandpa said they buried Aunt Jackie in hers. It was Mom's necklace that must have broken during the struggle. The pieces that Eddie has are my mom's."

Robert sat up straight and took a long deep breath. "Cal do you realize what this means?"

Cal shrugged.

"If this is all true and the prosecutor's office thinks they have a case, they'll charge Mona with murder. Is this really what you want to do?"

"What else can I do? It's the truth. I know she killed Jackie." Tears flooded Cal's eyes again as he spoke. "She used my dad and tried to pin the murder on him. Then, when Franklin dumped her like all the other Indian girls, she lied to Dad about being pregnant with his child and used him to get away from this place." He put his head down and began to sob.

Robert put an awkward hand on Cal's shoulder. "Cal, I'm-I'm—" he struggled, not knowing what to say.

A knock came at the door and the guard poked his head in. "The boy's mother is here. I need to take him back to the cell. He can't see her in here."

"We'll be just a moment. I'll come get you as soon as we're ready," said Robert with a forced politeness.

"She's back," Cal said, surprised, as the jailer shut the door.

"What are you going to do? Do you want to talk to her?" Robert asked.

Cal paused, wondering what she would say. "Yes, I think I would."

Robert nodded. "What do you want me to do?"

Cal pushed the documents toward him. "Take care of this. When I get out of here, I'm taking Rachel and we're leaving."

"Leaving? Where will you go?"

"I'll be eighteen next month. I'm taking her back to be with my dad in Spokane, and then I'll come back."

"Come back? Why?"

Cal tried to answer but he couldn't. He knew that nothing he'd say would make sense to Robert. "Please, just do this for me."

Robert agreed and then stood up, stunned, as Cal wiped his eyes with his sleeve. The lawyer left and came back with the guard.

Cal looked at the floor as the jailer led him from the room and back to his cell. When the guard took off the handcuffs, he rubbed his wrists and waited for his mother to come in.

The sound of the main cell door rumbled open and Cal heard Mona's soft monotone of a voice; the one she used in public. She walked over to the cell and waited until the guard left, then she asked, "Cal, are you all right?"

Cal wanted to release the pent up anger inside him, but instead the mass of sorrow flooded his heart. He lowered his head and began to cry.

"Cal, what happened?" she asked, reaching through the bars to try to comfort him.

Cal quickly backed away and tried to recover, then looked over at the other cell where the men had stopped their game and were watching them.

"What the hell are you staring at?" he shouted.

The men quickly turned back to their game.

Cal began pacing the cell as he wiped his eyes and nose. "I can't even look at you right now. I want to hate you but I can't, and that's what makes all of this so hard!"

"All what? Cal, I just needed to get away. I needed a couple days to—"

"That's not what I meant!" Cal shouted. "I don't care about your stupid trip to Salt Lake." He walked to the cell bars and stared down at her. "I *know* what happened. I know what you did. It was you."

"What was me?"

"You should be behind these bars, not me."

"For what? For bringing you here? Stop trying to convict me for making you leave your precious Spokane."

"You still don't get it, do you? I know what happened the night Jackie was killed."

Mona paused and looked at Cal with concern.

"And so do you, Mom. I saw the letters you wrote to Tim's wife. I know about you and that piece of crap Franklin Grayson. And I know about *me*."

"You don't know anything," she snapped, turning for the door.

"Why are you leaving?" Cal yelled back. "If it's not true, why are you walking out?"

She swung around, facing him. "I'm not going to listen to your lies. I thought that by bringing you back here, you'd see the truth. Of all the people in my life, I thought you'd be able to see."

Cal shook his head. "See what? They're not lies. Mom, stop running away. You can't keep running every time things go wrong. This isn't going away; it didn't the first time you tried to escape, and it's not going to, now."

"I'm not going to listen to this," she said as she reached for the door.

"I've told a lawyer and he knows everything."

"You did what?" she cried, turning back and grabbing the cell bars.

Cal reached for her hands and pulled her arms into the cell. Anger overtook him and he pulled her hard against the bars.

Mona screamed out, but Cal's rage kept him from releasing her.

"How could you, Mom? How could you bring us back to all this?"

Mona squirmed and cried out, "I did it for you!"

Cal thrust her back, hurling her to the floor. "You've done nothing for me."

"I wanted you to have a good life. I wanted you to have something better! I did it all for you. I did everything for you…" she hung her head and slumped against the wall as she sat there on the floor.

"That was an excuse to lie to Dad about me, but not for killing your own sister. Are you insane?"

The guard came in and went to Mona. "What's going on?"

Mona ignored him and stood up. She glared at Cal. "Someday you'll understand. It's not at all what you think."

"Understand? You killed your own sister. I'll never understand that."

The guard interrupted them, saying, "It's time to go."

"How do you live with yourself?" Cal went on. "How did you go all these years, knowing what you did? And how could you bring us here to go through all this crap!"

The guard tried to lead Mona toward the door but she resisted. "You weren't there Cal. You don't know what happened."

"You're still lying. Please, just for once, tell me the truth."

Mona pulled away from the guard. "I can't. You won't give me a chance."

The guard was now pulling Mona toward the door. "I have nothing if you don't believe me, Cal," she cried as the door slammed behind them.

Cal took a seat on the wooden bench and stared at the concrete floor. The musty smell of stagnant water and sweat penetrated his swollen nose. He sat wondering if he'd ever see his mother again. When the thought didn't sadden him, he was surprised and felt a little guilty. He didn't know what to do now. He couldn't go home to Spokane; his father obviously didn't want him around. But Rachel was here and he had to be there for her. Then Cal remembered with a chill that Rachel was actually only his *half* sister; then his thoughts turned to Lacey. If what Johnny said was true, then she, too, was his half sister. But the most painful part of all this came from realizing that Mitch was actually his half brother.

The intertwining of his life with those of the people of the Basin whirled in his head and made him so dizzy he had to hold onto the cell's bars for balance.

It was early evening when the rattle of keys woke Cal. He looked up to find Franklin standing at the cell door.

"Get up and come with me," he said in a gruff whisper.

Cal was apprehensive, but he had no choice other than to follow.

Franklin led him down a quiet hallway and through several doors to a large office. He motioned for Cal to sit on a small metal chair in front of a large mahogany desk. Franklin took a seat in the tall padded chair behind the desk and leaned back with a somber face, studying Cal as he sat there, defeated.

"You burglarized my house and I have proof. I confiscated the box and there's enough evidence to convict you. You're almost eighteen and you'll serve time. I can also put your mother away for murder."

Cal took a deep breath and just stared at the floor.

"Or we can make a deal. You shut up and give me the rest of the stuff, and I'll forget about everything, too."

Cal looked up at him with shocked skepticism. The rest of what stuff?

Then Cal heard a loud grinding from the office door as someone struggled with the doorknob. Cal turned toward the noise, then he heard thunderous pounding and Mitch's voice calling from the other side.

Franklin glared at the door and stood up. "You say one word and the deal's off, you hear?" he said, pointing at Cal.

Cal just sat silently, waiting to see what would happen next.

Franklin opened the door and Mitch burst into the room.

"Mitch, I can handle this. Go home," Franklin said sternly.

Mitch looked at Cal and then stood tall and crossed his arms over his chest. "Let him go."

Franklin walked back to his chair. "What?"

"You heard me. I said, let him go."

"Mitch, go home. I don't have time for this," said Franklin, still standing.

Mitch scoffed. "Yeah, you've handled the rest of this

real well, haven't you. I know what's going on. I know *everything* and I'm not letting you get away with it anymore."

An officer came into the doorway and Tim was with him. "Is everything okay, sir?" the officer asked, looking at the three of them.

Franklin shooed him away. "It's fine."

When the officer left, Tim stepped into the room.

"What do you want?" Franklin asked as he took his seat and rested his elbows on the large arms of his chair. He clasped his hands in front of him. "You have no business here."

"I don't *want* anything, Franklin. Mitch asked me to be here."

Cal looked at Tim and Mitch, confused.

"I've told him everything," Mitch said without inflection. "I know what you did. I've known for a while. I did everything I could to try and hide it, and I ended up killing someone because of it, someone who didn't deserve to die."

"Mitch, shut up!" thundered Franklin.

"No!" Mitch shouted back. "I won't. I'm not doing this anymore. You killed those girls to hide what you did. First it was Lacey's mom, and now I find out about Cal's aunt. When I found out you were Cal's father, I wanted him dead so I could keep it a secret." Mitch's eyes began to tear and his voice quavered. "I thought it was him on that motorcycle," he said, motioning towards Cal. "Doran had on Cal's jacket and was wearing a helmet, so I thought he was Cal. I wanted him dead so I wouldn't have to be embarrassed again about what you did. I killed someone innocent trying to protect you."

"Mitch, shut up NOW," urged Franklin.

"No. I don't care who knows. I refuse to be anything like you. I'm not going to lie and hide what I did. I'm nothing like you."

Franklin shook his head and sneered at his son. "No, you're definitely not like me." He turned to Tim. "I hope you're happy, manipulating some kid to try and make your life look better. You never really got over the fact that you had a half-breed for a kid. Now you have to pick on my family, too."

Tim gave Franklin a huff. "You're the only one who's got hang-ups, Grayson. I've never regretted anything I've done, but it seems to me you have quite a few regrets."

Franklin sat back in his chair unconcerned. "The only regret I have right now is the one standing in front of me." He looked his son up and down, then shook his head in disgust. "Get out of my sight."

Mitch sniffed and wiped his eyes, then shook his head, saying, "Not without Cal."

Franklin gave a disgusted laugh. "You can throw your life away if you want, but he's not going anywhere. He burglarized my house and he's going to jail."

Mitch took a deep breath. "He didn't take that box of letters. *I did*. I *gave* them to him."

Cal looked up at Mitch in shock. All this time he thought it was Lacey who'd given him the letters when it was actually Mitch.

"That's right. When I read Cal's paper at school, I started to figure things out. I didn't understand why you hated him so much. So I looked around through your old files and that's when I found the letters. I read them and figured out why you wanted him gone. You knew he was your son, and you knew he'd let your secret out. You knew that after all these years, everyone would finally know that you killed that girl. You tried to blame it on Cal's father, and now you're trying to take it out on him. I'm not letting you get away with it. Either you let him go, or I'll go to the newspapers and tell them what you did."

Tim stepped forward. "Now that Mitch has said that he gave Cal the letters, you have nothing to hold him on."

"I'm the law around here," Franklin growled. Then he shoved the chair back and stood up. "I don't give a damn what you do. You were around then, Tim. It was drugs from your Dad's pharmacy that doped David up. Nobody's going to believe anything you say. Besides, everyone knows I wasn't at the lake that night. I was cleared and there's no evidence."

"That isn't quite right, Grayson," Tim said. "You see, my daughter Lacey kept everything that belonged to her mother. You thought you'd stolen all the letters between Juanita and Mona, but there were several that you missed."

Franklin's eyes widened.

"You know which ones I'm talking about, don't you," Tim continued. "*You* wrote several letters threatening Juanita if she talked."

Franklin snorted. "There's nothing in those letters that'd stand up in court. I may have threatened her about telling everyone I was the father of some Indian kid, but I certainly didn't kill anyone."

Cal looked at the floor and felt his throat tighten,

knowing that what Franklin said was true. As much as he wished it wasn't so, he knew the truth.

"That may be true," Tim continued. "But do you really want to drag all this out in court? Have all these letters read aloud, in public?"

Franklin pounded his fist on the desk, making Cal jump. "What do you want from me?" the sheriff bellowed.

Tim looked at Mitch, who took a deep breath. "Just let him go," he said, pointing at Cal, "And leave him alone."

Franklin gave a mocking laugh. "Fine, I'll let him go. But this is far from over."

Tim directed Cal and Mitch to the door. "I'd think you'd want to see all of this go away, Grayson," he said before turning to leave with the boys.

"Get the hell out of here!" Franklin stood up and stared straight at Mitch. "I don't want to ever see *any* of you again."

Mitch stared Franklin down. Then he made a point of being the first one to turn his back on his father and leave the office. Franklin shouted after them as the three made their way down the hallway toward the exit. "This isn't over!"

But Mitch just kept on walking.

When they made it outside, Mitch's demeanor crumbled and he stood looking up at the sky in tears.

Cal stood watching him for moment, and then went to Mitch. "What're you going to do now?" he asked him quietly.

"I'm sure I'll be going to prison," said Mitch, wiping his eyes and trying to regain control of himself.

Cal saw his attempt to be steadfast, but felt an incredible sadness. He looked down and asked him, "What about tonight? Where will you go?"

"I'm going home," he said without hesitation.

Cal looked up, surprised.

"My mom's behind me. She's sick of all this crap, too. We're going to go stay with my grandparents and see what happens. Then I'm turning myself in tomorrow."

Tim came closer now and said, "It was a brave thing that you did in there, Mitch. There aren't many men who'd do what you're doing."

Mitch just shrugged.

"No. It is brave," Cal agreed, saying it quietly, almost to himself.

Mitch gave a long sigh and then looked back at the building. "I'd better go." He turned to leave, but stopped and turned back to Cal. Again, his eyes turned red as tears streamed down his face. "I'm so sorry about your brother."

The words hit Cal hard and he felt weak as he stood there, numb. Then he looked Mitch squarely in the eye. "I know," he told him.

Mitch started to speak, but then gave Cal a nod and walked away.

The sun had begun its fiery transformation as Cal walked with Tim to his truck.

Cal rode silently as Tim drove up to Bitter Creek to retrieve Cal's car. He wondered what Tim knew and what he should say.

Almost as if on cue, Tim cleared his throat and said, "I want you to know that I had nothing to do with Jackie's death," he said, breaking the silence. "Juanita stole the drugs without my knowledge. There was a lot that went on that I had no idea about. You have my word on this."

Cal nodded with raised eyebrows. "There were a lot more victims in this whole thing than just my aunt Jackie. The lies kept getting bigger. I mean, look at my life. It's all one big lie."

Tim let out a knowing huff and turned to Cal with a sympathetic look. "I guess you and I have kind of a unique relationship now, don't we. My daughter's your half sister."

"I suppose *unique's* a good word for it," Cal answered, "How long have you known?"

"About Lacey or you?"

"Both."

"I found out about Lacey years ago. I tried to keep it from her for a long time, but the rumors and stuff finally caught up to her."

"How long have you known about me?"

"Robert just told me. I'd had my suspicions ever since you moved back—your eyes gave it away—but I wasn't about to say anything." He paused and drove for a minute in silence. "It doesn't matter, you know. It may seem like it does right now, but in the long run, it doesn't. I love Lacey just as much as Shelly; it doesn't matter to me one bit. And it won't matter to David, either."

Cal felt the tears began to form. *But it does matter!* he screamed in his mind. He nodded to Tim and turned to the window as the tears fell, rolling from his cheeks and dropping on his jeans.

He was glad when he finally was alone in his car. He

sat in the dark for several minutes, letting the engine warm up. The valley looked small against the vast expanse of black sky, and he wondered if the pain would leave him if he drove his car right over the edge. Was it the only way out? Was death the only way anyone ever escaped or found relief? Cal sat contemplating the affect his death would have, then he sobbed into the steering wheel until he was too tired to cry any more. Then he slowly drove back home, not knowing what he'd find when he arrived.

When Cal walked into the house, Raymond stood pensively in the kitchen. He looked at Cal with questioning eyes, and Cal wasn't sure where to even begin.

"Where'd Mom go?" Cal asked, sure she was gone.

"She came home and said you were arrested. I drove over to the courthouse and they said you'd been released. When I got back home, she'd already left. I don't know where she's going this time." Raymond's face became pained. "What happened, Cal? Why were you in jail?"

"Didn't Johnny tell you?"

"I haven't seen him yet."

Cal immediately softened as he walked over to his grandfather. "I got into it with Franklin Grayson and he arrested me—"

"Are you all right?"

"Yes. No. Oh, Grandpa, there's all this stuff."

"All what stuff?"

"It's Mom. She lied to me for years. And then there's Jackie."

"What about Jackie?"

Cal paused and looked up at Raymond. He knew the

pain his grandfather felt when he lost Jackie. How could he possibly tell him that it was his own daughter who'd killed her? Cal shook his head and walked slowly into the living room. Raymond followed.

"Cal, please tell me what's going on," he pleaded.

"I really don't get it," Cal muttered.

"What's happened, Cal?"

"My life is—well, it's a joke. I can't even believe what's happened. The life I had before I came here is like a dream now. It was never even real."

"Cal, I know that Mona's drinking and the stuff with your father is making your life hard right now, but going away won't solve anything."

"Grandpa, it's a lot more than that. I found out some stuff today that—" Cal's voice began to crack as his emotions flooded him.

Raymond instinctively wrapped his bulky arm around Cal's shoulders. "What is it, boy?"

"I can't say it. I still can't even believe it's true."

Cal tried to stop the tears and choke back the sobs, but it was too hard. "I think Mom killed Jackie," he sobbed.

"What? But why?"

"She killed her because she wanted Franklin. She knew she was pregnant with me, and she wanted Jackie out of the picture."

"That's not true, Cal. She wouldn't."

Cal's tears subsided and he sat back exhausted against the soft worn fabric of the sofa. "I think she brought us back here because she was tired of running and knew that the truth would eventually come out once we were here again."

"But she loved David. She didn't want to marry Franklin."

"Yes, she did, Grandpa. But Franklin dumped her the same way he dumped every other Ute girl he slept with or got pregnant. She used Dad as an escape and Dad eventually found out. That's why they got divorced, and that's why we're here."

Raymond stood up and began to pace the floor. "But why would she come back, if she really did do this?"

Cal sat and thought. He knew deep down that Mona was the reason Jackie was dead, but like Raymond, he couldn't figure why Mona wanted to walk back into the middle of a place where things could eventually catch up to her. But then a chilling thought struck Cal with enough horror that he started to shake.

"Oh, God, Grandpa. Maybe that's what she wanted. Maybe she wants it all to be over."

"What do you mean, Cal?"

"She said that she came back here because you'd take care of us. Maybe she came back to put an end to everything—the pain, the memories. What if she wants to end it all?"

"End it all?"

Cal paused and then his eyes widened in fear. "She's going to kill herself." He then leaped to his feet and shouted, "Grab your coat, Grandpa. We've got to stop her!"

Raymond stood up but held his palms up, questioningly. "But where?"

"I think I know. I bet she went back to where this whole nightmare started."

17

Mona was exactly where Cal had guessed she'd be. She sat exposed to the cold on a cement block by the side of the lake. The glow from the streetlight showed the distinctive haze of her warm breath rising up in the cold night air. As Cal's car pulled in she stood up, stunned that they'd found her.

Cal walked over to her and asked, "What are you doing here, Mom?"

"Stay back!"she screamed as she pointed a small gun to her head.

"Mom, don't! You'll only make everything worse."

"I only wanted the best for you," Mona said, her voice becoming soft. "I lied to give you a better life. I've lived with the guilt my whole life, but I never wanted you to have that kind of pain."

"But don't you see? If you do this, you'll be causing so much more pain than from anything else you've ever done."

"Cal, I loved Jackie. But I was young and stupid. I thought it was the only way out. I just wanted a better life for you."

"Mom, please put the gun down," Cal pleaded.

"No. Not until you listen."

"Okay. I'll listen."

Mona lowered the gun. "I was so scared. Franklin used me and I had nowhere to turn. He convinced me that if Jackie were out of the way, it'd just be him and me. I knew I couldn't raise a baby alone. I honestly thought I loved him."

Cal's stomach turned at the mere thought.

"Afterwards, he dumped me and then threatened to turn me in. When Juanita stood up to him, she ended up dead. I knew he'd kill me too if I didn't get away. I know it was wrong, Cal. Everything I did was wrong."

Cal hung his head and let exhaustion fill every part of him.

"When David found out that he wasn't your real father, I knew it was over. I couldn't keep hiding. But I knew your grandpa would love you and take care of you. That's why I brought you back here. I know he loves you."

When she said that, Cal felt Raymond step closer to him. With the truth out, Cal felt both sadness and relief. He took a deep breath and looked at Raymond, who stood beside Cal with his head lowered. Cal turned and began to walk towards Mona, but then she raised the gun again.

"Mom, put the gun down. It'll be okay."

"No, it won't, Cal. It'll never be okay ever again."

"Sure it will."

She shook her head, unconvinced.

"Mom, you'll ruin everything for all of us if you kill yourself. Think about Rachel and what it'd do to *her*. You keep saying you did this all for me. So prove it and make this right."

Mona shook her head. "Make it right? How?"

"By telling the truth and finally letting everyone move on. You're the only one who can do that. Please, Mom. Do it for me."

Mona looked up at him with wet, swollen eyes. "I don't want you to hate me," She pleaded softly.

"I could never," Cal said.

Mona dropped the gun on the ground, looked up to the sky and then began to cry. Cal went to her and put his arms around her shoulders. He helped her get up and then turned back to Raymond, who still stood silently behind him. Raymond raised his head and looked at his grandson with an uncertain sadness.

Cal took a deep breath and let it out slowly. "Help me with her, Grandpa. And let's find Rachel. We're going home."

Raymond lowered his head and his shoulders began to shudder.

"Grandpa, everything's gonna be okay."

Raymond looked up at him with tear stained eyes. "I don't know if I can stand to see you leave."

Cal opened the car door and gently put Mona inside. He closed the door, walked back to Raymond and embraced him. Then he pulled back and looked him in the eye. "Grandpa, I'm not leaving."

"But you said you were going home."

Cal stopped and looked out into the night. Then he looked back to Raymond. "But Grandpa, don't you know? You *are* my home."

18

The morning sun peeked above the red rim of the basin as they made their way to Robert's law office in town. Raymond parked on the street in front of the small brick building that used to be one of the original homes along State Street in Roosevelt. Inside the carpet was green and worn, and the walls were covered with dark wood paneling and law degrees that were yellowed and curling up around the edges. Robert's desk was piled high with documents, handwritten notes, and cheaply framed photographs that were decades old. The lawyer had agreed to represent her, and Cal sat strong beside his mother as she signed her confession.

"Since Mona was only 17—a minor—when the crime was committed, the charge will be lowered to manslaughter and she'll spend very little time in jail," Robert reassured them.

Mona was expressionless as she finished signing the papers. Cal tried to smile at her in support, but he knew from her reaction that it came across as awkward and unsure.

Robert put the confession in a folder and then stood

up from the desk. "I need to make a copy of this and then I'll follow you over to the courthouse, and then we can take care of the rest."

"The rest" meant having Mona turn in her confession and be officially charged for the almost 20-year-old murder of her sister.

"I'll just be a minute," Robert said as he went to a back room with the folder.

Cal saw his mother start to get anxious. Her hands shook as she looked down at the legs of the chair she was sitting in, as if she were searching for something.

"I forgot my purse in the car, Cal. I need to wipe my nose. I'll wait for you outside," she said.

Raymond nodded, but Cal felt a sickening chill come over him as she walked out the door to the car. He felt that he should go with her, but the urge came too late. When he went to the door, Cal was just in time to see her start the engine and pull her car away from the curb.

"She's running," Cal called to Raymond. He burst through the door, hurtled over a shrub and ran to stop her.

"Leave me alone, Cal!" she yelled from the half-opened window as she tried to make the turn.

"Don't do this!" he screamed back to her. He ran to the front of the car and stood in front of it defiantly. "Quit running, Mom." Cal said and slammed his hands onto the rusted hood of the white Pontiac.

Their eyes locked and Cal could see that she was crying. He began to speak and try to convince her to stay, but then she turned the wheel sharply and gunned the engine, flinging Cal aside as she roared past.

Cal lay sprawled in the middle of the street as he watched her drive off into the early morning haze. He closed his eyes, trying to decide if he should cry. Instead, he pulled himself up slowly and picked the gravel from his palms. What she did didn't surprise Cal, but it crushed him. Even with the evidence he'd uncovered, there'd still been a lingering hope deep inside him that he'd been wrong and that she couldn't have done such a dreadful thing. But the truth was irreversible: she'd confessed.

He swallowed hard against the burning pressure behind his eyes and nose, sniffled hard, and then brushed the remnants of the road from his chest and pants. Cal walked back to the law office house where Raymond stood silently on the porch. They stared out at the day, both of them abandoned and defeated. Cal put his arm around Raymond's shoulders and heard the deep sobs of a father who felt he'd lost a daughter once again.

In the cold depths of the lake there was a hushed mumbling, the ending to a sad and lonely guilt that eventually took another life. An old white car rests upside down in the murky sludge, and holds the final act of the one who could have changed it all. There was no note, no explanation of why, and the reason seems locked forever in that rusting steel tomb. She'd eluded her demons by becoming one with the water that had been her murderous tool. And now she was trapped in the very place she had most wanted to escape.

Cal started to make arrangements for Rachel to be sent back to David in Spokane, but to his surprise, she refused to go.

"I'm staying here," she said, flatly.

"But I'm leaving for college and we don't know if Mom's ever coming back," Cal argued.

Rachel crossed her arms defiantly, shook her head and squinted her eyes. "Then who'll take care of Grandpa if I go, too?"

Cal was speechless. He looked at his little sister and smiled at the young woman she'd become. He grabbed her from her defensive stance and hugged her hard. "You will, God help him." Then he laughed when she tried to look offended.

The morning after Mona fled the Fort, Cal walked down to the lake with Raymond. They both felt a crushing weight of loss, but neither could find the words to explain their pain. The weather had turned crisp, and in the stillness, a light flurry of snow began to fall. Cal stood and watched the flakes land softly on his sweater; the entire valley was so silent, he could almost hear their fragile descent. He wrapped his arms around himself and stood there feeling even colder and more confused. He looked over to Raymond, who had put his head back, letting the snow cover his face.

As Cal watched his grandfather stand there with the snow melting on his cheeks, he saw a smile spread across his face, as though all of the turmoil and heartache were being washed away. Cal looked out over the glassy surface of Bottle Hollow as the flakes disappeared as soon as they touched the surface. As the light storm continued to wash over the basin, Cal felt as though it was cleansing his soul. The dark secret that had covered the Fort for so long was now released. It was over; the truth was out, and those still living had to decide if they would continue looking backwards or else step forward into a new day.

Raymond's face softened and he gave Cal a look of liberation. Cal understood; he took a deep breath and put his hand on Raymond's shoulder as they resumed their walk. Raymond seemed buoyant.

Cal felt it, too. His mind was finally free and he saw clearly what he needed to do next.

19

Cal sat on Doran's bench on the cliff, looking out over the burning horizon that was the start of a new morning. He took a deep breath. "It's weird, but for some reason I still like being up here, even after what happened to Doran." He kept staring out over the valley and then turned back when he didn't get a response.

Johnny sat on the tailgate of the truck and looked up at Cal. "It's not the place that took your brother. It was anger."

Cal turned back towards the basin and pondered the statement. He knew that it was true, and yet found it difficult that something so painful could be explained away so easily.

Johnny pushed himself off the truck and walked to the ridge, then peered out over the valley. "Besides, he's still here. That's why we put the bench up here."

"It's the perfect place for it," Cal said, patting the wooden seat. He sat for a moment and admired the view, and then he silently told Doran how much he missed him.

Johnny glanced at his watch and then turned to leave. "We'd better get back to your grandpa's. He's making chili and eggs for us all."

Cal nodded. "And I have to leave soon. I have a huge test tomorrow morning. I can't believe the week is already over." He looked out into the glimmering dawn and then whistled loudly.

The skip of small paws could be heard in the distance, and soon Doogie appeared, panting and happy.

"Come on, Doogie. Let's go," said Cal.

Johnny smiled as Doogie bounded around Cal's feet. "What happens when Mitch gets out? Who gets the dog then?"

Cal shrugged. "He asked me to take him. I didn't really think about giving him back."

Johnny laughed. "I still can't believe they let you keep him at the college."

Cal smiled. "He's great when it comes to meeting girls."

Johnny rolled his eyes. "So, did you ever get a chance to call Jovan down there?"

Cal turned to him surprised. "No. I guess I should. I don't know her that well, and I don't know—"

"Chicken!"

Cal laughed. "Well, hell. What am I supposed to do? Just call for no reason, and look like a total idiot?"

"Whatever. Suit yourself" Johnny pushed himself off the tailgate. "So, when are you coming back?"

Cal shrugged. "I don't know. It isn't that far, but I have work and school, so I rarely have two days off in a row."

"No," Johnny said, cutting him off. He stopped and looked down at the ground. "I mean when are you coming home? You know, for good."

Cal smiled and nodded. "Oh." He thought for a moment. The breeze picked up and wrapped around Cal like a down quilt. "Soon," he said, confidently. And it was home to him now. He had no plans of making a life anywhere else. "I also plan on making it home more often while I'm at school. It's just been busy. The only reason I got this week off was because I told them it was the Bear Dance and they were worried about it being some Indian religious holiday."

They laughed, then they both paused and continued to look out off the cliff, trying to lighten the crushing reason Cal was really there.

The cottonwood trees began to release their wispy clouds of seeds and there was a frosty sting in the air. Almost six months had passed since Cal went away to school. He'd never imagined or planned that it would be so long before got back. He'd started school at the University of Utah in Salt Lake City, and even though the drive was only a couple hours, it seemed that time got away from him. The real reason he'd come back was to testify at Mitch's sentencing hearing. Mitch did what he said he would do that day at the courthouse. He turned himself in and was convicted of Doran's murder.

There was no trial, but Cal found himself taking the stand and reliving the entire horrifying event. A knot throbbed in Cal's stomach, making his mouth water to such an extent that he felt he would lose it at any moment in front of the courtroom. But then it hit him; not the anger or sadness, but the baptism in the falling snow. Even with the pain he still felt for the loss of his brother, he shook himself free of the hate and drew in a calmness that enabled him to sit tall in that courtroom and tell the judge why Mitch should be spared.

His comments drew shock and hushed gasps from the audience in the courtroom, and Cal glanced up to see both Mitch's mother and Raymond in tears. They were on opposite sides of the courtroom, but their faces showed identical emotion. Cal talked about Mitch's bravery and told of his doing what was right, even in the face of losing both his father *and* his freedom. In many ways, Cal felt Mitch was also a victim. The pattern of lives ruined over what had happened decades before was something Cal wanted to see ended at last. Mitch sat with his face in his hands as Cal talked, but after the judge read the two-year sentence and Mitch was being led away, he turned back for a moment and nodded to Cal with a look of contentment that he knew would stay with him for the rest of his life. Now he too was free.

20

The morning of Cal's departure was windy, and even though it was March, the air was unusually cold and laced with a chill that bit through his jacket. Johnny watched as Raymond flipped the eggs and Cal put plates on the small kitchen table. Eddie, Puck and Fly arrived together. They were all still living on the reservation, and it looked like that's where they'd be staying. They seemed somewhat distant at first, like they were the first time they met Cal and Doran, but it didn't take long before they were laughing and talking about old times. Then Johnny pulled out a small vinyl photo album filled with photographs of tables, bookcases and bed frames.

"What are these amazing pieces?" Cal asked. "They're really beautiful. They look a lot like Grandpa's furniture."

Johnny smiled. "We made them. We sell them for quite a bit. Even the people off the reservation are buying our pieces. Some of our customers are as far away as Salt Lake City."

Cal looked at the others. "All of you are doing this?"

The group nodded in unison.

"Did you teach them?" he asked Raymond.

Raymond smiled. "I got them started, but they're much more creative with the wood than I am."

Cal turned back to the pictures. "What kind of wood is this?" he asked, marveling at the different shapes and colors.

Puck piped up. "It's juniper. It's the stuff that covers this area. It grows around here like weeds."

Cal smiled. It was hard to believe that this wood, with it's remarkable grain that danced with ribbons of character, came from the same scraggly trees that Cal always thought of as rangy and practically lifeless. His friends had found their place in the world and this made Cal feel good. So much of the pain of the past had faded.

Cal's new life at school helped a lot. What he learned that year on the Fort had served him well. Mr. Henry took Cal's writings and submitted them for the scholarship, as planned. Cal not only won that particular prize, but he got several other writing awards that paid for his entire education.

"My time on the basketball court is over. Now I want to be a force in the courtroom," he explained to his friends gathered around the table. "We need to know more about our tribal laws, and I want to help our people understand what they have and how to stand up for their rights." Cal paused and smiled at their intent interest in his plans. "I love my life at the University of Utah, and having the school's mascot be the running Ute is almost too ironic."

While they ate, Cal asked about Tim. The entire group smiled, including Raymond. "He's remarried and is living just outside of town."

"That's cool. No wonder I couldn't reach him," said Cal. "I wondered what he was doing now that Lacey is off at school. Didn't she go down south to Cedar City?"

"Yeah, but she comes home pretty regularly," said Puck as he smiled and nudged Johnny.

Cal looked at them surprised. "Johnny, are you and Lacey dating?"

Johnny didn't answer, but smiled and gave Puck a shove.

The group laughed as Raymond began to clear the dishes from the table. Cal was comforted by the news. He felt a strong connection to Lacey, not only because she was biologically his half-sister, but also because they shared in the discovery of what had happened that night at the lake, and their lives were somehow intertwined as a part of it.

When the facts came out about what had happened with his aunt and his mother, it didn't take long before many outside the community began to question the other tragedies surrounding the case. And with it came a hard look at the long and corrupt reign of Franklin Grayson. The entire unfortunate case played out on the television news and it was the front-page story of even the larger cities in the region. There was never enough proof of what took place to put Franklin behind bars, but it was enough to get him removed from office.

"He left in the night," Johnny explained, while the rest of the group nodded with pleasure. "No one has seen him since. I heard he went to California, but Puck heard from one of Mitch's old friends that Franklin tried to kill himself and was in a mental hospital."

Cal raised an eyebrow and shook his head sadly. He was relieved that it was all over and glad that Franklin no longer had the power to cause more turmoil, but Cal knew that no amount of pain for Franklin could ever erase what had happened or bring Doran back. For Cal, the thought of revenge was no longer sweet.

Johnny looked at his watch. "When do you have to leave? We have something we want to show you."

Cal nodded. "Soon, but first I have something for all of you." He reached into a worn paper bag leaning against the leg of his chair. He took out a large stack of papers bound together with rubber bands and proudly placed it in the middle of the table.

"I was going to wait until it was complete and in print, but I can't. I had to show you guys." And then he pulled out his wallet.

The group looked at each other, at the stack of papers, and then back to Cal, confused.

"These are some of the articles I've written," he said with a smile, knowing they wouldn't understand and then they'd be even more curious.

He opened the wallet and pulled out a check that he held up to show them.

Johnny turned the papers towards him and read one of the titles aloud. "I Am Nuchu." Then he read another. "'The History of Bottle Hollow.' Cal, these are all about us."

"Yes, that's right. They are," said Cal. Then he handed the check to Raymond. "It's five thousand dollars, Grandpa. I've saved up all the money I made from the articles and the awards."

The group all smiled and nodded.

Puck cleared his throat. "So are you getting that Thunderbird you were always talking about?"

Cal laughed, but then he paused for a moment before answering them. He drifted off in thought about how his dreams and desires were so drastically different now than when he first came to the Fort. He was aware and proud of that change, and he felt his chest expand as he sat up in his chair.

"No," Cal said. "I want us to rebuild the museum. You said we needed money before we could apply for the grant. So this can be a starting point." He smiled and waited to see their reaction.

Johnny looked up at him stunned. Then his face softened. "Really, Cal? You really want to give that money away?"

Cal nodded. "I'm not giving it away. I'm giving to something that means everything to me—to us. Don't you agree?"

"This is wonderful, Cal. It is what I've always dreamed of," beamed Raymond.

"It's what we've all dreamed about," Johnny said confidently. He smiled, then stared at Cal.

Cal gave him a knowing nod. "We can get all the plans and paperwork started. We should be able to begin building this summer," Cal said with an excited lilt in his voice.

"Enough," Fly said loudly. His demeanor, along with the fact that he actually spoke up, surprised them all and Puck let out a giggle. "We need to get going. We really do have something to show you before you go."

"Really now," said Cal. "Well, let's go see it, then." He half thought Fly was teasing him and was humored when he stood up with a flourish and directed the others to do the same.

"Come on," he ordered, returning to his traditional quiet tone. "It's time."

"Time for what?" Cal asked as he followed them.

At the door, the group grabbed coats and gloves and motioned for Cal to do the same.

"What's going on?" he asked with an inquisitive smile. Then he just bundled up and followed his friends out to the yard.

21

In the warm glow of the streetlight, Cal saw other people walking on the road toward the lake. He recognized some of the faces and they smiled at him. Johnny joined the march and motioned for the others to follow. Cal was full of questions, but rather than say anything, he simply followed along quietly. Puck beamed as though he was holding in every secret he'd ever been told, and when Cal looked over at him, Puck shook his head playfully and went to the other side of the group.

As they made their way up the hill, even more people came out of their houses and joined the throng. Many of the older people placed a hand on Raymond's back, but they stayed silent. He smiled kindly at them, as if thanking them for coming along.

When they reached the crest of the hill, Cal paused. In the valley was the lake that harbored the last breaths of the aunt he never knew, and standing next to it were dozens of people huddled around the glow of small bonfires.

"What's going on?" Cal asked Raymond.

Raymond smiled. "So many good things."

Cal stared at the bundled masses and picked out a familiar sight. It was Rachel, who smiled and waved at him to come down and join her. He felt a rush of emotion as he realized that Lacey stood next to her, and that she, too, was smiling.

"Grandpa, what *is* all this? Why are all these people waiting here?"

"They're here for you, Cal. They're here to celebrate something we should have done years ago, but we could never find the will. It took *you* to make us all see what was needed."

Cal shook his head, confused.

They continued walking toward the crowd. Rachel went to Cal and hugged him, wrapping her arms around his waist. When they reached the water's edge, Johnny and the other young men gathered around a beautifully crafted wooden bench. "What's this?" asked Cal, wondering why they'd make another bench for Doran.

"Isn't it beautiful?" Raymond asked, as he approached the group. He nodded his approval, saying, "It's perfect."

The back was high and polished, with the twists of brown and red streaks of the juniper wood. The arms were natural knotted branches, and the base was the cross-section of an ancient trunk, with glorious contrasting rings that revealed a long life. Cal admired it and stroked the smooth finish as he studied his friends' beautiful handiwork. Then he noticed what was carved into the back. In graceful, flowing script were the words:

"In Memory of Jackie Littlebear."

Cal was overwhelmed. The bench was so exquisitely

made, and the consideration and thought that went into it was even more touching.

Eddie went to Cal and patted the bench. "See? It's for my mom. It's her bench."

"Yes, it sure is." Cal smiled, knowing that this place had for so long held only memories of death. He hoped that now it would become a place to remember Jackie's life. A small twinge of sadness hit him and his smile faded.

Johnny noticed and spoke up. "Don't worry, we didn't forget the baby."

Cal looked up, stunned that Johnny had read him so clearly once more.

Johnny motioned to a section of the lake. "Come on. We'll show you."

They walked the path towards a bridge and Doogie trotted along, panting happily beside Cal.

Johnny led the way with long strides and a wide smile. Then he turned back to Cal and took a deep, satisfied breath. At the base of the bridge he stopped and the group gathered around again.

"We built this bridge over the summer. It's the access from the reservation to where the museum will be." Johnny stopped and smiled at the statement—*where the museum will be*. Then he pointed to the ground, where large, flat rocks were carefully set. "We made these stepping-stones in the sand. Lacey came up with the name 'baby steps,' so we decided it would make a good memorial for Jackie's baby." Then Johnny smiled at Cal.

Cal bent down and gently stroked one of the smooth stones. He looked up at Johnny and nodded his approval, then stood and walked along the stones and up onto the bridge. Raymond followed, and when they reached the crest, both of them looked out over the lake. Even with its serene expanse, Cal could almost hear the deafening last beats of a desperate heart.

The lake tugged at him, as though a part of him lay buried deep beneath its rolling surface. In the pull and push of the tides, the voices called to him. He strained to hear them, and wondered if he'd ever understand their whispers. He continued to watch as the onyx water lapped quietly along the red dirt of the banks. He thought to himself about his impressions of the Fort that day when he first drove into town, and wondered where that ugly, forbidding place had gone.

"You said so many good things were happening, Grandpa, and you were right," Cal said turning to Raymond.

Raymond nodded and gave his grandson an appreciative, heartfelt smile. "It all began with you, Cal."

Cal shook his head. "No, not with me."

"Yes, it did. You were the one who helped bring people together."

"No, it wasn't me. It was Doran. He's the one who never picked sides."

"Yes. He helped start it, but you're the one who carried it through. You could have left this all behind you and never looked back, but you didn't do that. And now the entire community is proud of what we are doing here. Things are beginning to heal, and even more good things will happen. You taught everyone how to forgive, Cal, and now we all can move forward."

Cal looked back at the friends who'd now become his brothers. They were unaware of his gaze as they stood laughing and huddled at the base of the bridge. The sight warmed Cal, and he had no doubt that his future was set. He knew his home would never be anywhere else.

He knew there was never any real escape from the Fort. It was what made him who he was. It was a part of him, and he a part of it.

He was Nuchu and by embracing it, he was free.